GHOSTS
of
GUATEMALA

To Hayley,

Stay alert in Antigua!

COLLIN GLAVAC

First edition

Title: *Ghosts of Guatemala*

Format: Paperback

This publication has been assigned: ISBN: 978-1-9991631-6-7

Title: *Ghosts of Guatemala*

Format: Electronic book

This publication has been assigned: ISBN: 978-0-9683310-6-4

GHOSTS OF GUATEMALA

COLLIN GLAVAC

The CIA never left Latin America...

Please sign up for our newsletter, watch the book trailer, and stay tuned for more at: www.collinglavac.com

For my father, who has always encouraged me to write, even when it was awful high fantasy.

Ghosts of Guatemala

"In 1954, the democratically elected government of Guatemala was overthrown by the CIA.

More than 200,000 people were killed over the course of the 36-year-long civil war that began in 1960 and ended with peace accords in 1996. About 83 percent of those killed were Mayan."

*1999 report written by the U.N.-backed Commission for Historical Clarification titled "**Guatemala: Memory of Silence**".*

https://hrdag.org/wp-content/uploads/2013/01/CEHreport-english.pdf Page 13.

Prologue

The gunshot slammed into Brian's chest with the force of a charging bull. It hadn't been the first time he'd been shot. But he'd also never taken a direct hit in the torso or lost any vitals before. The slug threw him against the veranda door he had just sneaked through, smashing glass and raking his arms as he crumpled painfully onto his back.

He managed not to moan — he was a professional even in the worst situations — but he couldn't stop himself from gasping. He was in shock. He knew he was in shock. He tried to kick it. Clear his mind, focus on the task at hand. He'd been shot. He needed to eliminate the threat. He had to finish the mission.

The searing pain was beginning to drip into his system now, a slow whine that overtook his adrenaline. As his pain tolerance started to be overwhelmed, he wanted to cry out, desperate for reprieve.

There was no one here to help him. If a mission went wrong, if someone was captured or killed, there would be no rescue. That's how the Firm's agents operated. That was how they kept the United States government far away from any political fallout. And besides, they never made mistakes.

Brian crawled painfully to cover, feeling blood smear against the shards of glass on the floor. He pressed a hand to his chest, not bothering to look at how bad the wound was. He didn't need to look at it. He knew what that kind of blood flow through his gloves meant. He managed to pull himself next to a cabinet, leaning his back against the wood, and tried to calm his breathing. His sigh turned into a cough. He raised his other hand instinctively to cover his mouth and he found he hadn't dropped his gun when he'd fallen. He held the reliable Beretta in white-knuckled fingers that refused to let go, shaking from the effort of his training that refused to abandon him against all odds.

He looked down at the glass. Some of it had been decorated with a metal coating. He placed his gun in his lap and retrieved a large piece, angling it to see where his attacker was hiding. It was dark and his vision was beginning to blur. His thoughts began to wander.

It wasn't supposed to be like this. It was supposed to be a simple hit: kill the head of an Antiguan drug cartel, snatch some information off a computer while he was at it. An upper level operative had confided in him that something was wrong with this cartel. Something about corruption. Something way above petty drug wars and trafficking operations.

He had slipped past security. Gotten into the estate. His target should have been here, caught unawares. A silent chuckle escaped him. Had he gotten that rusty? He coughed up blood.

As if to answer his unspoken questions, a figure emerged from the darkness. Brian watched it through the mirrored glass, but it was getting increasingly difficult to concentrate. The man had a large, imposing figure, made more so by the gun in his hand. Even as his consciousness ebbed and flowed, Brian couldn't help but admire what a well-tailored suit the man was wearing. He always tried to be an optimist. The man continued to walk toward Brian's hiding place, waving the handgun as he spoke. His low voice pierced the darkness.

"Looks like my deal is better than your deal, *mamón*. I almost feel bad. But business is business."

That was his target, no doubt about it. Sandor Puentes. But Brian didn't understand what the man was saying. He couldn't piece anything together. His mind was a fog. In his final moments, bleeding out, desperately attempting to complete at least part of his mission,

Brian thought of his best friend John Carpenter, and the painstaking Spanish lesson he'd received. He'd wanted to master at least one good swear word.

"*Que te folle un pez!*" Brian cried, bursting from behind the cabinet and preparing to unload his magazine into Puentes, brutal cartel boss of Antigua, probably one of the largest sex traffickers in all of Latin America. *I hope you get fucked by a fish!*

All people deserved justice. Some people's justice was death.

Gunshots tore through the air like vengeance.

* * *

"In here!" Juan Puentes yelled to the guards. *Where were the guards?*

He had heard his mother and father yelling, and gunshots. The deals they had made with the other cartels were holding strong. Who could be attacking them? His heart pounded in his chest, his soul itched for battle. If there was trouble, he would protect his family. He clutched his shotgun and bounded into the foyer where he was sure the commotion was. Guards flooded the room alongside him, some shining flashlights. *Idiotas*, Juan thought, pushing a guard out of the way. He flicked on the light switch, turning on the lavish electric chandelier.

Pablo and Isabella, his uncle and mother, were in the room, holding each other, shaking and weeping. Juan stared at them in shock. His eyes drifted over to his father's desk, and he saw a handgun resting idly there. He was hardly aware of anything else until his uncle spoke and pointed near the door.

"I'm sorry, *sobrino. Nephew.* Truly I am."

A man dressed all in black sprawled in a bloody heap on the floor. Blood and broken glass were everywhere. Juan didn't understand.

"I suppose it is not *sobrino* anymore, *mi hijo.*" Pablo's words hung, foreign in Juan's ears. *My son.*

It was then that Juan saw.

Sandor Puentes, his strong and determined father — his loving father — lay beside the other man, his forehead blown apart, mouth twisted in a sneer.

Juan let out a wail, overwhelmed by the sight of his father, firing his shotgun into the air. The ornate chandelier exploded in a shower of glass and crystal. Its shattered remains fell all around him as darkness covered the room once more.

CHAPTER 1

———————

Statistically, one hundred people a week were murdered in Guatemala. It was one of the most dangerous countries in the world, yet Antigua was known for its safety. That was because many cartels kept their children in Antigua. Teenage guards held shotguns guarding storefronts. They were never robbed. Who would be stupid enough to commit a crime with cartels keeping the city peaceful?

The government and local authorities were corrupt. This was known. Everything was owned and run by economic elites known as the *oligarcas familias. The family of oligarchs.* Mostly everyone else was poor.

Yet Antigua was called the 'Jewel of Guatemala' because of its beauty.

Pablo Puentes believed in Antigua.

Pablo was slightly shorter than average and had a squatter frame, olive-brown skin, and beady eyes. Anyone would recognize him as a Mayan. He was proud of this. He was one of many whose forefathers had originally flourished before Spanish conquest and colonialism had wiped the existing civilizations and created an underclass that lasted even today. But unlike the majority of Mayans in Guatemala who were poor and destitute, Pablo was wealthier than the city itself.

He lived on Cortega Street; one of the richest neighborhoods in the city, boasting a line of trees decorating either end, shading passersby from the sun. His estate was at the end of the street, vast, with ten foot walls keeping itself hidden away from peering eyes. Vines crawled up the towering walls and were lined with barbed wire. It surrounded the largest courtyard in Antigua. Guards wearing camouflage uniforms and colored berets patrolled the walls and the dozens of long hallways and luxury suites. They held wicked Remington Model 870 TAC-14 shotguns.

It had been two weeks since his brother, Sandor Puentes, had been killed. Pablo was now the new head of one of the largest cartels in Guatemala, and today would solidify his position more than anything he had done so far. But there was no wealth without danger.

"*Tío*, please," Juan Puentes pleaded, folding his arms to stop himself from using them as he spoke. He was trying to live up to his station and be the strong, imposing man his father had been. "Blackmail has never been our business. Business is our business, no? What am I missing here?" His beret spun slightly as he shook his head. It was white, the only one among the others holding that color, distinguishing him as *el comandante*. Many guards in the room wore the new black berets marking them as Pablo's chosen men, while still others sported the red berets of common guards.

Pablo couldn't have been more opposite, wearing a polo shirt with white and cream pants made of cotton. He sat with his legs spread wide and comfortable, elbows resting on the massive oak table. He radiated power.

"You are right, Juan. Business is our business. Every opportunity seized." Pablo raised a fist and clenched it. "You are thinking of money. This is a small thing to think about. I have money. You have money. We all have money. But now I have something no one else does."

"Then keep it. Don't give it away."

Pablo smiled and shook his head like a man who refused to share a secret. "To become invincible, I must declare war."

"Yes, but *tío*, this opens another front in a war we don't need to-"

"And there is no need to call me *tío*. *Uncle*. I much prefer being your father."

Juan grew quiet. After his father died, Pablo had quickly married Isabella, Juan's mother. Pablo was now both his uncle and stepfather.

Isabella sat beside Juan, cradling a laptop. Her slender frame was cloaked in a loose, blood-red dress. She gave her son a sympathetic look, then spoke softly to Pablo.

"Juan is right that these are not simple cartels, or even politicians to threaten or bribe, *mi amor*."

Pablo pointed an index finger down at the table and opened his mouth to make a point, but Isabella continued.

"I am not saying no. You decided this. Juan is simply being cautious. There is a reason he heads your security."

"I am not being cautious," Juan snapped, immediately regretting the rudeness shown to his mother as he caught her glare. He touched her shoulder lightly in unspoken apology before turning back to Pablo. "I am asking you to be more ambitious. There is more we can do with this information."

Pablo raised a hand to cut off Juan's protests. It was clear Isabella would not sway him either. He had decided. Pablo reached for a small gray cell phone lying in the middle of the table. He opened it solemnly and handed it over to Isabella.

Isabella's eyes flicked from her laptop screen to the phone. She punched in a number, then handed the phone back to Pablo.

They waited as it rang.

Pablo did not put the phone on speaker for the benefit of his wife or stepson. He shared so much with them and kept few things even from his guards. He had a reputation of being strangely open and keeping little to no privacy. Yet even Pablo wanted this conversation to be kept from his family. This moment would be his own. He held the phone close to his ear.

The line continued to ring.

Juan pursed his lips, eyes fixated on the phone. Isabella's face was a mask, unreadable.

There was a click. Static, then a breath.

"Go ahead." The voice on the other end was hard and flat, and full of contempt.

Pablo smiled. His voice would not be the one they expected, and he reveled in this surprise; the tension before a magician turns his hand.

"Your man is dead."

There was silence on the other end of the line.

"But perhaps you already knew that."

Some static and a shuffling sound.

"Who is this?" It was a different voice now. Another man's voice, hard, short, strong. A voice that gave commands instead of taking them.

"They call me the *patrón* of Antigua," Pablo continued. "I have always liked the title."

"Pablo Puentes."

He was surprised how quickly the man had identified him. He had hoped for a little more playfulness in this exchange. "It seems you have heard of me."

There was a brief pause, and Pablo thought he could hear the chattering of a computer keyboard. The voice spoke again.

"We know you front one of the largest illicit cartels in Latin America, dealing primarily in cocaine and sex trafficking. You extort protection money from half of Antigua. Money laundering. We know you have members of the *oligarcha familias* on your payroll

— the respected López family voted to suppress the anti-corruption commission. We know you are currently located at 117 Cortega Street. We know your wife, Isabella Muñoz, 43, and stepson, Juan Puentes, 27, and son Pablito Puentes, 8."

"It seems you know quite a lot about me."

"We even know you killed your brother Sandor Puentes. Does Isabella know that, Pablo? What about Juan? Mr. Puentes, this is an office of the United States of America's Central Intelligence Agency. We don't know a lot about you. We know *everything* about you."

Pablo had to admit, some of this was concerning. But a fire was lit in his mind and though Pablo's fists clenched, his smile did not waver. Instead, if anything, his determination was steeled. His voice cut the air like a knife.

"Do you know about this, Mr. Central Intelligence Agency?"

Pablo turned to Isabella, smiling, and nodded to her. She smiled back and took his hand and gave it a firm squeeze. Then she took a breath, shook herself, and sent a simple email to the man they were speaking with.

Pablo waited patiently. There was the sound of keyboards now — he was sure there was more than one — and hushed whispers saying something incoherent. Finally, the voice replied.

"You think you're clever, Puentes? You're not. We know about this."

Pablo put one of his hands up, as if making a sign of surrender, even though the man on the other end of the line couldn't see. He was enjoying himself. "Alright, alright. It seems there are no secrets. This is good. I hate secrets." Pablo leaned forward in his chair and bared his teeth. "I'm sure the American people know about this if it's no secret."

"If you send any of this information to the-"

"It is too bad you cannot do anything."

"Pablo, it appears you misunderstand the sheer power of the United States of America. Within hours, a Reaper drone loaded with

Hellfire missiles can be called to strike wherever we choose around the globe. Its blast is a focused fifty-foot kill radius. You and your family can run. We don't miss. It doesn't leave dirt in its crater because the thousand-degree Fahrenheit chemical reactions are too hot. It makes glass. I have 117 Cortega Street prepared for a priority cue. All I have to do is give the word."

"I don't think the Guatemalan government would like that very much, or the United Nations for that matter."

"For Christ's sake, we bankroll the United Nations. All I have to do," the man broke up the sentence for emphasis. "Is give. The. Word. Do you know what the word is, Pablo? The word is *go*. I know my drone pilots personally. Maybe they should get to know you too."

"My brother used to say it's not what you do, it's who you know."

Silence.

"I disagreed with him. It is what you do. That is why he is dead and I am alive. *Señor*, I have a very long list of emails for respected American journalists who are very good writers, and they write for very curious citizens. If I am killed, these journalists will receive the same information I sent to you."

More silence. Pablo thought for a moment that the line was dead. He continued anyway.

"My brother did not know what I could do. But you, you know what I can do. Perhaps you will be safe."

The silence continued for a moment, then there came a sound of exasperation.

"What do you want? What bizarre stroke of madness made you think you could get something out of this?"

Pablo shrugged. "Maybe send some money. Maybe do some favors." He leaned forward again. "But whatever you do, or do not do, does not matter. You cannot kill me. That is what you did not know. Now. You. Do."

He ended the call. Pablo snapped the small cell phone in two pieces and tossed the remains on the table in front of him. Juan let out a breath of air through his teeth. Pablo gave him a sideways glance and winked. Juan probably hadn't liked the way he had spoken about his late father. But Juan was his son now. He would be stronger. He would be part of something much bigger.

Isabella stroked his leg, bringing him out of his reflections. "You have become the most powerful man in Guatemala, *mi amor*."

"No," said Pablo, stroking her cheek, although she wasn't wrong. "I have become the most powerful man in America."

CHAPTER 2

Chief Operations Officer Mike Morrandon didn't know anyone who enjoyed bureaucracy, but everyone seemed to accept its necessity. He recognized it was the best way to keep power in check. He might even agree that it stymied corruption. But even the Romans had bureaucracy, and America wasn't about to be outdone by another empire, collapsed or not. Yes, bureaucrats were downright miserable people. And the CIA was a bureaucratic nightmare. He just hoped his meeting wouldn't be akin to a gladiatorial match. After all, he'd been the one to request it.

It didn't help that it was early in the morning. An earlier start than he was used to. Not that he usually slept well, but he was sure his colleagues weren't enthused about the morning's efforts either.

His cell phone reception was knocked out as soon as he'd driven close to Langley's CIA offices. The jammers were a basic precaution but an important one. The jammers added a helpful warning to American citizens as they drove by. If anyone was using their phone at the time, they'd know that the CIA was there, and the CIA would know you were, too.

He pulled into the parking lot after flashing his badge at the security guards manning the gate. Once parked, he made his way across a manicured lawn and up the steps to one of the imposing office buildings. A sharply dressed man and woman in matching suits, shades, and wired earpieces opened the double glass doors for Mike. He nodded thanks to the impassive bodies and passed over the threshold into the CIA's Special Activities Division (SAD) building. The acronym seemed apt as a small group of intelligence personnel hurried past him, murmuring to one another. Any hint of a personality was sterilized by the seriousness of what they all did for a living.

As far as Mike was concerned, the CIA *was* Special Activities. SAD was a department formed for the express purpose of giving the CIA an arm's length from any sensitive operations or public scrutiny, or anything the international community might not find particularly appetizing.

Needless to say, the department was huge.

All the offices at Langley were modern, clean, and constantly reminding anyone walking the halls that they had the best money could buy. He used to be amazed by it. He used to try and keep track of it all. But that was long before he had learned a thing or two about what money was able to do. He had encountered it directly, and more than once. Offers of payment or promotional whispers if he would lean this way or that, or send a team to check something out as a personal favor. He had always politely declined, forwarded the name off to Internal Affairs, and kept his head down. Nothing had happened in the three cases he'd experienced — at least visibly — but that was as much as he could do.

And that was money, something the average American consumer could understand, but it wasn't a budget. Budgets were different. Budgets were giant slices of a great big money pie that could hardly be fathomed by a single person. The Central Intelligence Agency had a budget of fifteen billion dollars. That was on the books. Mike would never know the exact number. In fact, it was possible that no one would ever know the exact amount, which was probably seen as a strategic win by many and a bitter foxhole by others. The last estimate, by an associated team conducting an audit that Mike happened to be privy to, revealed a figure at least quadruple of that on the books. But Mike — or anyone — hardly knew what that meant because of all the offices under, associated, and otherwise attached to the agency. It made Mike think of barnacles stuck to a harbor front or, perhaps more aptly, suckling piglets to a sow.

The CIA had become a sprawling monster with offices other offices didn't know about, positions other positions made up, and people that other people thought were inactive, elsewhere, or altogether dead. The only semblance of control came from oversight meetings, such as today's. They were a pain. They were sometimes too passive, and sometimes were corrupt. They also happened to be the only thing standing between fair use of powerful tactical units — like the one he was in charge of — and schoolyard bullies like his colleagues. Everything was off the record in the Special Operations Group as far as the CIA was concerned. Mike had learned to play ball.

He made his way up an elevator after passing through another security checkpoint, then found himself interrogated by a harsh secretary who refused to blink when he spoke. Eventually, he was allowed into the head offices of the Special Operations Group. For better or worse, this was his wheelhouse.

The spacious meeting room held plenty of tables surrounded by chairs, but only three were occupied. He was the last to the party, he noticed, although as he walked over to the chair left for him it looked like his colleague Paul Locklee was just getting settled himself. The man sat the Latin American desk for Special Operations. And he looked like he hadn't slept a wink.

As Mike approached, Locklee met his eyes with a furious glare.

Mike couldn't remember a time he'd truly gotten along with the man. Maybe it was because Locklee was the opposite of Mike in too many ways to reconcile. Locklee was built like a string bean on a diet, while Mike had started putting on a little extra after his metabolism had decided to kick him to the curb. Locklee was white, his ancestry looking like it lingered from some Danish isle or the other. Mike was a dark shade of black. Locklee dressed decently, but had a greasy gray ponytail that betrayed any common sense of style the man might have had. Mike's hair was trim, but he couldn't remember the last time his shirt wasn't wrinkled and felt lucky if his pants weren't stained. Locklee was a bastard who was dangerously good at his job.

So was Mike.

At a certain point the differences came to an end, even if he wasn't happy about it. They were all bastards when it really came down to it. Anyone working in the CIA probably thought that, but anyone working farther toward the basement knew it. SAD might be under the CIA, but the Special Operations Group didn't have windows.

Locklee was mad because he'd come to Mike with a mission request that he'd rather keep the blinds on, and Mike had called upon the faithful bureaucracy, which his boss Linda Kim represented, to let the sun shine in.

"Mike. Paul." Linda nodded curtly to them each respectively.

Linda was an older-than-middle-aged Korean woman who had carved a tight and successful career as director of the CIA's Special Operations Group. She could be a pain, but she was his boss, and it was times like these he appreciated how tight-laced she was. He suspected that respect was mutual, though he doubted she'd ever admit it. Apparently she'd had enough time to enjoy half a cup of coffee.

And there was one other person at the table. A stranger.

"I don't think either of you have met Sara Burnes. She's PAG. Works the Latin American desk over there."

Mike and Locklee both frowned in unison.

PAG stood for the Political Action Group. When they bothered to think at all, the American public always believed black operative organizations like Linda's Special Operations Group were the scary ones. Things like assassinations and sabotaging infrastructure across international borders came to mind, to assert American dominance and eliminate threats around the world. And they'd be right. But this didn't compare to the scale of what the Political Action Group's operations involved. They moved slowly over decades, methodically moving the global theatre toward the goal of American supremacy.

There was a reason SOG and PAG didn't usually mix.

They were on the same team, but worked two different angles. The SOG conducted more surgical, often militaristic missions; the PAG leveraged political situations and instances of diplomatic subterfuge. That was fine by Mike, as long as no one got in his way. He didn't like playing games to achieve his goals. But perhaps she would prove to be a pleasant distraction from all the nasty business that had fallen into his lap.

Pleasant distraction indeed.

She was undeniably attractive. She had the face and body of a world war propaganda pinup. White skin, bright blue eyes, light brown curls and not-too-thickly applied red lipstick greeted Mike with a smile. Too put-together for the hour.

"Nice to meet you," Mike said, his even tone a practiced neutral. He was careful not to betray any of his thoughts.

"Thank you for having me," Sara responded sweetly.

"What the fuck is she doing here?" Locklee asked, stabbing a finger at Sara.

Mike frowned again as Linda bristled. Sara's smile, however, remained plastered on her perfect unmoving face, unfazed as she spoke.

"We're hoping the Guatemalan government doesn't become a problem for us. For anyone. Perhaps we can pool some of our more specialized resources." Sara didn't take her eyes off Mike as she spoke.

Ah, he thought, *there's the kicker.*

Mike's position was highly enviable. He was head of a special, off-the-record Latin American task force known as Blackthorne. He could coordinate efforts across Latin America, initiating everything from intel-gathering to target elimination. He had agents scattered in various countries, ready at any moment to receive a phone call and execute his orders. If there was a person of interest in Latin America or a situation that needed follow-up, he was the CIA's most effective tool. That also meant he was usually saved for a last resort. He got the tough missions. He liked it that way.

He wasn't all-powerful. Linda was still his boss and had to approve everything before Mike could make a call, but he was used to intelligence personnel like Sara shimmying up next to him, or trigger-happy officers like Locklee using his team at every chance provided.

"I'm sorry, aren't you the folks who overthrew this same democratic government back in the good ol' days?" Locklee asked.

Sara shrugged. "That was a long time ago. I'm not quite that old, Paul."

Locklee looked like a tea kettle put to boil. He opened his mouth for another retort. Mike had the distinct feeling that he was back in high school.

"Now, people, let's play nice," Linda said flatly. "We're all here for the same reason. This Puentes character poses too great a threat to ignore. Paul, give us the briefing."

Locklee stopped his seething to adjust his wiry glasses, suddenly all business. He pulled out a thin file folder and lifted a couple pages, half reading from the page, half putting together his thoughts into words as they came.

"Two weeks ago, Blackthorne sent one of its agents to eliminate Sandor Puentes, a cartel lord in Antigua, Guatemala. His illicit affairs were well known and increasing in volume. Unfortunately, our agent was killed in the process."

His name was Brian. He was a good agent. And the mission was at your request, Locklee. Don't forget that. I sure haven't.

"Follow-up revealed Sandor Puentes had been eliminated after all, assumed to be the casualty of a coup by his younger brother, Pablo Puentes. Unfortunately, Pablo has become the new threat. At twelve thirty-three A.M., my office received a call from Pablo Puentes," Locklee said, glancing up from the printout in front of him. "In a surprise move, he has declared war on the agency, providing blackmail in an attempt at immunity."

Mike already knew where this was going. He didn't like it, but he had to leave things to Linda.

"Well, I can't say I'm a stranger to how these things work," Sara was saying. "It has a simple fix. Eliminate him and be done with it."

"Thank you for your input, Sara, but you're not here in an advisory capacity," Linda said pointedly.

Mike rubbed his forehead, feeling his wrinkles furrow with idle disappointment. There seemed to be too many of them recently.

Locklee crossed his arms. "The blackmail means we can't just take him out. He claims to have a kill switch; if he dies, the blackmail is released. What exactly are you bringing to the table, Sara? Or are you just here for the show?"

Linda's anger was palpable. "Paul, that is-"

She was cut off by a rude snort from Sara. "Our shows are a little more entertaining than this one." Her eyes flashed dangerously. Locklee seemed to back off, visibly giving her some breathing room. "We admittedly have an interest in the situation in Antigua," she said slowly. "Pablo has just inherited his late brother's illicit empire and could threaten our allies in the *familias oligarcas*. We are hoping the situation is stabilized once you folks are done."

"Once Pablo is dead, you mean," Mike said.

Sara closed her eyes and smiled, nodding in agreement as if he were a small child finally understanding the lesson she was trying to teach. When her eyes opened, she was looking at Locklee.

"Tell us about the blackmail, Paul. I'm curious."

Mike turned to his colleague, who was glaring back at Sara. Locklee finally pulled away and looked to Mike and Linda.

"It pertains to Sandor's assassination. He's wanting to reveal to the world and his government that an American assassin performed operations on foreign soil, killing a Guatemalan citizen in his home."

Mike scoffed. "They won't be able to prove any of that."

"Oh, I'm sorry, Mike, do you want to be the spokesperson for the legal shitstorm that will be hitting the fan? Or do you want to be the one who helps solve the situation?"

"By killing the brother now? Locklee, really, do we just keep knocking them off until there's no one left to complain?"

"*That's your fucking job!*"

"Enough!" Linda hissed.

Mike and Locklee shut up and snapped their attention to Linda without another word. Linda disregarded them, turning to the PAG woman instead.

"Sorry, Sara, I'm going to have to cut things here. Mission details are SOG only, and it looks like we have plenty to talk about."

Sara gave a little sigh, but she shrugged off any annoyance with a little shake of her heavily hair-sprayed head. "I understand. Good luck to you," she said to Linda while standing up, then turned to Mike and Locklee. "Gentlemen. Don't take too long." Her eyes hovered on Mike's a moment longer before she turned to leave.

Was that flirting? Or a threat?

Both made him uncomfortable. Locklee scowled and Mike quickly averted his gaze to focus back on his boss when Linda cleared her throat.

"This is embarrassing, to say the least," she snapped. "Blackmailing the CIA on top of everything already? The boys upstairs are on my ass because of the botched op. PAG is on my ass because an American agent has been exposed in an assassination attempt behind Guatemala's back. And it's no concession that our attempt was a failure. I am *not* going in front of some oversight committee and being told that Special Operations needs to pull out of Guatemala, and that it's time to simply ignore the drugs and sex trafficking that is ending up in goddamn America."

Linda didn't yell when she was angry. She didn't need to. Mike sucked in air as she continued.

"This is what is going to happen. Puentes will be removed. Blackthorne will complete this mission without a hitch. I want this kill switch — whatever form it might take — deactivated beforehand. And after all is said and done, I'm going to tell this PAG bitch she can do what she needs to in order to smooth things over. She will pass it up the chain that there's no problem here. Understand?"

They were silent for a moment.

"Thank you. Yes," said Locklee.

Mike didn't like that. Locklee agreeing with his angry boss was one thing, but being polite was another. Something was off. They were jumping from one failed mission into something that felt even worse. The man wasn't telling him everything. Luckily, he had other ways of getting the information he needed.

"Mike?" Linda prompted.

"Fine. If this is the way it's going to be, fine."

Locklee leaned back, seeming a little too relieved. Mike savored the pause.

"But no one is going to stop one of my agents from having a conversation with Pablo."

Linda narrowed her eyes, but didn't disagree with him. He appreciated that. Linda was hard but fair. His suggestion would be a lot more difficult than what Linda had been thinking. A simple hit and run now required a full-on interrogation, probably kidnapping the target, maybe coercing other guards or family close to Pablo. It could be messy. He didn't care. He owed it to Brian. Mike might be a CIA desk-jockey bastard, but he could give the dead agent that much.

"Fine. Just get it done. I don't want a repeat of last time."

Mike nodded and muttered his thanks as Locklee piped up.

"What, wait-"

"Is there a problem here, Locklee? I mean, aside from all the other problems we're dealing with?"

Locklee went a little red in the face, but held back whatever he was about to say.

"No. Never mind."

"Good."

When it was clear there was nothing left to discuss, they all stood and walked away, separately, without further comment — Linda back to her office, Mike and Locklee giving a wide berth between each other and avoiding the same elevator. If anyone had been watching, it would have seemed like an ordinary business meeting. But then, for members of the CIA's Special Operations Group, it may as well have been.

★★★

As soon as Mike was a mile away from the agency, he placed a call to his trusted assistant, Barker. He was a strange young man, but clever and loyal. Mike tried to look past Barker's more disturbing qualities.

"Chief?" came Barker's muffled reply. He was probably just waking up. "How was the meeting?"

"Shit. It's just as I thought. Locklee wants to nail the younger Puentes brother this time. Send another of our agents in for the kill."

"For the kill, or to get killed?"

That wouldn't normally be an appropriate remark, but Barker was too good at what he did. Mike let him have it. "We're being set up. It's Brian all over again."

"Right. But why? What's his angle?" Barker's tone betrayed too much curiosity over any concern he might've felt.

Mike frowned. "I don't know," he said, although it pained him. Mike clenched the car's steering wheel.

"Chief?"

Brian had been a good agent. A good man.

"We'll find out for sure," Mike said. "Linda approved an interrogation of the target."

A pause. "What? Sir, why?"

"Because I said so," Mike growled. "I want information. And Locklee doesn't know we already have someone on the inside."

"Yes, sir. Should I send the order?"

Mike rubbed his chin. "Yes. But she won't be alone. We're not doing another solo op." He paused, thinking about who he had scattered where in Latin America. Who would be best for the job? He'd need someone who could infiltrate; someone who could move through the region like they were part of it, and wouldn't think twice about getting answers from Puentes. All his agents fit the bill. But there was someone who Mike knew would want a chance at revenge. Someone who would do anything to see the mission through and get some answers. And that made all the difference.

"Barker?"

"Yes, sir?"

"Get me Carpenter."

CHAPTER 3

———

John Carpenter didn't dream often. But when he did, they were always full of dread.

He was jogging along a beach, and although he couldn't say where it was exactly, he somehow knew he was somewhere in Latin America. Sweat stained his armpits and chest. The beach was empty except for a lone figure up ahead, directly in his path. He moved to jog around them, but the man followed his movement. He slowed so he could meet the man. The man turned away, pulling ahead. John sped up again. Faster and faster. Legs pumping furiously. He knew who that figure was. It was his friend. His best friend, Brian. It had to be. And he had to stop him. But Brian kept running.

"Brian!"

John tried to call out but the wind was blowing hard in his face…

"Brian!"

And the sun had disappeared and his words were snatched away…

"Brian!"

Then he was in Washington. He knew it was Washington. He was running again, forgetting suddenly why he had been so worried — he was jogging along a paved path through a park, along the water near the Washington monument, birds chirping and cawing from their trees. He pulled up short when he reached a bench. There was a paper coffee cup sitting there, as if waiting for him. Another was spilled on the pavement in front of the bench. But no one was there.

The birds in the trees exploded in every direction, cawing and chirping frantically at some unseen threat. John spun around, reaching towards the back of his waistband for his gun. But there was nothing there. It should've been there. He always kept it there. And his phone was ringing. He didn't dare answer it. If he answered it, he'd know some horrible truth...

John's eyes shot open as the phone's ringing continued, slipping from his dream and into reality. His phone didn't ring often. But when it did, he had to answer it. Answering his phone was his job.

It was sitting on his night table, a cheap prepaid phone. The noise stopped after the second ring. As if the caller had hung up. Or hadn't meant to call at all.

John sat up in bed, snatching up the phone and blinking a couple times. Early morning light was just beginning to creep into the room. He was usually an early riser, but sleep had become a difficult thing the last little while.

He snapped open the phone.

There was a single line of text from an unknown number displayed.

Antigua, Guatemala.
54 Hernandez Street.
13:30.

So much could be said without two people ever speaking. John had never been a man of many words. It was fitting that he didn't need many to tell him what to do either. As long as they were precise, direct, and put him to work.

He memorized the information. Then he snapped the phone shut. The message would delete within a minute. He swung his legs over the side of the bed, resigned that he wouldn't be going back to sleep. A phone call put everything else on hold.

He was going to Guatemala.

***

John was on a plane out of Augusto C. Sandino International Airport in Managua, Nicaragua within hours. He had enjoyed the surfing, its beaches, and even its jungles. But now it was time to leave. Now it was time to work.

Normally he'd be at relative ease. The flight was short — a hop and a skip over Honduras and El Salvador, and he'd be making land. Flying didn't gave him nerves and it wasn't the upcoming mission either. No one ever truly lost the adrenaline that came with the start of a new operation, that little spark of excitement could never be shrugged off. But he didn't have the pre-op jitters. That's not what was bothering him. John was too experienced for that.

He didn't need reminding. Turning thirty he could handle. Pushing forty put a different spin on things. The gray in his hair was stubborn but he said a silent prayer for avoiding going bald for this long. He caught his reflection in the plane window and tightened the cap he was wearing. The Canadian pin stuck to its front flashed, glinting sunlight off a blood-red edge.

It was a good country. He wore the hat to emphasize his Canadian heritage, which was always a safer bet when traveling. And although lacking in the accent and boisterousness, he was also half-American.

His parents had divorced long ago. He had been born and raised in his mother's country, getting his high school diploma on the east coast of Canada. He hadn't had any true ambition to pursue post-secondary, even though his mother had pushed him to do so. John had been average all his life. Still was in many ways. Taller than many, but still passing for average. Average weight, although muscled more now. Average looks. He had a strong jaw and gray-blue eyes that pierced like a hawk's, but spotting him in a crowd would leave him forgotten.

His only distinguishable personality trait was his seriousness. People described him as cold. Grim, even. John knew he didn't empathize the same way as others, or process emotions as readily. But he still felt average in all the other ways. He didn't feel like a special person. Not really. But his training begged otherwise.

It had started when his father intervened, after his mother's prodding to get John somewhere further after high school fell flat. His father was a hard Oregon man and was determined to find something that would be good for his son. The U.S. Navy was offering generous scholarships and was hungry for young, able-bodied men. John had never had many friends so the move hadn't been hard, but it had changed things with his mother.

It had been a rash decision to join up, but it was an attempt to beat back the feeling of being nothing but average. He could never have been prepared for how it would change him, or for the path it would set him on. Part of the attraction came from a place of unbridled and unabashed masculine desire. The image of the strong, crisp soldier in uniform, taking orders and fighting against all odds for victory and glory. The Navy was more than these things, of course. A part of young John Carpenter must've known. The other part signed up anyway.

The experience had been a cruel shock for John. He was able to fit into the soldier's mold well enough; orders and discipline weren't a problem. But the culture was. Americans were different than Canadians. Louder, prouder, and meaner in his initial experience. But besides Americans, soldiers had a different way of life than any civilian could imagine. The social aspects were the hardest. John had never drunk more in his life (and never could outmatch himself after). Partying altogether had been a foreign concept for him. Previously he'd been considered somewhat of a loner. He liked the physical activity of it all; being active and pushing himself spoke to both his natural resolve and his testosterone. But the boredom was a brutal reality of the soldier's life. He had heard about it, but living it was something else. Still, he seemed to have a better mental discipline to handle it than many of his compatriots. He'd also seen combat. Two battles, one of which he hardly felt he'd participated due to orders that placed him far from where the real fighting took place; the other had been a true skirmish experience, brief but dangerous. Both instances left him unsatisfied to be called a combat-veteran.

He'd been happy to bring some stability to troubled regions. There were murmurings that the military did more harm than good, but he had to content himself with his own efforts as an example of something worthwhile. But besides hopefully helping the local society, his tour had an important perk.

Travel.

He'd expected to be in Africa or the Middle-East, but fate had placed his company in Latin America — a region containing a plethora of countries he knew next to nothing about.

He fell in love.

It had been a reluctant rise to appreciation. The absorption of culture and climate and society was slow but sure. The cuisine may not have impressed him, but the people and geography had.

He was in Panama first, then Nicaragua, then Guatemala. He picked up the language, the feel, the nuance in each region as best he could.

Better than most. It was clear he worked harder at it. Practicing language amidst the boredom. Refusing card games in favor of language lessons and a local explaining any and all cultural particularities.

The brass took notice. After his mandatory tour and his eagerness to stay on, a few officers had thrown his name around and suggested he get further education and training. They didn't want him stuck and plateauing. They told him he was ripe for potential. Some of them joked they didn't want to see John end up like them.

One of those officers knew a Navy SEAL trainer and put in a word, just to see what would be good for John. But the trainer wasn't interested in asking around or moving John elsewhere. He'd either take the kid on or stay out of it.

John took the plunge.

It was the most challenging thing he'd ever done in his life. It would probably remain that way. If John had thought Navy training was tough, becoming a SEAL was pure hell. He was broken down and built back up, stronger in ways he couldn't imagine ever becoming. Sometimes he thought about the training. Other times it seemed like a strange dream. Either way, it was simply a part of him now. Who he was.

It was also hard because he had found his passion for Latin America, but had to leave it behind. The SEALs allowed him to enroll in college classes, perfecting his knowledge of Latin-American culture, religion, and of course, the language. SEALs were encouraged to have college degrees and John's education was considered an important asset for the team, so it was fully paid for. Say what one will of the military; it took care of its own.

Graduation was a double blessing. A completed degree to the delight of his mother, who was becoming less estranged, and the perfect capstone to the accumulation of all his training: the Navy, SEALs, and a diploma in his hands. He could achieve a good position and pay, and live the good life.

But it was hardly a year before he was pulled by a strange detachment. Definitely not the Navy, much as they'd like to have him back. He was overqualified. And it wasn't the army, or another

Navy branch. No, these recruiters spoke and acted like civilians. But John could sense they were equipped with military minds.

He was never told it was the CIA. He'd never asked. He'd been told they'd never speak again if he did. If he accepted their offer of recruitment, he'd work for America and would undergo another round of specialized training to expand an already extensive record. He was a prime candidate.

He would've said no, but was offered generous pay and further education options on their dime. He didn't need more money. The education was a nice perk. He had hesitated. Then they laid the perfect bait. His job postings would only be across Latin America. Freedom of travel throughout as long as he came when called and performed as necessary.

He took the bait. They weren't surprised. It was what they did for a living.

Training had been brutal again. Different than what he'd gone through with the SEALs. More psychological than anything. More covert. More focus on solo ability. And once it was done, he had become a killing machine.

He worked for a group only known to him as the Firm. He knew his handler's codename, Esteban, and a few other agents who he worked with on missions. His regional residences varied across Latin America. His comings and goings were indeed loose, thankfully. But when orders came — always by cell, always brief, always direct — he moved. He tracked. He killed.

This time should've been no different.

He loved Guatemala. It was a beautiful country. For all its poverty, corruption, and unstable infrastructure, it was welcoming, warm, and bursting at the seams with joy. The people were the happiest he'd ever seen. And Antigua was one of Guatemala's gems. But Antigua meant something else to John. Something darker.

A week ago, John had sent Brian an email. Agents were not supposed to contact each other, but the job was a lonely one. John was a solitary creature, but for the first time since he could remember, he had made a good friend. He didn't want to lose that. The emails they shared were brief, devoid of any work details, and encrypted. If the Firm took issue, they would shut it down. The messages were almost certainly monitored. That was fine.

Last week John had sent Brian an email. He had received an almost immediate response.

Asset is KIA. Cease email.
—Esteban

John rested his head against the plane window, closing his eyes, letting the rhythm of the plane's engines lure him into calmness. He couldn't avoid his sadness, but he could avoid that feeling he got when he remembered. It was a haunting feeling, the undeniable wrongness of a good friend who was no longer alive, removed altogether from his life. Memories remained. Nothing else.

Brian had died in Antigua.

He didn't know how. It was classified information. John had been kept in the dark. He was always kept in the dark. It wasn't usually a problem — it had never bothered him before. Not really. Not until now.

He'd always done his job. Done his job well. Now…

Now it was personal.

And John had a good feeling this operation would be linked to whatever Brian had been ordered to do. It might even be the same mission. The Firm had an interest in Antigua. He didn't know what it was, but he'd find out soon enough.

And then he'd get the answers he needed.

CHAPTER 4

The master bedroom in Pablo's compound was the size of a small apartment. A massive king-sized bed sat in its center, on a round hand-woven carpet spilling out from under the claw foot legs propping it up. The colors were a rainbow of purples and reds and yellows, looking like a flattened egg from some fairy tale. The bed matched its sentiment with white silks flowing from the brass canopy. The bed was raised four feet off the ground and seemed difficult to climb into, but there was a helpful stepladder at the side for just this purpose.

It was the first time Marcela had been in the room. Black bereted guards had opened the great double bay doors for her and as she entered across the threshold, she knew she had made some progress in her mission. Years of training and experience couldn't stop her heart from pounding.

She noticed Juan first, sitting in a cushioned chair next to the bedside. His legs were crossed and his hands clasped, chin resting upon them. He was desperately trying to look comfortable amidst the men flanking him. It was then that she noticed there were guards around the entire room. Everyone was watching, and it was not only odd but disturbing.

The bed loomed before her. The silk canopy bed curtains were translucent enough for her to see Pablo sitting cross-legged on a pile of pillows, naked. His bare chest looked broader and thicker without one of his usual thin cream shirts covering it. A similar effect fell on his shoulders and arms, making them look stronger and larger as they rested at his side.

She could hear the sounds of sex. A woman's moaning, lips kissing, skin rubbing, the light wet smacking sound of fluid and flesh. Marcela didn't have much of a chance to think about it.

"Strip," Pablo commanded.

Marcela did as she was told. The room was hot and stuffy with all the bodies in the space, but she felt cold as the last of her garments were removed. Nakedness would always remain a vulnerability for most. But not her.

My body is a weapon, she reminded herself. It was an old creed, but it carried on because it was true. The last of her clothing fell to the ground. Pablo smiled.

"Juan, *mi niño*, what do you think of her?"

Juan looked at Marcela with a cold expression, brow furrowed and lips pursed. As he examined her up and down his eyes lingered on her small breasts. She saw his imagination working behind his eyes; a fantasy playing out in his mind. But Juan simply blinked and said, "She is very beautiful, *tio*."

"You must get used to calling me *papá*, *mi niño*, just as Pablito does. Maybe he can help teach you."

Juan bristled, but nodded.

"Or maybe Marcela will. Marcela may call me *papá*." Pablo reached a hand out to Marcela, emerging through the curtains. For some reason this lazy gesture was terrifying. For an instant Marcela felt a shiver run up her spine, despite the heat of the room. She composed herself.

Working for the Firm required her to do many difficult things, some monstrous enough to make her reconsider her humanity from time to time, let alone working for the Firm. The temptation of fleeing had crossed her mind, embarrassingly, more than once. But these were the times she cleared her head, remembered what she had committed to, remembered the underlying reasons why she began, and the ultimate end goals that drove her on, staying her course.

She took Pablo's hand, feigning shyness, and let herself be led up the stepladder and into the massive bed.

Being a female agent meant she used sex as leverage more than if she were a man. This bothered her on some level; it felt demeaning that for all her abilities it often came down to the shake of her ass to disarm a target. But she was also aware of the variety of ways to work a target, and men couldn't do what she could. She was prepared to do what was required of her. What disturbed her most now was not sex — far from it — it was the absurdity of the way Pablo ran his master bedroom. She managed not to glance at the guards around the room. Marcela had been exposed to some strange kinks in the past, and a few had even been surprisingly appealing, but this made her feel distinctly uncomfortable.

"You look better without clothes, *mi querida*."

Marcela made herself blush and covered her breasts, playing the shy maiden so many men enjoyed. But Pablo did not bite.

"Maybe we should have you naked all the time. What do you think, Juan?"

Marcela turned to see Juan staring back at her through the translucent silken sheets.

"I think that might be too much." He frowned. He was handsome, Marcela had to admit, but he was also wicked.

Pablo shrugged. "Maybe, maybe not." He leaned in to whisper to Marcela. His breath was hot and smelled of crisp mint. "I don't hide anything. That way everyone is kept safe."

The blankets stirred and Pablo lifted them, revealing Isabella's head at his crotch. The woman's long black hair was a tangled mess, but even then she looked composed and beautiful. She licked her lips and brought herself to sit naked on her thighs. Her breasts hung lightly and Pablo cupped one as he put an arm around her.

It was fitting Isabella was here. It had been she who had hired her.

"It seems Marcela is still shy," Pablo said to Isabella. "Why don't we show her we are all family here?"

Isabella moved toward Marcela, groped her lips with her fingers, then moved onto her neck and bit her ear, hard. Pablo began to probe Marcela's waist. His fingers walked down one at a time, inching lower and lower. He exhaled a deep, quiet chuckle of satisfaction into her ear.

Marcela kissed Isabella and felt pleasure begin to ebb at the touch of Pablo's fingers. Pablo said he had no secrets, but she knew a couple managed to remain hidden. She would fish out the information she needed and disable the kill switch. She would get what she wanted, and maybe more. So she spoke on cue.

"Oh, *papá*…"

Ringing the walls of the room, guards stood and watched impassively.

***

Later, when Marcela had retired to her room, she checked her special prepaid cell phone hidden among some clothing in a bottom drawer. She checked it constantly throughout the day, but hadn't received word from the Firm since she had arrived almost two weeks ago. She had done her job. But it felt hollow. She had integrated into the Puentes estate, and tonight had been proof of that progress, but the winds of what Pablo was up to were changing.

She didn't expect communications with the Firm to be any different this time. Instead, there was one unread text. Her eyes lit up with disbelief at the words on the screen:

Backup en route.
Rendezvous at birdfeeder 13:30

Relief washed over her. She'd find a way to slip out and meet her backup at the safe house. It was time to finally get this mission underway. With talk of a kill switch and Pablo taking on the United States, she had a hunch what lay ahead. She licked her lips, committed the message to memory, and watched it disappear from her phone.

CHAPTER 5

———

La Aurora International Airport was large by Latin American standards, but small in comparison to most first-world countries. Located in Guatemala City, it was the closest airport to Antigua, but John would still have to drive an hour to get there.

He had no trouble with security, his passport quickly ushering him through. He pushed against a crowd mostly made up of tourists, noticing many Guatemalans as well. They were lighter-skinned than most people assumed, ancestors of Spanish invaders who would eventually dominate the country and its native inhabitants, the Maya. John picked out any Mayan descendants with ease. They were darker and usually squatter, but they weren't part of the crowds of landed travelers or those getting ready to take off. They were pushing baggage and cleaning supply carts, pointing directions, and running the airport's stores.

He was tempted to stop for a coffee or something to eat, but decided to press on without. The sooner he arrived at his destination, the sooner he could rest if he needed to.

The sun shone bright and hot, nearly blinding him as he exited the airport. Nicaragua had boasted the same sunshine, but he had traveled while it was still dark and he'd been cooped up in a plane.

It was surprisingly refreshing. He blinked a couple times, breathing deeply, but was suddenly interrupted by a coughing fit. Guatemala was dusty, and the dust was irritating to tourists, foreigners, and natives alike.

"Hello. Do you need a taxi?"

John wiped his mouth and looked up at a short man with a plain face. He was shorter by John by a foot and was unmistakably Mayan. His accent hung heavy over his English.

"*Si, graçias,*" John said, looking for the man's cab. "*Me voy a Antigua.*" *I'm going to Antigua.*

The man smiled, whether from John's practiced Spanish or from the declaration of a hefty cab fare, he couldn't tell. The driver gestured to a car not far from where they stood. John was glad he didn't have to hail one. The man moved to take John's bag, but John waved him away.

"No, *graçias.*"

The man shrugged, opened the back door of the cab for John, then made for the driver's seat. After a bit of honking and cursing, they managed to squeeze out of the airport's parking and pulled onto RN-10. Traffic crawled at the same pace the sun continued its lazy ascent.

John tried not to yawn as he pulled his bag off his back and moved it onto his lap. He didn't own much because he was always traveling, whether by choice or by duty. Some things he kept at his different residences, but even then he'd never been much of a materialist. He wasn't the kind to get attached to a trinket or keepsake. Everything he carried was all he needed: different passports, money, cellphone, earbuds, some clothing, toiletries, a couple small pill bottles, fake wallet with a few American bills, and a reliable Glock 19, complete with silencer and ammunition. His life. Everything sat neatly in the bag except the fake wallet and gun. Those two he always kept on his person.

They passed much of the drive in silence. John watched drivers and passengers slowly creeping by on the road, and he took in the smell of diesel and hot asphalt. There were a few used American orange school buses belching black smoke. Some still had the names of American school districts painted on their sides. Guatemala could be dangerous for the unwary, and he wasn't about to get in any trouble before his mission even began. John remained alert.

After an hour and a half of driving, they finally pulled into Antigua. John felt the weather changing as they drew up into the mountains. Most people (especially tourists) assumed Antigua was hot like most of Guatemala. In reality, it could be chilly, earning the city the title of 'Land of Eternal Spring' because of how similar the weather felt. The sun shone a deep yellow, illuminating the colors of the city. John loved the pastels and vibrancies of buildings and people alike. Houses were bright blue, orange, and pink. Mayan women wore colorful traditional dresses as they moved through the streets. The cab pulled under the *Arco de Santa Catalina*, one of the most famous landmarks of the city of Antigua. Most people didn't know of the hidden passageway within the arch. It had been used by cloistered nuns who were not allowed to be seen in public, allowing them to cross the street from their convent and teach at a school on the other end of the arch. John couldn't help but smile when he saw it. The saffron arch, complete with its old clock face, was so iconic, finding its way onto many postcards.

His eyes continued to peer past to an even greater sight. Beyond the view of the city, among the white clouds, rose the dormant *Volcán de Agua*. It sat mysterious and magnificent, defiant of man's creations, a constant reminder of nature's power.

The cab driver flicked his gaze to John in the rear-view mirror. He looked back at him, but the man quickly looked away, back to the road. John was slowly inching his hand to the gun in the back of his waistband when the car abruptly turned into an alley and jerked to a stop as the driver put it in park.

"Aquí estás, señor. Antigua." Here you are, sir. Antigua.

"Graçias. ¿Cuánto cuesta?" Thank you. How much?

The driver spun towards John clumsily in his seat, pointing a gun at him all the same.

"Dame todo." All of it.

John looked calmly at the barrel of the gun and then up at the man's eyes. He knew there was a chance of being mugged on the way over. He hoped his seasoned Spanish would distinguish himself from a mere tourist and hoped the long cab ride fare would be enough to satiate any greed that violence could relinquish.

Petty thoughts didn't eliminate the threat.

"Ahora mismo!" the man yelled. *Now!*

"Si. Bueno," John said, slow so as not to startle the man.

John wasn't scared.

His adrenaline was flowing to be sure, but he didn't fear for his life or for injury. If anything, he felt an anxiety that the mission would probably fail with him dead. But he was pretty sure he'd live through this one. His backpack, though small, was bulletproof.

Many people were skeptical when it came to Kevlar and other bullet-proofing products. Many didn't think bullet-proofing could stop point-blank bullets. Most of the time that depended on calibre. The average bullet-proof vest wouldn't stop a rifle's round at point-blank range, but John's level IV grade armor plate was one inch of ceramic, Kevlar, and ultra-high density poly-ethylene. His bag insert was more than enough to save him from a petty 9mm round.

Just as John's hand clenched the familiar grip of his own gun, a motorcycle engine revved loudly as it pulled up next to the car. The driver didn't have time to turn to see it.

His head exploded as if a small bomb had sat in the middle of his skull. Brains and blood plastered the passenger side window. A small bullet hole centred on the window.

John hadn't drawn his pistol. He did now though, keeping it close and hidden next to his leg.

A woman in a black leather jacket sat on a motorcycle just outside the car, her helmet hiding her face and a gun smoking in her hand. She turned to John.

"*Vamos!*"

John's expression relaxed at the sound of her voice, his shoulders easing slightly, and his breath returned to its steady intake. He knew who she was. He tucked his gun away, opened the door, and mounted the motorcycle, careful to tighten his pack first.

She tapped her helmet, revved the engine, and they flew from the scene.

"We were supposed to meet at the safe house," John said as they took a sharp turn at a street corner. "What are you doing here?"

"Saving your life!" Her voice was muffled by the helmet but it remained sharp against the wind. "You are lucky I spotted you in that cab when you pulled into Antigua."

"I was fine."

"You almost got yourself killed! I'd have to take care of Pablo myself! You're supposed to be my backup!"

John frowned. "Am I being targeted?"

Marcela scoffed. "No. You are just a dumbfuck."

John suppressed a smile. "Alright. Okay."

They tore past a fleet of tuk-tuks, the open windowed vehicles veering precariously on their three wheels as they tried to get out of the way. Marcela turned immediately to take a corner, speeding past *Iglesia de La Merced* — a massive baroque church that served as one of Antigua's most notable landmarks — then darted through and out of an alley, nearly plowing through a group of tourists and Mayan vendors. She slowed once they were far from the scene, slipping into the town and taking the street as if they were out for a leisurely ride.

"Good to see you again, Marcela."

John felt her soften, tension leaving her grip on the motorcycle's steering and leaving her tone as well. He knew she was smiling through her helmet.

"Welcome back to Antigua, John. I hope your stay is better than your arrival."

He grimaced but didn't reply.

She turned once more onto Hernandez Street, pulled to a curb, then pulled the key from the bike, leaving the engine to die. John dismounted and followed her, already moving to a small nondescript apartment.

54 Hernandez.

No one was in the building when they entered. He suspected the rooms were all vacant. Marcela pulled off her motorcycle helmet and shook her head, letting a shower of dark hair fall down her back without breaking her stride. She climbed a flight of stairs and stopped at one of the doors. She pulled a pair of keys from her pocket and inserted one into the lock.

"Our place is safe, but drafty."

She opened the door then closed it before John could take a step forward. Somewhere the door made a barely audible click, and she opened it again to let him through. Then she closed it behind them, deliberately. John gave her an inquisitive look.

She pointed. "See the stove over there?" Directly across the room, a quaint stove sat in the apartment kitchenette. "If the door opens, it arms the stove. High pressure propane. *Boom*." She blew into his face and flicked his nose. He swatted her hand away. "Leaving the door open or closing it once keeps it armed. Goes off in one minute. Disarm it by opening and closing again."

"Thorough." Such measures used to surprise John. Not anymore. He smiled inwardly at the wave of nostalgia and focused on committing the safeguard to memory.

"Excessive." She gave him a mock sigh, then winked. "But yes, thorough."

The apartment was barely two rooms, and sparsely furnished. Whites, creams, and pastels colored the walls, and the place reflected a normalcy so obvious it was almost suspicious. Marcela tossed her backpack on the kitchen table and put her motorcycle helmet next to it.

"You've been here before?"

"*Si*. For communications when I first got here. Periodically since. Not often."

John threw his own backpack on a kitchen chair. "How long have you been in the city?"

"Too long." She counted out two fingers and held them up. "Almost two weeks."

"Undercover?"

She nodded. John blew out some air. Going undercover for a long period of time took its toll. They were both trained in it, but both also preferred simpler missions.

She held out her phone to him and he took it, passing his own over. They put their numbers in so they could text each other any information they'd need to share. It was always better to share information in person when possible, but both their phones were equipped with two-way encrypted text software, and a removal app. Marcela couldn't see the text he'd received from Esteban even if she wanted to. No tracing. No saved messages. As soon as he had his phone back, John turned to business.

"What did Esteban tell you?"

"What you'd expect."

That meant nothing.

It definitely wasn't his real name, but Esteban was who John knew to be their handler at the Firm. He'd heard the man's tight voice over the phone for mission briefings and in-op situations, but John had never met Esteban in person. At least, not that he knew of.

"Ah, Esteban. Ever cryptic. He loves playing the spy."

John thought about that. "He's cautious."

Marcela shrugged. "He can be cautious once he's in the field. Speaking of which." She glanced at her phone and gave it a tap. "I have to get back soon. My excuses only last so long."

John took the hint. "Let's get briefed, then."

John swept through the safe house and investigated, seeing what was at their disposal. He found a laptop in a desk. When he turned it on, he found it didn't have much on it, but it held one of their decoding programs. He mentioned it to Marcela but she waved him over, distracted by something.

She had found a prepaid cell phone in a glass jar of rice. John made his way over and plugged in his earbuds, giving one to Marcela while she checked for messages.

"You have one new message," the voicemail responded in an automated female voice. "Message will expire in twenty hours."

Marcela punched a number to proceed.

"Please enter your password."

She input the code that agents had received for that week.

Esteban's hard monotone finally came through the phone.

"Target is Pablo Puentes. Capture, interrogate, and eliminate him. He has a kill switch. Unknown location, unknown style. Locate and disable it before dealing with Pablo. I want this done in under a week. Plan at your own discretion." The message ended there.

John's brow furrowed as Marcela deleted the message and returned the phone. He tucked the earbuds away.

"A kill switch?"

She slacked her jaw and gave an unflattering impression of Esteban's low voice, drawing her chin all the way to her neck. "'Unknown location, unknown style.'"

John hardly reacted, but Marcela was used to the stony expression so many others found unnerving. In the few opportunities they had worked together, it always surprised him how comfortable she could be. He enjoyed the opportunity to plan and talk aloud with Marcela. Especially in light of Esteban having a habit of providing the bare bones of what he wanted them to do. This mission in particular had some less than desirable parts to it.

"We'll have to figure out how to deal with that."

"That's not the only thing we have to worry about."

John inclined his head for her to continue. She replied by rummaging the cupboards, finding an electric kettle in a bottom drawer. She bent over to pick it up. A younger John would have gawked, but instead he looked away. When he turned back, she was eyeing him suspiciously as she filled the kettle with water.

He cleared his throat. "Tell me about Pablo."

"Pablo Puentes isn't your average cartel leader," she said while she untied the laces of her boots. "He has recently inherited his empire from his brother Sandor, who was very respected by friends and foes alike. He was like a bee." Marcela plucked at her jacket. "Mind if I take this off?" she asked.

John shrugged and she pulled it off, revealing a tight tank top underneath. John waited for her to continue, but had to eventually prompt her. "Like a bee?"

"Yes…you know…a bee." She managed to pull a boot off and got to work on the other. "Always jumping from flower to flower. He was very social. Always with people, always at parties."

John nodded. "A social butterfly."

"Bee, butterfly, whatever." She took a breath. "Pablo is similar but more…" she frowned, thinking of the word. "Unpredictable. He will be hard to catch, John."

"Good thing there's two of us."

"We need two of us. To find and disable this strange kill switch, and to capture him. Not a one-person job. Besides, it's not as if I requested you." She sighed. "I'd have called for one of the new guys. Break him in a bit." She grinned mischievously and gave John a teasing wink. John pretended to forget his age for a moment.

Marcela found a teabag and mug and poured the kettle.

"Alright. What else?"

"He has guards watching him at all times."

"Alright. Guards are no problem."

"Guards *are* a problem, Carpenter," she said as she stirred sugar into her mug. "Guards all the time. *Veinticuatro siete.*" *Twenty-four seven.* She lifted her tank top a couple inches and used it to fan her midriff. "When I say all the time, I mean *all the time.* He's indifferent about privacy. Trust me on that."

"What's wrong with that? You seem indifferent about privacy."

Marcela paused just as she was licking her spoon. He smiled sheepishly and she tossed a boot off the floor at him. It was so quick he took it full in the gut.

"I can't get him alone. Pablo may be a rich and evil man, but even so, why can't he enjoy a glass of wine alone with his sweet Marcela?"

"Maybe he doesn't trust his sweet Marcela," John coughed.

She shrugged. "He likes me very much, but do not confuse that with love. He loves his wife. He loves his little *hijo.* He does not love me. He trusts me, but he does not listen to me."

"Tell me about the son."

"Which one?" she asked. John spread his hands and shrugged with them. She tapped her spoon on the tip of her lip. "Juan is his son by his wife, Isabella. He is *el comandante* of the guards. He is strong, but inside he is just a little boy trying to make his *papá* proud." She put a hand over her heart in mock tenderness.

"You're sleeping with him?"

She raised her eyebrows at that but nodded, showing no shame if she felt it. Sex was as much a part of their work as anything else.

"And Pablo doesn't know? What about these constant guards?"

"As I said, Juan is *el comandante* of the guards. It seems there are some ways in and out that are unseen. That doesn't change the fact that they watch when I sleep with Pablo and Isabella."

John paused for a moment, caught off guard. He changed the subject quickly. "Tell me about Isabella, then." Marcela didn't seem to notice his discomfort.

"Not much to tell. She was married to Sandor, and is now married to Pablo. She was the one who hired me."

"She hired you for Pablo?"

Marcela shrugged. "They are adventurous."

John rubbed the stubble on his chin. He was trying to figure out how to work all this.

"Is there tension?"

"Oh yes. Between the two men. Pablo has inherited Sandor's power and Juan is treated like a little boy."

"We can use that."

"We can."

"Okay. Back to Pablo. He's never alone."

Marcela looked at him more seriously than before. "Never. He lives in a heavily guarded compound with heavily guarded guards. And so do I." She chuckled to herself. John waited patiently for her to continue. "He leaves by helicopter sometimes. I assume for business. Colombia. Who knows? Oh, and he will go into different towns around Guatemala, sometimes as if he were *nómada*."

"Is he paranoid?"

"No." She shrugged. "He's confident. He wants to be with his people. Mayans."

John didn't point out that that would include Marcela.

"Overconfident?"

"Sure." She shrugged and took a drink of her tea. "You could walk into his compound and he wouldn't care. He knows he is safe and knows people fear him. He has bought all the right people." She took another hasty drink of her tea and pulled out her phone. She gave it a tap, then tucked it away.

"I have to go soon."

John glanced at the ceiling for a moment. The plaster was ugly and eroding.

"We'll need to go through the house. Room by room if we have to," he said. "It won't do for me to stay on the outside. You'll need me to help you with the legwork."

"You'd like that, wouldn't you, Carpenter?" She tossed him another look that briefly tested his willpower. "I've been doing plenty of legwork. Speaking of which. I can't forget these."

She walked over to the corner of the room where a shopping bag sat.

"What's that?" John thought it was probably weaponry. She may have been wanting to smuggle something in for the coming job.

"Shoes!" Marcela exclaimed. She pulled out a pair of lavish-looking heels. She laughed at the blank expression on John's face. "I am a status symbol for Pablo. He gives me money, I go shopping. I kept these here in case I needed an excuse for being out. Do you like them?" She bent her knees as if she were posing in a picture, holding the shoes next to her feet.

John frowned. "Do we have anything on the kill switch?"

Marcela scrunched up her face, stuffed the shoes into her backpack, and returned to her mug of tea. "I don't know where it would be. But I haven't exactly been able to search every room. Juan probably knows about it." She held up a hand to stop John from interrupting. "Pablo was angry a few nights ago. I pushed him for information and he hinted at it. Said he had something that would 'crawl into my enemy's camp and eat them from within' if he were killed. He wasn't just spitting *veneno*. He's actually a very calm man, John." She took another drink of her tea, then began to put on her new heels. "Pablo's language is not sex. Surprising, I know. But now we know that. We will speak to him another way. Something closer to his heart."

"Which is where I come in." John leaned back on the edge of a kitchen chair. "I've been trying to come up with a plan this whole time, but you already have one."

She had been leaning on the edge of the kitchen counter but now stood up, determination in her posture. "We will get you close to his son, Pablito."

"Juan's younger brother?"

Marcela shook her head. "Cousin. Pablo says he had a lover but they couldn't be together. So she left him with the son. Tragic." She rolled her eyes. "I suspect this mysterious lover may indeed be Isabella. Juan has whispered his horror at such a possibility of it to me before. But who can know?"

"More tension."

Marcela rubbed her hands together as if she were starting a fire.

"I will tell my sweet Pablo that Pablito should have not just a good English tutor, but a tutor to teach him even better Spanish. The language of business and the language of his *papá*." John opened his mouth to protest the likelihood of such a plan, but Marcela knew the situation better than he could ever know. "Don't worry," she said, "I'll make sure you have an open position. Tutors come and go."

John's concern was replaced with a rising realization. Marcela must have known what a treat this would be for him. "Marcela, you've left me hardly any work. I'll get so caught up in teaching I'll hardly remember to do anything else."

"John Carpenter, as fluent in death as he is in Spanish," she shot back.

The lack of response from John made her realize that her words were harsher than she meant them to be, but they'd been said.

Marcela finished drinking her tea and placed the mug in the sink.

"Would you mind washing that for me, John? *Graçias*." She looked at her phone again, beginning to rush.

"Marcela."

"What?"

"How did Sandor Puentes die?"

"Some killer. Professional. They killed each other."

John held his breath. "What was your mission? Before I got here."

She froze for a brief moment, then slowly put her phone away. They weren't supposed to talk about previous missions or assignment details. And John wasn't one to break rules.

"Did it have anything to do with-?"

"Yes," she said, locking eyes with him as she moved closer. "Brian."

A chill went down his back. His whole body tensed as he watched her every move.

"Esteban wanted me in position," she continued. "Information gathering. Regarding the killing." She held up a hand before he could start. "I didn't find anything useful. Yes, I would tell you if I did." She brushed his shoulders as if dust had collected there. "But now the mission has changed."

"Maybe we'll get some answers," John said.

Marcela smiled up at him and swung her jacket and backpack over her shoulders.

"Put on a fake moustache and a flower shirt. Reacquaint yourself with the city," she said.

His voice struggled for a moment and came out softer than he meant. "It's not my first time in Antigua, Marcela."

"No, John, it's not." She winked at him and made her way to the door. She opened her mouth to say something then seemed to change her mind. John spoke instead.

"Marcela?"

"Yes, John?"

"When we interrogate Pablo, I'll be the one doing it."

She pursed her lips, then shrugged. He nodded slowly to her and she nodded back, opened the door, and left. She opened and closed it again for him on the other side to disarm the trap.

He stood there longer than he meant to, his mind swirling with all but forgotten memories, and thinking about how Marcela could disarm him easier than the stove.

CHAPTER 6

In his past visits, Washington D.C. always seemed cold to John. In part, that had to do with the bad weather that always seemed to plague him when he visited. It also had to do with the nature of most of his trips. D.C. was a place for debriefs, clandestine meetings, and generally grim news from some official or another. He was rarely in the city to celebrate, or even to rest.

It was too early in the morning for most Americans, but the persistent culture of jogging was not to be underestimated. Men and women, usually in pairs and always in tight, bright clothing, ran their routines, following trails and winding pavement through the pines that surrounded the lake.

His friend finally appeared through the mist and trudged slowly over to the bench where John was seated. Geese honked indignantly as he moved past them. He held two non-descript Styrofoam cups.

"I got you a coffee."

John accepted it silently and wondered how he had made it. Brian sometimes spiked his coffee with too much sugar or cream just to spite him. But Brian wore a look on his face that said there wouldn't be any jokes today. He sat down solemnly.

"Thanks for coming."

"Of course." John tried to lighten the mood, even against his better judgement. "Is this a job interview? It seems I forgot my resume."

This was the part where Brian would comment that his resume was too thin, or that he wasn't actually hiring but just liked to interview people. He seemed to try at a smile, but it didn't quite push through the veil of darkness that hung heavily over him. Instead, he just repeated himself again.

"Thanks for coming, John."

Brian's hair was a mess and his coat was rumpled. The tie underneath was loose and wrinkled, and his collar had a small but apparent coffee stain. The man was a mess. John hated small talk and he was no stranger to talking shop. "What is it, Brian? You don't have to ease me into anything."

That seemed to spur something in his friend. He reached down and picked up a stone and tossed it into the water. The geese honked. Brian turned to face John and forced eye contact, as if he were searching for something hidden there.

"How many people do you trust? Completely and utterly?"

"Two," John answered, without hesitation. He had thought about this question before but no one had ever asked him, nor had he answered aloud. It gave a different weight to the words but didn't change them.

"Am I one of them?"

"Yes."

Brian stared a little longer into John's eyes, then seemed to give a sigh of relief and slouched back into the bench. They sat in silence for a while. John took a sip of his coffee and watched a couple joggers run by as Brian stared out over the water.

"Are you surprised?"

"With what?"

"That I trust you?"

Brian kept his gaze on the water. Finally, he spoke.

"One."

"What?"

"You. That's my number."

It was John's turn to be silent. Something was amiss. These weren't two friends meeting any longer. These were two co-conspirators. Two brothers, bound by whatever words were spoken next.

"Thinkers and doers," Brian muttered under his breath. He looked at John, who raised his eyebrows in response. "You remember what we said about thinkers and doers?"

The topic was a constant thread between the two of them, something old friends would say idly that would signal one another. John recalled a memory of the two of them from years ago.

***

It hadn't been the first time they had met, but it had been one of the first times Brian and John had had a good and proper conversation. They had been training for the Firm. Their unit was going through testing to see if they had what it took. They were both cautious in their ways, as most people in their unit had been, but soon their differences had given way to commonalities and friendship. John had joked about how he hated academics and ivory towers.

"You mean, like me?"

John had blanched. "What? No. I didn't think…"

Brian had laughed at that, a sweet and friendly sound that could pick him out of a crowd. They were in the unit's mess hall, grabbing an early dinner before hitting the books. They were cramming for a test the next day and Brian had asked if John would be interested in quizzing him for practice. John had decided to ask the man about himself.

"Well, I wanted to be a lawyer, but I knew school was going to be long and expensive. So I enlisted in the reserves, hoping to pay for schooling that way," Brian explained over a plate of roast beef, beans, and potatoes. John had opted for a tuna sandwich and a mug of tea. "It was a lot of schooling. A lot of textbooks, a lot of memorizing, a lot of time spent doing thinky-things." He went cross-eyed and puckered his lips.

John balked at that. "Okay, but you're not an egghead."

"Nah, no, I suppose I'm not." He stuck a fork laden with mash potatoes back onto his plate as if to make a point. "I ended up eventually interning for the JAG corps by the time I was in second-year law. I finished, became a Legalman, but after deployment and active combat, my stream changed. So I might be a nerd — maybe — but I don't have a stick up my ass."

"But you're a squid."

Brian scowled. The term 'squid' was usually thrown at members of the Navy by other branches.

John smiled. "So am I."

Brian perked up at that and prompted a fist bump.

"Did you like being in law?"

The question seemed to catch the man off guard and he had to use a napkin to mop up some gravy as he dropped a forkful of food onto the table. "I suppose I technically still am, I just haven't been in that world for a long time. I suspect I won't be returning anytime soon. This new life we've chosen and all." He seemed to brood on that for a moment, but his train of thought changed tracks. "I had friends who became full-blown lawyers. Let me tell you, there are very few lawyers who actually enjoy being a lawyer. And the ones who do are the most suspect."

"Of what?"

"Of being evil."

John laughed, but stopped when Brian's expression didn't change.

"I'm serious, John, it's a devious business. You're taking people's money in their times of greatest crisis. It's profiting off of suffering.

Plus the job constantly reminds you how shitty people are, how corrupt things can be."

John thought about that and frowned. "I've heard similar things from a couple lawyers my father knew. I remember them coming over for dinner and the old man asked them point-blank how they could do what they did. The two of them shrugged and said the pay was good and that they were good at it. No different than anyone else."

"Bastards."

"But-" John pressed on even though Brian had opened his mouth. "*But*, they also said how they don't have to enjoy fighting for what was right. Lots of people don't like their jobs. Doesn't mean they're not important. Doesn't mean they shouldn't do them."

Brian grunted. He seemed placated somewhat, but John had never seen him so worked up. He supposed he didn't know him well enough, but Brian was so good natured, almost a class clown.

"I didn't know you felt so strongly about it."

"That's alright. I usually forget how pissed off it makes me." He smiled then and John felt relieved. He didn't want to mess up a potential friendship so early — or lose a study partner who knew international law better than he ever would.

"We need people in law, don't we? I mean, would you disagree?" John asked.

Brian moved his tongue around his mouth for a moment and seemed to suck something out of his front teeth. "Yes and no. We don't need lawyers. We need *good* lawyers. Not good at the job, but good at being decent people. We need people who won't protect corruption for a paycheck."

"I can meet you on that." John took a sip of his tea. It was bitter, but sugar would have ruined it.

"What about you, John?"

John explained that he had been a U.S. Navy SEAL, but he had done some teaching — languages, mostly — and studied world cultures. It was his passion. He was a bit of an expert when it came to Latin America, and usually tried to remain humble about that fact, but Brian made him open up. John had to stop himself from reciting parts of his final paper.

"And now you're here."

"And now I'm here."

"A teacher. Culture. Latin America."

"That's right."

"Mucho gusto, señor."

His accent was awful. John laughed.

Brian grinned. "Well, it seems like you were pretty far up that ivory tower yourself."

John finished the last bite of his sandwich and shook his head while he chewed. "I said I *could've* gone on to become an academic. A professor, or something similar. Maybe an ambassador." He shrugged. "But that felt…I don't know."

"Like bullshit?"

John shrugged again, but smiled. "Yeah, I guess so. It wasn't me. I wanted to do something else."

"When we sat down, you were talking about how much you hate thinkers, John, right? Well,

I'm not the first to say this, but there are two kinds of people in this world: thinkers and doers. Thinkers sit around and get fat on their thoughts. Doers get things done." Brian wiped his fingers, which had gotten gravy and potatoes on them, then pushed his tray forward. "Maybe that's too harsh. Look, we need thinkers. We need people with their theories and imaginations and ideas. But damn it, man, people have to *do* something about their thoughts! You can't just have them, you have to live them!" For a moment, Brian seemed more a preacher than a military man. "It wasn't the paperwork, and maybe it wasn't even the nastiness surrounding the job. I just didn't feel like I was doing enough."

He stared off a bit and John didn't have anything to respond with. It almost made John feel like he was doing things for the wrong reasons. But his course was clear. He had decided to go through with the training and join the Firm.

John finished his tea, Brian dropped off their trays, and the two of them moved out the doors. The last bit of evening sunlight shone on them as they made their way across the training grounds and to the library. Both were dreading the coming evening and it had become apparent that their meal was largely for procrastination purposes.

"What the hell are we doing here?" Brian laughed.

John laughed too and knew he had made a new friend.

***

The park bench was uncomfortable and John was cold. He remembered reading in some book that city benches and stairs were purposely made uncomfortable so people would spend less time loitering and to dissuade homeless incursions. The city armed its public places against its lower classes. He frowned at the thought. Brian hadn't moved or said a word.

"Thinkers and doers," John said softly, hoping to prompt Brian.

The man took his time and took a long sip of his coffee, but finally spoke up when he seemed satisfied that John was truly listening. "We were two thinkers in a group of doers, convinced we were doers. We would always talk about thinkers and doers, but there's another important type of people in this world." He paused. John didn't say anything so Brian continued. "There are people who do the right thing, and people who do the wrong thing."

John grunted, not sure where this was going. He sipped the coffee Brian had given him. It was made right, but had already started growing cold.

"People think about doing the right thing, but then they don't. I suppose there are people that think wrong and a group of people that act wrong as well. That means that out of these four types of people, there's only one worth their salt."

He turned to John then, and his eyes were flaring in such a way that John leaned back without thinking.

"We have to be the people to do the right thing, John." Brian brought his coffee to his mouth and tilted his head back, eyes closed, drinking deeply. He must have finished half his coffee in several long gulps, making a little gasp when he finished. John noticed there were dark circles and bags around the man's eyes.

"What's going on, Brian? What's happened?"

"I got an assignment."

John was silent. They weren't supposed to talk about their missions.

"Standard stuff. But then I get a call from someone. Telling me to swipe information while I'm on the job."

"Esteban?"

"No, it wasn't him. It sounded like this guy didn't trust him."

John gave his friend a hard look. "You have to report it."

Brian nodded. "He had clearance."

"You still have to report it."

"Shut up!" Brian snapped. He took a deep breath. "Sorry. I didn't mean that. Sorry."

John kept quiet for a moment. "Talk to me," he said eventually.

"He explained some of the situation. But I can tell he's still keeping me in the dark. He's cautious. But he told me things. Things that I'm not supposed to know about. I think that's why he told me. I think he was trying to protect me...I don't know. The worst part is, the things he told me seem to check out. So he asked me to swipe some information during the mission. Said it would prove what he was saying. He even said I could look at the data first if I didn't believe him. Destroy it or turn it in or whatever I wanted."

"What…what things did he tell you?"

Brian shook his head. "No, John, I'm not telling you anymore. Not unless you're in. And if you're in, you lose everything."

It was a rare thing for John to feel anxiety. But there was an unsettling feeling dawning over him. He put his coffee down next to him and moved closer to Brian. John knew this would be his only chance to bring his friend to his senses.

"Brian. You've always picked fights. Most of the time with the wrong people. Don't do this."

His answer was a snarl and a glare. "You'd have me let them get away with it?"

Now it was John's turn to be mad. "I don't even know what *it* is! You're asking me to give up everything for some mystery you don't even have all the facts about!"

Brian looked away. Suddenly he tossed his coffee cup on the sidewalk. What remained of the brown liquid oozed out onto the pavement, briefly steaming in the morning mist. John thought the man would get up and leave, but he didn't. A couple of joggers in tight bright clothing moved past, avoiding the now cold puddle of coffee.

"All I'm saying is, have all your ducks in a row. That's it. I'm not worried that you're picking a fight. You can handle yourself. I'm worried that you don't know who you're fighting and what you're fighting."

Brian seemed to have calmed down. It didn't make John feel any better. He had probably already said the wrong thing.

"Damn," Brian said. "I spilled my coffee."

The air between them was tense, but John couldn't help but laugh. Brian joined him and wiped tears from his eyes. John hoped they were only from laughing, but at least he was smiling now. They could always talk. It was something John always appreciated about his friend. John was as antisocial as they came, but Brian could have him laughing and opening up over drinks in minutes.

"Your love of Latin America…it's an asset, John. My lawyering, well, it's a liability," Brian said when they were ready to return to the topic at hand.

"That's not true." Even as John said it, he wasn't sure he believed it. Brian was a stickler for the truth, asked too many questions, and picked fights when someone was wrong. The bigger it was, the bolder he became.

"You love culture and languages. Spanish most of all. You told me once that operating in Latin America has been as much a vacation to you as it is work."

It was true that he had said that. A long time ago, but it was still probably true.

"I don't love or hate this job any different than you, and I sure as hell didn't enjoy being a Legalman before this, John. But my love is for justice. Pure and simple."

"This sounds like a rabbit hole, Brian. What happens if you jump in?"

Brian folded his hands and furrowed his brow. "I was asking myself that for hours after the call and began to understand what I was being asked to do. But then I realized I was asking the wrong question. There's a more important one."

"What's that?"

Brian smiled, but it was unkind. "What happens if I don't?"

***

John shook himself out of his reminiscing and took another sip of his half-empty beer. He was at a little street-bar, cooling off in the midday sun. The beer was getting warm, mostly from his grip. But the sun was shining, he was in Antigua, and there was work to do. These were the things that made up a perfect day. He stood up, deciding it was time to get a move on. But he didn't feel like moving on. As he stood, he accidentally knocked the table and the beer tipped over. He caught the glass but the beer spilled, lost on the hot pavement.

"*¿Señor?*"

The barman had come outside for a smoke. He gestured to his empty glass.

"*¿Otra cerveza, señor?*"

John looked at the empty glass. The afternoon was warming up and he'd only enjoyed half the beer. He could always use another drink…or two. The barman finished his smoke, put it out, and took John's empty glass. He gave him a little wink, but John shook his head. "*No graçias,*" John said.

He pulled his bag over his shoulders and left money on the table. He had to get moving. There were worse things than spilled beer.

CHAPTER 7

Pablo's compound boasted an almost mythical reputation among the ordinary people of

Antigua. It seemed to float above the humdrum of regular life and inspire a sense of holiness. Perhaps not in the same way the *oligarcas familias* were revered; their wealth and power allowed them to carve up and rule Guatemala like the Spanish once had. Nor in the same way the Catholic Church still dominated a majority of souls in Latin America.

Tourists would marvel at the decadence of the compound, wondering who lived there surrounded by such wealth. Antiguans would marvel too, but they knew who lived behind the well-guarded walls. They also knew what built them. When tourists would inevitably ask about the compound, guides and other folk would give a measured glance and say '*drogas*'. The only way to afford something akin to a castle in Latin America was the drug trade, or something similarly illegal. It seemed strange for crime to be on such public display and the knowledge of it to be so open. But nothing was to be done about it, which helped build the perception that this was indeed the way things were done, and the way things would continue to be.

Which was of course a calculated play by many cartels and rich families alike. Pablo Puentes went a step further. Everything he did, he made sure was public. This included his crimes. For what reason would he worry about a witness? Because everyone knew everything about him, there was no need for secrets. They already worked for him and respected him, and if neither of those, they feared him.

Pablo was also not some mob boss or a simple mover of *drogas*. He was a *patrón*. He protected his people, paid his people, and cared for his people. He was sophisticated. He loved the arts. He donated bushels of cash to the Catholic Church. He supported the right people and politics in the *oligarcas familias.*

Even so, there would always be a little thorn that needed removing. *Una espinilla. A pimple.*

The compound's courtyard was a gorgeous mosaic of foliage, with clay tile around a small pond, and of course, guards and servants. An expensive patio set and a chiminea sat in comfortable positions in the shade around the courtyard. Sweat stained the chests, armpits, and backs of the laborers maintaining the estate's oasis. Amongst the courtyard's foliage, a gardener worked methodically, hacking at an overgrown wild tamarind with a machete. Another cleaned the pond, another pruned one of the three small lemon trees. More privileged servants were making sure drinks and sweets were prepared for the sunny afternoon; they were afforded the kindness of working in the shade. Guards stood in a measured spread across the walls and doors. The courtyard was always bustling with work, but when Juan and a group of guards moved into the space, dragging their heavy boots and leading a man with a bloody nose along by his belt loops, everyone stopped what they were doing. They stood to wait for their *patrón.*

Pablo took his time. Once satisfied his people had waited long enough, he strode out onto the balconied veranda attaching the courtyard through glass doors to his villa. The courtyard was his favorite place. It was open, beautiful, and full of happy people. These

71

were things that mattered, and the best way to express that was to show it and share it.

There were two types of wealth in Guatemala: *dinero nuevo y dinero viejo*. New money and old money. *Dinero viejo* came from farming, which dominated the corporate landscape and maintained control through land-ownership. Land owners kept the lower classes and Mayans under a thick thumb. *Dinero nuevo,* on the other hand, could be liberating for the common man, and was a different sort of beast. They took Latin America by storm with drugs, and more recently sex trafficking. Old money patriarchs would play down their wealth. Passing by someone with *dinero viejo* wouldn't bring cause for attention, or the knowledge of how rich and powerful that person was. *Dinero nuevo*, on the other hand, loved to flash it.

Pablo didn't think much of these distinctions. He was content as long as he took care of his people. His brother hadn't done enough of that. Guatemalans were no stranger to corruption. So Pablo gave justice whenever he could.

The best way to deliver justice was to hold court. Where better to hold court than in the courtyard?

Court was now in session.

The man brought forth was one of Pablito's tutors. Pablo's expression darkened. A man who had done wrong, who had been close to his son. That was unacceptable.

The guards held the man tightly in front of Pablo, propping him up slightly.

"Diego."

The man's eyes were heavy. One was bruising over. "Yes."

"What's this I hear about you? It is concerning."

The man looked away, but Pablo grabbed him by the chin and jerked his face like it was some mechanical part, forcing the man to look into his eyes. The man didn't reply. Pablo looked to Juan and his men. Juan gestured to one of the guards that had brought the prisoner.

"*Patrón* Puentes, this man was touching one of your women," he said.

Pablo's eyes widened in shock, an almost comical look plastering his face.

The man struggled against the two guards holding him. "No! I would never be so stupid as to do that, *patrón*!" His squirming made Pablo think of a wriggling fish caught in a net.

"He did, *patrón*," the guard spoke again, grunting with the effort of holding the man in place. He spoke hastily, as if he were concerned Pablo would think he wrong. "One of the captains. His girlfriend, *patrón*."

"Not yours!" The man cried again. "Never one of yours!" One of the guards punched him in the gut and he wheezed as the wind left his lungs. Pablo raised a hand to stop the man from receiving more blows and the guards halted. Pablo walked over to the man, his interest piqued.

"And why would you touch something that was not yours, Diego?"

Diego struggled to get the words out around his gasps for air. "Because…I was drunk…I…"

"There are more important things in this life than this *lujuria*, *señor*," Pablo said sadly. "Family. Honor. And there are better things in the next." Pablo fingered the golden crucifix hung around his neck. A servant was pouring a glass of juice from a pitcher and Pablo pointed to it. The glass was brought at once and Pablo gave it to Diego. He drank deeply.

"I wanted…I want what you have, *patrón*."

"Oh?"

"We know…you have us watch…I only wanted…"

Pablo had begun to raise a glass of juice for himself but brought it down hard before it was brought to his lips. "I am allowed these things because it is fair, *señor*. It is just. They are my right. I am married. I have a family. A business. You, what do you have?"

"I am smart, I-"

"*Tonto del culo.*" Dumbass.

"...I work hard for you."

"I work hard too! And I pay you well. I pay everyone here well!" His voice rose to a roar as he gestured grandly around the courtyard. Some of the servants flinched, but many of the guards nodded.

Diego seemed to have realized the dangerous path he was carving. He changed his strategy. "Forgive me, *patrón*. It will not happen again."

"You say this in your moment of desperation."

"No! I...I am a good tutor to your son. I made a mistake."

Pablo seemed to consider this for a moment. "Yes." He took the glass of juice from the man and flung it across the lawn. "But I need men who are honest, before they are caught."

Pablo pointed to a gardener, nearly hidden by the branches of the tamarind she had been pruning. It took her a moment to realize she was being summoned. A guard whistled to spur her to move faster. She rushed over to Pablo, keeping her eyes downcast as she approached.

"The captain's girlfriend is mine, *señor*. I make sure she is safe. I love her as I love all my people. My children." The man's eyes grew wide as Pablo continued. "And now I have a dirty little thief trying to steal a woman from one of my good citizens. From one of my *guerreros. Warriors.* Disrespecting a woman. Disrespecting me."

"*Señor* Puentes, I did not...I did not mean to steal from you."

"Okay."

"Or disrespect the woman. Or you."

"Okay."

The man began to stand, uncertain if he were free to go. Pablo looked at him curiously. The man began to turn away. Pablo snapped his fingers.

The guards who had been holding the man earlier flanked him once again, grabbing his arms and neck. They ignored his cry of protest as they forced him over to a tree stump.

"Your words are good, but your actions are not," Pablo said darkly, looming over the man as he began to sob.

"Don't kill me. Please don't kill me." The words were almost a whisper.

Pablo laughed. "Don't be crazy. I am not a murderer, *señor*!" He took the machete from the hands of the gardener standing timidly next to Pablo. She twitched as the tool was taken from her. and slunk a few steps away when it became clear that Pablo had no further need of her, relieved. "I am a simple man, carrying out God's word. 'Thou shalt not steal', no? 'Thou shalt not covet'. 'Thou shalt not have any god but *me*'." Pablo's eyes flashed dangerously.

Diego was brought to his knees and his arms pulled across the wood. He saw that the tree stump was stained a dark brown which seemed to unnaturally wash over the color of the bark. Sudden realization burned Diego like a brand as he struggled against his captors again, to no avail.

"You have taught my little son some math, no? Pablito is very good at counting, but sometimes he only counts to two. He will run around the house and garden, yelling 'One! Two! One! Two!'" Pablo smiled. "It is so funny."

Pablo brought down the machete and lopped a hand clean off the man's arm.

"Yes!" Pablo yelled wildly.

The man screamed. Blood spurted from the stump of his arm, as if someone had only recently turned on a hose.

"That is one! *Uno, señor*!"

"Please…"

"You have two hands, *señor*! You will still be able to touch. To *steal*. We must rid you of your other hand!"

"No, please, *señor*, *patrón* Puentes, *please*…"

Pablo looked almost sad as he raised the machete again. "It is okay. This way we will make sure."

He brought down the machete in a crushing arc and sliced through flesh and bone a second time. The man wailed again as his hand flew from the tree stump. He fell backward onto his back. Pablo snapped his fingers and guards pulled the man from the ground and forced him into a chair.

"*Dos.*"

Pablo retrieved the hands and laid them out tenderly on the table in front of the man. Diego was sputtering, saliva flying from his lips as he drifted in and out of pain and shock.

"Oh…I can't…it hurts…"

"Of course it does. If it didn't, I would be very worried." Pablo walked to where the glass of juice had been thrown, retrieved it, and summoned a servant to pour more. Once the glass was full, he offered it to the man. The man shook his head, crying, but Pablo made him drink. He coughed against the liquid as it dribbled down his chin.

"Now…will you let me go…?" The words were slurred, barely distinguishable through his moans.

"Have you learned your lesson?"

"Yes…"

"Are you sorry?"

The man's face was red and dripping with sweat. "Yes," he wheezed.

"Good."

The man seemed to catch enough of his breath to stand, but he still stumbled as he found his way out of his chair. Pablo stood as well, but didn't take his eyes off the maimed man. He was surprised the man had somehow managed not to pass out. "We are done with you, I think."

"Please...I can't...my hands..." The stumps had stopped spraying blood, instead opting for a steady stream.

"Yes, I will let you keep your hands." Pablo snapped his fingers and a servant came with a cloth bag, picked up the hands off the table and put them inside, then gave the bag to Pablo. The *patrón* hadn't looked away from the thief, examining him as if he were some exotic curiosity.

"Here. You want these?"

Pablo held out the bag. The man was sobbing.

"Take them."

The man waved his stumps. Blood sprayed across Pablo's clothes again. The garish red splash of blood on Pablo's white shirt made him seem as if he were wearing an abstract art piece. He didn't grow angry at the stains. He seemed to enjoy them, baring his teeth in a vicious smile, a drop of blood oozing down his lips and carving a line down onto his chin. He hung the bag around the man's neck.

"You are free to go." Pablo stroked the man's cheek tenderly. "No more stealing now, *amigo*."

The man stumbled to the courtyard gates, tripping before he reached them. He used a stump to break his fall, his muscle memory forgetting he had no hands. He cried as his bleeding arm smashed into the ground and his whole body spasmed from the pain. He tried to grab the arm that had broken his fall with his other stump, again his body unaccustomed to the missing parts.

Pablo shook his head at the pitiful man. Juan was grimacing.

"Is it too much for you, *mi hijo*?"

Juan blinked and narrowed his gaze, clearly uncomfortable that Pablo had seen his discomfort. He yelled at a guard and pointed to the bleeding mess flopping before the courtyard gate. The guard moved to pick the man up and carry him over his shoulder, exiting the compound.

"No." Juan twisted his neck for a moment, cracking his neck. It made an audible click before he continued. "We have another."

Pablo was determined to work on his new son. He needed to be stronger. Sandor had worked too much with tallying numbers, secret emails, and out of country business trips. He had sold himself out. It happened all the time, and it was sad. Pablo would give the young man the business and family values he desperately needed. Respect for tradition and culture, love for family and honor, understanding of how power worked.

He accepted a cloth from a servant and wiped his face as he turned to meet the next man they brought into the courtyard.

He was walking by himself instead of being dragged, meaning this man probably hadn't done anything wrong. At least not yet. He was nondescript. Clearly strong from the way his arms and chest pulled at his plain black shirt, but not large and menacing like most of his guards. A short, salt-and-pepper stubble of a beard around the man's stiff jaw reflected the precision of his short, graying hair. If the man had any striking feature, it was his eyes. Pablo met them as the two moved toward one another in unspoken mutual agreement. Pablo's beady dark irises met a piercing gray-blue stare that made him think of some predator, a hawk or a panther.

The man was silent for a long moment, staring down Pablo. He felt a hint of discomfort, but then he smiled inwardly, thinking this is how most people felt with him. He motioned for the man to speak before his patience was tested.

"*Patrón* Puentes." The man gave a respectful nod.

Puentes would have preferred a bow, but the respect shown was acceptable. The man was clearly a *gringo* after all, but not as painfully so as he had initially thought. He had moved with a familiar ease and didn't glance around nervously like so many tourists or others who didn't know their surroundings. The man's perfect Spanish confirmed that this was no aloof *idiota*. His words were firm and solid as a rock.

"My name is John Carpenter. I would like to tutor your son."

CHAPTER 8

The bloody lines on Pablo's shirts were disconcerting, but only somewhat.

Target acquired.

Although it would still be a couple days before the plan's execution to kidnap and move Pablo to the safe house, it was nice to have the target in plain sight ahead of time. John had done one too many jobs working off nothing but a fuzzy surveillance picture.

On the other hand, John wasn't used to being this...personable with his target. This would be, he reflected, the first time he'd be going undercover in years.

Protocol was straightforward: have a plausible cover story; take on a position that was meaningful but not crucial in the life of the target; establish a semblance of routine.

Strike.

Protocol was also unfortunately limited. It relied upon the creativity of fieldworkers to see to the viability and successful execution of actions. At least he had Marcela to help with that.

Speak of the devil.

Marcela slipped out of the estate doors and delicately made her way down the courtyard steps. She was wearing a skin-tight pink dress, the hem fluttering well above her knees. Her new heels clacked loudly as she made her way over to Pablo, towering over him.

"I like the new glass on the entrance, Pablo. I never saw the old entrance, but this seems very nice." She moved closer to him, lips almost pressing to his ear, one hand on his chest, the other moving down his back. "Like you, *patrón*."

Pablo grinned.

She looked at the blood on his outfit.

"Diego," Pablo said, shrugging.

"Ah." She looked at John with curious eyes, as if she had never seen him before, maintaining their covers.

John liked working with her. She was younger and, admittedly, friendlier than he'd prefer, but he couldn't deny her skill and ability. In this case, he was experiencing a rude reminder of just how efficient she could be.

'Don't worry. I'll make sure you have an open position. Tutors come and go.'

He didn't know she would be quite so brutal. Or so dramatic.

But, he reminded himself, she'd been here longer than he had. She knew the landscape, and he'd follow her lead.

Pablo hadn't taken his eyes off John. He finally broke eye contact and snapped his fingers at the gardener who had given him the machete. He passed the weapon off. John saw horror linger under the woman's eyes, but she hid it well. She eyed the blood dripping slowly down the length of the metal, but held the handle firmly and moved back to the tamarind she had been working on before. Pablo wiped his hands on his pants, leaving soft streaks of red where droplets had flown before. He picked up a small cookie from a plate sitting on the table beside a cup of juice and took a small bite. He considered it for a moment before he returned his attention to John.

"Cookie?"

Fuck no.

Pablo didn't wait for him to answer. He took his cookie and popped it into Marcela's mouth. She bent at the waist and kissed him delicately on the cheek. John was stunned by her Barbie-doll act. This wasn't the Marcela he knew. He noticed the guards watching her from nearby. One man in particular had a particularly severe look on his face. Stern, but hungry. John guessed the man was Juan. And the look on his face made the tension in the air palpable.

Marcela licked her lips, then took a seat on one of the patio chairs, examining her nails and looking bored. Pablo retrieved a new cookie for himself, and switched to Spanish as he spoke.

"You want to teach my son?"

"*Si*," John replied easily, eager to return to business. "I teach langu-"

"What is your nationality?" Pablo gestured to John's entirety with his cookie.

"Canadian."

In truth he was a dual citizen. His mother was born in Newfoundland, even speaking Newfoundland English; his father was from a hard Oregon line of woodsmen and trappers turned military and administrative. John's childhood would always be Canada. His adult life was the U.S. of A. Just as American tourists pinned Canadian flags to their bags to avoid local harassment, John almost always used his Canadian identity whenever things called upon him to be a bit more personable.

"Canada. Where's that?"

John almost rolled his eyes and began to explain, but then Pablo took a large step and grabbed his shoulder.

"I'm joking, of course. America's hat, no? But we all know who wears the pants." He winked and John gave an uncomfortable smile until his shoulder was finally let go. He didn't like how friendly Pablo was. This man had chopped the hands off a man moments ago and was now joking about national geography. He was erratic. Unpredictability was always a problem when it came to any operation. John didn't need things to be any more complicated.

"You military?" Juan asked, his eyes investigating every inch of John's person.

The man had been lingering closer as they spoke. He was tall and hard-looking. The kind of mold infantry divisions liked to use for recruits.

The question made a cool line of unexpected adrenaline creep up John's spine. If he was blown this early...and in a courtyard of shotgun-wielding guards...

Pablo gave his stepson a chiding glance, but Juan didn't break his gaze.

"I'm just asking, in case. He seems military. And you are of interest, uncle."

Pablo smiled, but it still held some tension. "I am, I am. *Señor* Carpenter?"

John decided to ignore Juan completely so he could work Pablo.

"Sort of. Coastguard, years ago. Put in the time." He shrugged. "Gotta love the water."

I joined the SEALs. I sat in a bathtub of ice for two hours and learned to force my heartbeat to compensate for heat loss. I carried two men on my shoulders on a Swedish beach in a training accident...

"Ah. And then?"

I was pulled for a new unit specializing in Latin American affairs. Intel gathering, assassinations, even sabotage. I had the knowledge background, the language, and the military expertise. They liked that. According to records, I'm either dead or don't exist.

John tried his best at a lazy smile. "*Gringo* vagabond."

Pablo broke into a grin then, and John knew he'd won the dangerous man over. Juan still scowled, and John made a mental note to tread lightly around the man so as to not further raise his suspicions. The operation wasn't supposed to take too much time, but he'd have to spend a few days establishing himself.

"I teach English and Spanish, *señor*. A couple other languages, if you prefer. And Latin American history and culture."

Pablo narrowed his eyes. "And how much Mayan do you know?"

John held up his thumb and forefinger an inch apart from one another. "*Poquito*. I am ashamed to say I have a limited Mayan vocabulary, and most of it is K'iche'. There are so many different dialects." John meant it. "But the language is not everything. *Maximón*, for example, has always fascinated me."

Pablo nearly beamed at the mention of *Maximón*. "You are infatuated, sir. With our country."

"I am." It seemed some things John couldn't hide, even from this cartel leader who had no secrets.

"That will work well, *Señor* Carpenter."

"*Mi tío*," Juan interjected again, "We cannot just have men off the street come in and work for us."

Pablo made a raspberry sound with his lips. "We do it all the time. Relax, I am not giving him one of your funny hats to wear. Besides-" Pablo pushed his stepson aside gently as he waved for a few guards to follow him as he began to lead John inside. "There are no secrets here. *Señor* Carpenter would have to be an *idiota* to enter my estate and try to cause me or anyone here harm. Or have *los cojones* the size of melons." He winked again at this.

John soon saw what the man meant. As he passed through the door and into the villa, he saw there were cameras mounted above the door, and in half the corners once he was inside. Guards stood at attention in between adjoining rooms. It was strangely militaristic… or prisonlike. It leant the compound an impenetrable air. But then again, it was too open. Obsessively safe. Eyes everywhere. Orwellian.

No secrets indeed.

They moved through a couple rooms that left John wondering how much wealth someone needed before they felt happy. He couldn't even think of what the rooms would be used for. They had couches, chairs, TVs, tables — normal things, although much more lavish — and art. Statues and busts and paintings on every wall. Through a window John caught sight of a helicopter resting on a pad beside the compound.

The kitchen was slightly plainer. A servant was pulling fresh bread from the oven, making John's mouth water. He hadn't realized how hungry he'd become.

"Isabella," Pablo said softly, interrupting John's thoughts about food.

A middle-aged Mayan woman was sitting on a chair near the door working away at a small compact laptop, face tight in concentration. She looked up quickly at the sound of her name. She gave a smile for Pablo, but pursed her lips and shut her laptop at the sight of John. She curled an eyebrow at Pablo.

"New tutor," Pablo said, shrugging.

"*Buenos días*, Isabella," John said smoothly.

She didn't seem particularly impressed with him. Isabella looked him up and down, stood from her chair, and shared a kiss with Pablo. He curled an arm around her even as she began to depart.

"*Buena suerte*, tutor." *Good luck.* She gave Pablo a knowing look before leaving. His eyes lingered on her.

"*Papá!*"

And there was the boy of interest. He squealed as if seeing his father for the first time. He sat at the kitchen table, coloring a strange creation on a piece of paper with multicolored crayons strewn about. A cup of juice sat precariously close to the table's edge. Pablo moved it away from the edge and poked at the child's ribs. He gave a little shriek.

"Pablito. I have someone new for you. A tutor who will help you with language. And to appreciate our culture."

"A tutor? Like Diego?"

"Yes, like Diego."

The boy frowned. "They took him away. I thought he was funny."

"I thought so, too."

"What happened to Diego?"

"He left."

"Where?"

Pablo looked like he was considering what to say. He exchanged a look with John.

"I chopped off his hands!" Then he laughed and tickled Pablito, and the boy was laughing, and the guards smiled. John frowned.

Then the boy looked up at him. He was cute and skinny, with dark hair and his father's dark Mayan eyes, but held none of the sinister lingering notes that rested behind Pablo's. He seemed so small, not because of his size but because he was surrounded by things too large for him to understand. John felt bad for the boy.

Yet as John looked back to Pablo, he saw something equally disconcerting there.

Love.

Pablo obviously loved his son. The way he rubbed the boy's head, helped him reach for a crayon, pointed at his coloring, eyes lingering on his every move.

Pablo's attention abruptly snapped back to John.

"The carrot and the stick."

"*Perdón*?"

Pablo grinned. "Sometimes Pablito needs the stick, but I always prefer the carrot."

"Ah." *A spoiled child*, John thought. He shouldn't have been surprised. He had suspected his student might end up being a challenge one way or another.

Pablo snapped his fingers at John and pointed to Pablito. "Go. Teach."

John nodded and sidled into a chair, hardly missing a beat at the sudden command to begin work. Pablito looked at him suspiciously at first, in that way all children have of newcomers, then gave an exaggerated wink. He must have picked it up from Pablo. John nearly shuddered at the gesture.

"What…is your name?" Pablito asked in tentative English.

"John Carpenter."

And I'm here to kill your father.

CHAPTER 9

The hotel they had chosen to meet sported a roof terrace veranda, small round tables, and chairs situated for customers. A hand-painted wooden sign hung on the plaster wall saying '*solo clientes*' to dissuade any street urchins or tired tourists. They had a stunning view of all three of Antigua's volcanoes: *Volcán de Agua,* the 'Volcano of Water'; *Volcán de Fuego,* the 'Volcano of Fire'; and *Acatenango*, translating roughly as 'wall of reeds' or 'reeds of corn'. Marcela watched her coffee swirl before carefully putting the cup down on the table where John sat. She eased into the chair across from him. She didn't say anything for a while, and he tried to enjoy the peace.

They were both wearing basic disguises, John sporting a mustache, sunglasses, sun hat, and flowered shirt; Marcela wore sunglasses and a wig. They weren't completely alone but everyone else was out of earshot. It was the perfect kind of place to discuss sensitive things. They'd done a quick sweep anyway just to be sure, looking like they were simply arranging the chairs and table umbrella the way they'd prefer. In some ways it became safer than their safe house. They didn't want to be going in and out of there too often.

A Yamaha motorcycle spat down the cobblestone street, four people precariously riding on its back. John could make out the whole family: the father drove with hands on the throttle, his young daughter sat behind him holding onto his waist, while the mother sat at the back, her focus dedicated to the screen of her cell phone. A toddler sat wedged in front of the dashboard, legs flying free. None wore a helmet. A couple of tourists struggling to cross the street leapt out of the way as the motorcycle revved up to speed. John held back a smile, but Marcela caught him.

"You're not allowed to laugh at that," she said, jokingly.

He arched an eyebrow and took a sip of his coffee. It was hotter than he thought and he ended up burning his tongue. The roast itself was almost perfect, but no one made coffee better than Tito, his favorite barista back in Nicaragua. John sighed. Just one of the many things left behind. The little things were always the best, so losing them was always the worst.

He frowned at the cup in front of him and took the bait. "Most people say I don't laugh enough. Shoot me for trying."

Marcela grinned to spite him. "I've never said that."

"That's a lie."

"That's our trade."

He grew quiet at that. Marcela didn't seem to notice. She only kept smiling. Marcela seemed comfortable and at ease with everything, never wavering. All the more troubling when it came to more serious matters.

"Why aren't I allowed to laugh at the tourists, *señorita*?"

"Because you're a *gringo*! That's why." She grinned again and reached for her coffee.

John grabbed the table and moved to give it a shake. Marcela yelped and lunged for her coffee cup, plucking it off the table before it could spill. His own coffee suffered for it. Some of the hot liquid found his hand and he tried to shake it off. There were no napkins, so he let the liquid dribble off the table. He shot her a dangerous look, but to her it was the equivalent of a pout. She laughed.

"Don't try and pull *mierda* with me, Carpenter. You'll get burned if you do."

"Don't laugh at the *gringos,* Marcela."

She rolled her eyes. "As long as you remember who the *gringo* is, I'll remember to hold back."

John enjoyed the good weather for a few minutes and let her keep smiling. Both put him in a good mood. But then he gave her a look that meant it was time to talk business.

"That man. Diego. I know that was you."

She shrugged and bent her hands at the wrist and waved them around, laughing. He frowned.

"You look like you've just eaten a lemon," she said.

"And what do I usually look like?"

"Like you've eaten half a lemon," she snorted. "What else do you like to eat, John?"

"Beans and rice."

She laughed at that. Anyone living in Guatemala ate that every day. It was a painful staple for some. Marcela could've sworn she saw a smile threaten to creep up out of the depths of John's soul. But she returned to what he had said before.

"I didn't think it would be like that, honestly. But does it make you feel any better if I say he was a bad man? He was touchy, you know."

"What did you do?"

"Whispered in Juan's ear. One of the only things I've been able to do the last while." She looked off at *El Volcán Agua* for a moment, the giant dormant volcano that crept above Antigua's horizon. "I'm anxious, John."

"I know."

She was in a tight spot and he didn't envy her. Not only was she a coveted mistress of Pablo, but she circumvented him to work Juan as well. That would be a dangerous enough position, but she was also an undercover Firm agent. It took its toll, no matter the training. She'd do it for a year if she had to. But no one would want to.

"We find out how the kill switch works, disable it, then smuggle Pablo out to the safe house. We extract the information, and then it's a matter of simple disposal." John shrugged. "Then we can both spend some time enjoying the sun."

She grimaced. "Alright. I'm hoping to get something out of Juan."

John nodded. "Fine. But at a certain point it might just be better to get rid of him. It's not like you're going to turn him."

Marcela tried not to be offended, but he was right. Juan wouldn't turn on his uncle just for a bit of sex. She could get information from him easier than Pablo, but it wasn't as if he was telling her whatever she wanted, either.

"Just kill him once we're able to go after the target," John said. "We might as well cause some disarray in their ranks. It'll delay them in their search once we snatch Pablo."

She nodded, failing to hide her reluctance. She didn't hold sympathy for Juan, but she had hoped to get something more from him. It seemed a waste. "And the kill switch?"

John sighed. "That's the tricky part. Juan?"

"No." She frowned, feeling bad that she didn't have more to give John. "He knows it exists, but I don't think he knows what that entails. Not really."

"Damn. Okay."

Juan shouldn't be the reason they were grasping at straws. "They're giving us nothing."

"Coming up with something is our job."

Marcela opened her mouth, then closed it. John watched her chew on her thoughts, allowing an uncomfortable silence to hang in the air between them before she spoke again.

"Do you trust Esteban?"

Marcela's words rang in his head like a gong, shattering the silence. Marcela had a knack for saying perfectly blunt things that caught him off guard. Did he trust Esteban?

Esteban had Brian killed, he almost said, but he didn't know that for sure. Instead he started thinking about what trust meant. Then he quickly shut down that rabbit hole of thinking.

"I trust him to give us orders."

"That's all you need?"

"That's all *we* need." He moved to refocus the conversation. "Why don't we do a quick computer hack?"

"You think they're stupid enough to keep kill switch information readily available?"

"No. Maybe." John licked his lips, took in a breath and let it out. "Probably not, no. But I'd just like to have something to work with. If Esteban wants to keep us in the dark, fine. We'll gather our own information."

"Makes you miss the easy missions, eh?" She mimed a rifle and pulled its imaginary trigger. "Pshew." She let the recoil rock her back in her chair. "Takeout."

The joke in the business was that most ops, like assassinations, were like fast food. It was sometimes messy but it was quick, and usually you didn't even have to deal with the trash afterwards. John didn't think the joke was very funny.

"There is a laptop sometimes kept in an office space. Isabella spends time in there. She uses it more than anyone else. But, of course, there are guards."

"I can take care of them long enough for you to get in a wig."

She blew air out of her lips, making them vibrate. "Definitely not takeout."

John nodded and drained most of his coffee. The term 'wig' was either short for 'earwig' or 'wiggle', but either way it referred to a program developed by coders at MIT in the late 90's. It copied everything off a computer in thirty seconds or less, indiscriminately leeching files, pictures, and browser histories. The CIA quietly bought the program and passed it onto the Special Activities Division for field-work. The SAD added a quick brute force hacking program to accompany the wig and created a slick device to house it. It looked like a simple USB stick. Pop it into a computer, copy the data, and walk away.

The catch was threefold: one, it didn't download things, it only copied them. That was necessary for such a quick transfer time; two, it didn't distinguish different files from one another. There were some basic quick-find abilities for keywords and the like, but one usually had to sift through a mash of data manually, so it was hard to isolate anything. Essentially, all the raw data was compressed together, presenting a seemingly random pattern of gibberish. A decoder program could help parse the information and make some sense of it, but that took time to read; third, and most importantly, the data corrupted when files were transferred; the data could only be used directly off the device itself.

It was great for when operatives knew there was something incriminating on a hard drive, but didn't know what it was and had the time and personnel to comb through it. It was also best used on small data banks. Luckily, they had a decoding program on their safe house laptop just for this.

Gathering information on the Puentes family was what Brian was secretly asked to do. John suppressed a shiver as he considered the similarity.

"Anything else?" he asked.

Marcela tapped the side of her coffee. "Cameras. Although Juan's hinted no one really bothers to look at them closely."

"We can mess up a camera or two."

"Okay." She grimaced. "Getting in and out with a wig will be really hard, John."

His brow furrowed and his eyes narrowed ever so slightly. This was becoming unprofessional.

"Yeah well, we'll do it."

"Don't worry about it!" She suddenly straightened in her chair. She put something on the table and pushed it toward him. It was a wig.

He moved to take it but she snatched it back up, looking at it.

"It's already done."

He cocked his head, not understanding at first. She let a self-satisfied smile creep over her lips as his expression changed.

"How…when?" John was genuinely speechless. He tried to compose himself and Marcela giggled softly as he did so. He sunk a little in his chair.

"Yesterday, when everyone was in the courtyard."

"But you were in the courtyard." *You were hard to miss*, he thought.

She waved a hand dismissively. "Before that. Isabella usually has her laptop with her, but she was absent. I went into the computer room on the pretense of trying to find a pen and paper." She batted her eyes and turned her head, doing an exaggerated impression of innocence. "I enjoy drawing in my spare time, *monsieur*."

"That's…why are you speaking French?"

"French like art."

"What?"

She waved his question off. "The point is, I have the wig. How'd you like to do some sifting?"

"That's…quite impressive, Marcela."

She blushed a bit at the compliment. "My charm." She batted her eyes again, but then grew more serious. "Honestly, the guard didn't even ask. I wasn't doing anything dangerous, after all."

"And Isabella wasn't there? I saw her in the kitchen with her laptop when I went inside."

"Not when I was there. Even the rich and powerful need to *pipí*. A tragic flaw. Care to do some sifting?"

He hesitated. It felt so easy. But then again, going through all the data was going to occupy all their time, and probably wouldn't give them anything useful. Such was the price of having too much information.

"Yeah. Okay." He took the wig and pocketed it. Hopefully she didn't stiff him with too much of the work. John finished the rest of his coffee, then stood up to leave. He was surprised when there was a touch on his arm. Marcela gave him a look that he couldn't quite figure out, which made him uncomfortable.

"I said it was impressive, but I also meant to say good work." He still didn't know what she wanted. He patted his pocket with the wig inside. "Thank you."

She nodded, taking the compliment with sincerity. Her mouth twitched as she held his gaze.

"*¿Le puedo comprar una cerveza?*" she asked. *Can I buy you a beer?*

It was out of the blue. If John didn't know better, he'd think she was hitting on him. Maybe he didn't know better. She saw him thinking.

She spoke again, softer. "*Solo quiero hablar.*" *I just want to talk.*

He had work to do. But there was something in her tone. He ordered another coffee and sat back down. Marcela ordered a beer. He looked at her expectantly while she drank from the perspiring bottle. She put it down hard on the table when she'd finished about a quarter of the liquid.

"How old are you?"

John wasn't sure if he should be amused or insulted.

"Old enough that you shouldn't ask."

Marcela started to smile but then it was washed away by something. She looked out over the street, surveying locals and tourists as if they were part of a play, existing only for her entertainment.

"John, I'm thinking about what happens after this."

She wasn't looking at him. John took a sip of his coffee and fidgeted a little as he realized the sun had gone down a bit. It wasn't really cold, but the afternoon was slipping away.

"You know?"

"What do you mean?" he asked.

"After the mission. What then?"

Then we get another mission. We keep going.

He was silent for a moment, not knowing what to say. He didn't know what she wanted to hear either. He tried to bring something gentle into his voice.

"Are you getting cold feet? About our work?"

If an agent got wind that another agent was even considering desertion or anything like it, they were to contact a handler immediately and the situation would be dealt with. Everyone knew what that meant. On the other hand, it wasn't unheard of for an agent to retire from fieldwork and be moved to a different branch or posting. Or so John had heard. He didn't know for sure.

Thankfully, Marcela rolled her eyes.

"No, no. I don't mean us. I know we keep going. That's not what I mean."

"Then what do you-"

"I'm talking about after the mission, after Pablo, what happens? A cartel leader is dead and now there's a power gap left over. That's what happened in the first place, no? We are here to destroy an evil man. There's no questioning that. But I want to know that there's a bigger and better plan for after."

"Sounds like you need religion."

Marcela snorted beer, coughing.

"I just want to know that the powers that be have a plan. God. CIA. What's the difference?" She wiped her nose. "You know, these stupid *chicos* have no idea who and what they're up against."

"The CIA? Or the cartels?"

"Ha. I meant the cartels. And the rest of the corruption in Latin America, really."

John thought about that. "I think they know, but I don't think it will make them act any different. We are what we are."

"You really think that?"

"Yes."

She took another swig of her beer as a couple of noisy motorcycles tore by.

"I know we're one piece of a puzzle. I just want to know what the puzzle looks like. Then I could be satisfied."

"What if you don't like what it looks like though?"

She ignored him. "What do you think, after Pablo?"

"I don't."

"I'm serious."

"So am I."

"We all know that." She winked at his soured expression. "But that's all we know. How much do you know about me? About why I'm doing this?"

Now that made John distinctly uncomfortable. More than before. "I wasn't going to ask."

"You should. It's important to ask. We're partners."

"We're not supposed to be personal, Marcela," he said tightly.

"Shut up. Really. Just shut up. It's not like we're sleeping together. I've put in my time, and I got that wig. Give me a break."

She said it so matter-of-factly. Again, John wasn't sure how to feel or what to think. So he did the only sensible thing. He closed his mouth and sipped his coffee. He was surprised she jumped right into personal storytelling without preamble.

"I do what I do because of my background, and what happened with my family. When the civil war began, they sided with the landowners. The landowners and government were backed by the Americans."

"But you're Mayan. That seems strange to me."

She pointed a finger at him while she drank. She finished with a sigh that was a bit too loud. "There's the rubbing."

"The rub."

"Hm?"

"You mean to say, 'there's the rub'. Not 'rubbing'."

"Yes, yes. Thank you for the grammar lesson, *profesor*. But you have to understand that not all Mayans were rebels. Just as not all landowners stayed with the government. Like all things, it is more *sutil* than that. More messy. Let me explain.

"My mother and father were both Mayan. They came from hard-working farmer lines, typical old-country types. My father was always a farmer and continued to be a farmer. My mother became something of an administrator, helping with our farm and others. They did well for themselves, especially because of her work.

"Now, their farmland wasn't their own. No Mayan farmer owned their own land, as far as I ever knew. It was on one of the *oligarcas familias's* lands, the Bello family. One of their big trades for hundreds of years was brewing, and they needed barley and wheat."

She sported one of her mischievous grins. "There was a big joke all the time about one needing beer and drink to be '*Bello*'. I always thought that was funny."

John smiled at that and prompted her to continue. She raised her beer in a 'cheers' gesture.

"They did well for themselves, so there was always a need for farming, and yes, administrators like my mother. And this meant we did okay as well. But a lot of other farmers and other Mayans didn't like arrangements like this one. It was, and is-" She made a triangle shape with her fingers. "*Pirámide*?"

John scrunched up his face, not understanding, then realized what she was getting at. "Oh. Feudal. Feudalism"

She snapped her fingers and nodded, taking a swig of beer.

"Exactly. Like European kings. They brought it here." She demonstrated further with her hands. "Landowners at the top, farmers at the bottom. Mayans are always at the bottom. No one liked being on the bottom, but my parents didn't seem to mind too much. They had an arrangement that they thought was fair. But not the others. They didn't like that my mother was administrating for the Bellos. She was becoming in the middle, above them, in many ways managing their farms.

"Then came communism."

She spat out a mouthful of beer over the table. A tourist must have noticed from across the terrace, instinctively reaching for his camera to take a picture. But Marcela took off her shades and shot him a glare so dangerous he awkwardly made it seem as though he was looking at the café sign, allowing his eyes to wander aimlessly until they returned to focus straight ahead. He went back to his business. She replaced her sunglasses and continued, hardly breaking her stride.

"As you know, the Mayans revolted against the landowners and the *oligarcas familias,* and the government. My parents did not. They weren't demonstrators or joining the soldiers or anything, but it was clear they didn't take the side of their fellow Mayans and farmers. And so, my mother was beaten to death in one of the Bello's estates one evening after a mob broke in through the windows. A week later, my father was hanged. Communism preaches equality. Well, we're all equal in death, no?"

John swallowed and bit the inside of his lip. Everyone had secrets, and everyone had skeletons in their closet. Hearing what they were made all the difference. Saying them out loud and having someone listen. Nobody seemed to understand that.

Her calm made him all the more disconcerted. But this was who they were. Two agents sharing a *café* and *cerveza*, looking like two friends or lovers enjoying the fading afternoon in Antigua.

"On the one hand, yes, I'm working against my nature, my heritage. On the other hand, I've never had that heritage. I've never been a poor farmer. Instead, just a girl who had her parents killed. America gave me my life back. More importantly, America gave me a purpose. I won't have something like that happen in my country again, John."

"And I can see how useful you are to American interests in Latin America."

She shrugged, but it was in agreeance.

"Pablo is Mayan," he said, hoping he wasn't breaching further into personal taboo.

Marcela looked at him then, her eyes growing hard. Harder than he'd ever seen in her. Then they lightened, full of laughter again, as if nothing had happened.

"Sure. I'll even admit it's a bit personal. Is it going to impact the job? No. I left any dreams of *venganza* like that behind a long time ago. There's a reason for why I do what I do now. Build a better world by stopping those who would make it worse. Say what you want, I fight for America because I do believe in America."

John gave that some thought. It was interesting. Watching things like Hollywood movies tended to paint the big bad empire up against justified rebels. John knew his history. Many people, Mayans, Latin Americans, or otherwise, didn't see the uprising that way. They saw the Americans backing a brutal capitalist dictator and crushing natives who'd been stamped under the thumb of colonialism for years. They saw their last chance of hope lit by the civil war and snuffed out by foreign money. Thousands of dead Mayans slept restlessly in mass graves.

But as she'd pointed out, it wasn't as simple as America/Latin America, capitalism/communism, Mayan/landowner...now it was a different ball game. Somewhere along the road, the line grew even more blurred than that. Drugs and sex trafficking cartels entered the picture. Marcela was describing the damage that justified creating units of their own. But there was something to be said about what that was doing in the long run, what it meant to be a part of it. He had no doubt they were shaping the world, though it wasn't something he often thought about.

Marcela looked at him expectantly. He leaned forward slowly, deciding he wasn't going to comment on what she'd said, or mention more history. But he could be personal. Maybe just a bit.

"Y'know, the best advice I ever got was from a fellow SEAL of mine on our way to an operation." He saw her lean forward for the details but he looked up and smiled. "No, it doesn't matter where it was, or when it was, or even what happened during the mission. But it was one of those ops that just didn't feel right, you know? Something just stunk."

"Like this one."

"Like this one," he agreed.

"Okay."

"Well, he was this kind of idiotic guy we all pushed around a bit, but it was all in good fun. We were a team. He wasn't so stupid anyway — he was a SEAL after all — but it was just how he would talk about girls, or he'd say how much he hated reading. Just these things that made him seem like a dumbass. Looking back on it now, I think he did it for our benefit. It makes me feel stupid realizing that now instead of then."

"Okay. What did he say? Your *amigo*?"

John flushed a bit, realizing he was rambling. Usually he didn't have more than one coffee in an hour. But he knew he couldn't just blame the coffee either. He had a tendency to bottle things up. He wasn't sure how else to do things.

"Right. We're about to hit the op and one of the other guys brings up what's on everybody's mind. The mission's shit. Something is foul. Maybe our orders are wrong." John closed his eyes, remembering. "And this idiot-guy, he walks right up to our naysayer, looks at him for a time, then smacks him over the head. The naysayer tries to say something, but gets clocked again. The idiot turns to the rest of us, and keep in mind, we're less than a day out from hitting the field, and he says something to the effect of this: 'Forget about the politics. Don't think about the politics. It's all bullshit. Both sides. It doesn't matter. We're not here for that'.

"And so we all shut up and did our job. Even the guy who got hit didn't say anything."

Marcela pursed her lips and blinked a couple times. John couldn't tell what she thought of the story.

"I feel like that doesn't answer the question that we have to ask ourselves."

"And what's that?"

"Why we do what we do. How many times a day do you ask yourself that? I have my reason. I just told you. What's yours?"

John thought for a moment. She hadn't been the first one to ask. Brian had asked him the same thing once. So had a close cousin of his. And no, he didn't ask himself that every day. Not until Brian. That had changed things. But he wasn't ready for that now. Not that he'd admit that.

"Maybe I'll tell you once we're done. For now, I'd like to start on that data."

He got up and stretched his arms. He could see her figuring out whether she should push him for a better response, but soon saw her decide it was best left alone. She nodded instead, something sad hiding behind the way her neck moved, stiff and controlled, less a gesture of agreement than a gesture of reluctant compromise. He put a hand on her shoulder as he walked by and lingered there, just a second too long, then gave it a short squeeze.

Marcela noticed he'd hardly drank his coffee, and watched him walk away.

CHAPTER 10

John rolled up to Arrivals at the St. John's International Airport Newfoundland,

Canada, and managed to wait a minute before a car behind him honked. He looked in the rear-view mirror to see a big woman with bright red hair giving him the finger from a black SUV. John recalled driving an SUV once, in a presidential parade greeting a foreign dignitary from Peru. They were unnecessarily large vehicles, and even at the time he had felt sheepish driving the hulking car down the streets of Washington. He gave the woman a frown and kept his foot on the brake.

He kept scanning the crowd coming and going through the airport doors. He was struck by the variety of people. Colors of brown and black, Asian and Caucasian features. Sikhs and Muslims wore turbans and hijabs respectively. When he was in the States, there was white and there was black. The racial divisiveness was palpable on the streets; he could *see* racism. Recent headlines from the Canadian Broadcasting Corporation (CBC) had recently reminded Canadians that no, America was not the only country with severe racist issues; but even so, seeing this swath of color and multiculturalism made John think of one thing: home.

He found himself staring at a group of young women in absurdly tight jean shorts when a knock on his window broke him out of his reverie. His hand started to go to his hip in reflex, but when he looked to the window, a young handsome man in a clerical collar and cassock was grinning and waving at him. John smiled back at his cousin Connor and rolled down the window.

"I feel so pompous still wearing this — I didn't have time to change between flights! The lady on the plane next to me kept trying to quote scripture and asking me questions. I was just trying to watch the movie."

John popped the trunk and the priest put his travel bag in the back. The SUV lady honked again and started yelling out her window.

"This isn't a parking spot, fucker! Move!"

"Sorry, we're just leaving, ma'am," Connor said to her.

"Fuck off and move!"

His cousin made to say something else, but John rolled down his own window.

"Ignore her and get in."

Connor looked at the woman, then looked to John, then made his way to the passenger side. John leaned over and popped the door open for him.

"That woman is crazy," John said, looking in the rear-view again.

"Must be Lutheran."

John choked on a laugh. Connor barely had his seatbelt done up before John floored the gas and tossed the man hard into the seat. Another honk followed them as they pulled out of the airport and cruised into more regular traffic. Connor let out a whoosh of air.

"Sorry. American driving. Keep forgetting to tone it down." John gave a wink.

"No kidding. When did you get back? How long are you back for?"

"Few days ago. Visited Mom and some old friends."

"You have friends?"

John laughed. "Acquaintances, then. I'm here for the week, then off to Latin America."

"Again."

"Again," John agreed.

"I didn't think you were allowed to tell me where you were going?"

"You're a priest. You're not allowed to tell anyone what I tell you."

Connor wagged a finger. "Only in confession, cous." But then Connor said, more seriously, "I'd never say a word."

After one of John's early missions, his unit's commanding officer had been convinced they should all see the Navy shrink. The mission had been rough and although some of the team may have needed it, John felt the provision was more of an annoyance than anything else. If he'd been ordered to he would've complied, but it just so happened that his cousin was visiting a seminary just out of town and John, wanting an excuse to see Connor anyway, convinced his CO that the priest would do better for him. He was fully licensed for trauma therapy and had treated vets with PTSD. Skeptical at first and going through hoops with the Navy shrink and chaplaincy, John finally received permission to see Connor as his therapist for certain matters. John signed a non-disclosure document regarding mission details and he followed it to a tee.

"This time it's a vacation," John said as he changed lanes and pulled onto the highway.

"Speaking of which, how was yours?"

Connor hung onto the handlebar above his window. "Hardly a vacation, mostly work."

"But Ireland."

Connor grinned. "But yes. Ireland is gorgeous."

They spent the rest of the ride home catching up, making jokes, and mostly talking about Connor's continually budding work in Ireland. They had relatives out there — closer to Connor than to

John by way of Connor's mother and John's aunt — and he had been studying and taking some classes that seemed fairly serious in the world of Catholic clergy. When John had jokingly asked him one night if he was learning exorcism, Connor had looked at him straight in the eyes and said, quite seriously, "John, I learned that years ago." Then, he had smiled and finished John's beer for him.

The small town of Trinity was a kind sight for travel-worn eyes. Connor made the obligatory theology jokes as they pulled past the sign advertising the town's name and John rolled down the windows after keeping them up on the highway. Cold salt air flushed through the car and both of them kept a comfortable silence, letting the wind do the talking for them.

John was turning as if to take them to Connor's small condo inland when his cousin asked if they could stop by his church instead. John had shrugged and turned the other way, bringing them closer to the sea, and eventually pulling up to an old but functioning church, home to a shrinking parish. Connor unlocked the side door meant for staff as John stretched his legs on the sidewalk. He was happy he didn't have to ask Connor to start the cappuccino maker after they had gotten to the office.

"This thing is the best," John patted it affectionately as Connor found the mugs.

"I swear I didn't raid the donations for it."

They sat in comfortable chairs and spoke some more about nothing. In one of the silences, John's eyes drifted over to the kneeling bench that sat in the corner of the office. There was a more proper confessional in the church, but Connor had once told John that some people preferred the comfort and softness of the office. John recalled himself saying something more rash at the time, calling a comfortable confession stupid, and Connor had been angry with him for one of the only times John could remember.

Connor had gotten up for a second cup when John spoke.

"Can I do a confession?"

Connor turned around and put the mug down slowly. He seemed surprised. He looked at John carefully.

"Sure." He nodded. "Yes, of course."

John put his own mug down on the cappuccino maker's table and then slowly brought himself to the kneeler. It was uncomfortable, which made John smile a bit.

Connor had unbuttoned his shirt but now buttoned it back up and put on a stole — purple for sorrow and penance — and brought his chair over. Connor gave John a moment to let out a breath. Anyone who had performed confession knew it was not an easy thing.

"Bless me Father, for I have sinned."

"How long as it been since your last confession?" Connor began. He didn't know. John racked his brain.

"Since Ecuador."

Connor nodded, but he didn't say anything.

"I want to…I want to tell you about my father."

Connor was silent.

"As you know, my father was a hard man. I never thought of him as a bad man. Scary maybe, but not bad, not…evil. But well, I had an argument with a colleague and it made me think about something coming back from Washington and…" His words were getting all muddied.

"What did you and your colleague argue about?"

"Ethics." It was always ethics with Brian. And really hard philosophical ethics too, nothing surface-value that could be quickly thought about. "He was going on about duty to law, which I agreed with, and then duty to do what's right, which I agreed with even more. But then we veered off when he started talking about laws that weren't right. I argued his points. It just kept going and going and he wouldn't let up-"

"I've been there."

John was irritated Connor had interrupted him now that he had found his train of thought, but continued without hesitating. "You don't know my friend. Not like I do. I wanted to go and enjoy the town a bit." He had been in its capital, Quito, but wouldn't be able to reveal the location for his cousin's benefit. "He just kept going and I couldn't even remember what I was disagreeing with. It seemed like he just wanted to argue, even though he's such a funny guy, he just gets in this mode and goes after the jugular. He finally said something about how we always have to do what's right, even when we want to do wrong to make right. Sometimes it's hard to do what's right to make right, but we still have to stay that course. Or something similar to it. But I disagreed. I said sometimes we had to do what seemed wrong. We kept going back and forth, again and again, and I was pissed, I was royally pissed off. Because Connor, really, our jobs don't make us knights in shining armor. Quite the opposite. You, maybe, but not us."

Connor made a noncommittal noise in his throat, and John continued.

"This friend of mine has a whole romantic ideal about goodness, not unlike you do with forgiveness and grace, but I can at least respect you because you live it. You're a priest. He isn't. It all just got me thinking about my father. I think that's what struck a nerve." John took a moment to regain his thoughts, but Connor must have thought John was nearing his conclusion.

"Are you confessing your argument with your friend, that you mistreated him? Or that your anger was unjustified?"

John's face was flushing slightly; just discussing the argument was making him mad and Connor's interruptions didn't make it any better. "No, my father said something similar to what I was arguing for, and that made me feel ashamed, I suppose. And I've been holding onto it for a long time. I stayed ignorant because I thought that was better. But my friend had to fuc...excuse me, he had to push me, and said that we have to be exposed to knowledge even if it's hard. Because the truth is right. Well, my father did something pretty bad. I don't even have all the details. I didn't follow it up. I didn't want to know what he'd done."

"This doesn't sound like your confession, John. This sounds like your dad's."

"Yes, but-"

"And although I'm sure God appreciates the sentiment behind confessing for him, he must do it himself-"

"Let me confess!" John yelled.

The rage that had boiled over was gone as quickly as it had come. Connor remained silent. John loved him for it, but also hated it.

"I'm sorry."

"It's okay."

"I didn't mean to yell like that."

"And I shouldn't have interrupted."

"Okay."

Connor sensed something else lurked beneath John's confession. Being a priest, he must have an ear for what hid under a man's words but rested in his soul.

"Do you want to stop? We can come back to this another time. You can confess something else."

Yes. "No." *Please God yes, I want to stop.* "Confession wasn't made to be easy, was it?"

"No. Okay, John. Continue."

He swallowed. There was a lump in his throat that refused to move. His stomach felt like it had on his first high-altitude high-open jump. Ten thousand feet out of a transport plane, over Perris, California. Over a hundred miles per hour. Arching his body to stabilize. He focused on the feeling, followed it, and found it taking him back to a memory.

"My father was reading the paper as he always did in the morning. He was always up before me. I walked slowly into the kitchen, still tired, said good morning, and got myself a bowl of cereal. My father was having the same. The milk kept dripping off his spoon. I hated that so much. I don't know why I remember that." He swallowed again. John thought Connor would say something like, 'go on', but he didn't. Connor was better than that.

"It wasn't until I had sat down with my bowl of cereal that I noticed the gun on the table. I had been pouring milk, I think, and it spilled, and it made me notice something there. It was my father's gun." He closed his eyes for a second, then opened them again, seeing the gun. "I must have been staring at it, because my father started talking. And he never spoke during breakfast or while reading the paper." John had probably inherited some of his father when it came to keeping dreadfully silent so much of the time. His lack of humor, his mild-manners, and work ethic had always been commented upon and linked to his father. Even now, he knew he was speaking more than he usually did.

"I wanted to ask what the gun was doing on the table. It frightened me. I wouldn't say so, but it did. That bothered me almost as much as the gun. My father must have sensed it. My fear. *The gun bothering you, John*? I never thought of him as a dangerous man, but he was a hard man, a tough one. Ice always seemed to linger under his words when he spoke seriously, which was most of the time.

No, I said, *but why is it on the table?*

Because it's served its purpose, and now it's yours.

"This was about a week or two after my mother and him had formally divorced, and my father had been acting more erratically... more rash than usual. No one seemed to pay this much notice because my father was so rigid that now he only seemed to act normal. But this normalcy hid a looseness I slowly began to think of as concerning."

John wasn't thinking about the words much anymore, he was seeing everything play out in his mind's eye and he spoke as it came, ignoring his blunt ineloquence and stupid sounding mimicry of him and his father talking. It was his confession anyway, he could say it as he liked.

"I finished my cereal by then — I decided it'd be best to finish eating and leave the kitchen — but my father wouldn't give me that. *Sit down.*

"I obliged. I sat gripping the empty bowl in both hands, looking down, thinking I could make a show of spooning some loose pieces of cereal in the small puddle of milk left behind. I don't know why that seemed to be a helpful option. I just wanted to avoid his eyes.

"My father picked up the gun.

"My heart leapt into my throat. He looked at the gun strangely. For a moment I thought he was going to shoot me. Or himself. Or me and then himself.

But instead he just kept staring at the gun. Like it was an old friend. He didn't usually smile in the way he did then. He didn't smile much at all. When he did it always seemed kind of sad. Then he spoke.

Do you know why I divorced your mother?

"*No*, I said. I didn't want to know. I convinced myself knowing wouldn't put things right and would only make things worse for me. It wasn't my business.

"He put the gun down and looked at me then. I must have let out a breath.

I divorced your mother, he continued, in a way that suggested this was more for him than for me, *because she was disloyal. Do you know what I mean by that, John?*

Yes, I said. I think I knew. I had already heard enough.

She cheated on me, John. She decided she needed a different man to make her happy.

"I didn't say anything. This was none of my business. Shame burned my ears anyway. I could feel them going red.

'Do you know who she was with, John?

No, I said, in a whisper.

John was breathing hard now. His blood pressure had been rising as he reached the part he didn't want to tell Connor but he needed to say. Connor was still silent, waiting.

"At first-" John cleared his throat, then mustered himself to continue. "At first I thought he was done talking. Then his eyes grew mad and he slammed his palms on the table, scaring me half to death. My spoon and bowl flew off the table and cracked on the floor.

The fucking priest.

"His face came to me, then. Father Neil, an average sort of man, middle-aged, shorter than most, silly moustache. He always greeted my mother and I warmly, and always said goodbye to us the same. Mother would attend his study groups and socials. Once or twice, I knew, she had called him on the phone, but the snippets of conversation I had heard were never...scandalous? Even so, all these thoughts became tainted as I saw his kindness become flirtation, his closeness become sexual advances.

So this morning, my father continued, when he had composed himself. *I walked to his house. It's not that far, really. Ten blocks. I counted. I rang the doorbell, and he came to the door wearing a funny housecoat, and he looked angry because it was pretty early, I suppose. And do you know what I did?*

"I didn't answer again until my father made it clear he wouldn't continue without me uttering something.

No, I said, I didn't know.

"My father grabbed the gun and slid it across the table to me.

I caught it mid-slide, without thinking. My father smiled. It was a proud smile this time. That chilled me. Oh God, that chilled me to the bone."

John bit back tears and they pooled painfully behind his eyes. He thought Connor was breathing hard. He couldn't tell.

"My father finished his coffee. He finished reading the paper. I sat there holding the gun. It felt warm to me. I don't know if it was, but I always remember the gun being so warm in my hands."

You might need this one day, John. Sometimes a man has to do an awful thing to make right.

There was a long pause. John couldn't hold back the mucus beginning to run down his nose. He broke the quiet with a hard sniff. Then he continued.

"I have the gun, Connor." Tears were welling in his eyes now, and he couldn't stop the words coming to his mouth. "I have the gun. I was going to throw it away, it's cursed, it's got bad blood on it, but I kept it because I thought one day I might need it. One day I might need to do something so awful that I'd need some help."

Silence. John took the opportunity to wipe his eyes. Connor cleared his throat but still said nothing, as if thinking.

Finally, his cousin spoke. His voice was hoarse but measured. "You have to get rid of it, John. Your sin is linked to the gun. You'll be harboring this guilt and this burden until it's gone. It's a psychological thing, forget about theology for a second."

"I know, I know. But I came for forgiveness."

"And God will give you that, and I will too. But you know you won't be able to forgive yourself until you throw that gun away and let go of what your dad said. You can see that, right?"

John nodded. With his tears gone they were replaced with a steely resolve. "I can, Connor, you're right. But I didn't come to ask forgiveness for keeping the gun. That I will take care of in my own time."

Connor stumbled for a moment, confused. "Did you just need to get it off your chest, then? I can give you a blessing and forgive any other sins you feel-"

John cut him off, albeit softly. "I ask for forgiveness because I didn't do anything. When my father told me." He paused. He didn't know what that meant, not really. Whether it meant telling his mother or going to the cops, or telling his father he was wrong. "I should have done something. And Connor, I promise God, and have you as my witness, that I will never let that happen again. I will not stand by in the face of wrongness. Even if it's hard."

Connor let the words linger. John thanked him silently for that.

"Okay, John. Is there anything else you wish to confess?"

"No. There's too much on the list, so we'll just knock that one off."

Connor laughed. John tried to as well, but a gross chuckle came out instead. His throat still hurt. His mother had once said his jokes were the best because no one expected them. That made him sad.

"You'll really forgive me for this, Connor?"

"Yes," his cousin said without a hint of hesitation. "God will, too."

That was something John felt he could never fully understand. Forgiveness, and given so freely.

"Then I ask it, humbly. From both you and of God."

Connor seemed to straighten as he acted *in persona Christi*, extending his hands above John's head. "The Lord God hears you and forgives you, John Carpenter. I absolve you from your sins in the name of the Father, and of the Son, and of the Holy Spirit."

John's voice was a whisper.

"Amen."

CHAPTER 11

———

"*Profesor* Builder?"

"Yes, Pablito?"

John and Pablito had been working at English conversational skills for the better part of the afternoon. Papers and a few pencils were strewn about the kitchen table. Pablito swung his little legs back and forth methodically in his chair, like he was pumping for momentum on a swing. John had learned the boy was rather cheeky, considering he had already earned himself a nickname.

"*La siesta?*"

Cheeky, but also lazy.

"No, Pablito, we must finish this last worksheet before taking a break."

Pablito gave an exaggerated sigh as if he were an old and weathered man. He picked up the pencil he had put down and carefully worked it into the crook of his hand, taking the time to get the grip just right.

John had put together a lesson and was pushing Pablito to make use of the English he knew in conversation, but decided to move on to some worksheets he had found off the Internet after the boy had started to get frustrated: fill in the blanks, word matchup, and spelling. John preferred to have more personal tutoring, but the sheets were a helpful change of pace, and sometimes seeing the words could make a big difference.

That being said, John had to remind himself that he wasn't here to teach, he was here to gather intel. But that didn't mean he couldn't do a good job of blending in.

"I want to play with my friends," Pablito said, whimpering as he painstakingly worked at the sheet in front of him.

John nodded but didn't reply. Pablito's friends would include many kids from the wealthy elite *oligarcas familias* or from other cartels — whether allies or rivals of Pablo's. Pablito may have private tutors, but he wasn't totally sheltered. He had his own bodyguards hovering at all times and Pablo would never truly fear for his safety. Much of Guatemala was dangerous, and kidnapping was a profitable enterprise. Antigua was ironically safer than most other cities precisely because so many cartels kept their families in Antigua. With so many cartels about, nobody wanted to make a move against them.

"Maybe your papa will let you play with your friends later," John said in English. "But you will have to ask him."

Pablito gave another soft, sad sigh. "*Papá* is at *Maximón*. He won't be back tonight. He sleeps at his summer home because it is closer."

John's eyes went up a bit at the mention of *Maximón*, the strange Catholic-Mayan deity and spiritual practice many Mayans followed. With Pablo out of the compound, John might have a little more flexibility to snoop around, even if the guards were watching at all times.

John sensed the boy was getting distracted. He didn't like sitting for long if he could help it either.

"Okay. Let's go for a walk."

Pablito squealed and launched out of his chair. John tidied up the papers in a neat stack, then led the way out of the kitchen.

"Where are you going?" The guard standing at the doorway snarled, even though he must have heard John perfectly well.

"A walk."

"Where?"

John frowned. He didn't like the idea of going to the courtyard, although that was his initial thought. The image of bloody arm stumps came to mind. It didn't disturb him as much as the thought of Pablito witnessing such acts did.

"Just the side of the villa. Some fresh air."

The guard thought for a moment, then nodded. "Okay." He let John lead Pablito out of the kitchen, but followed close behind. After moving through a couple of hallways they walked out the door into the sun air and dust of Antigua. John skirted the courtyard and moved to the side of the house, which was still larger than most backyards in North American homes.

"Can we play a game?" Pablito asked in Spanish. John didn't like how he kept switching over to his native language when he was trying to teach him English.

"What would you like to play?" John asked in English.

Pablito tapped his upper lip with his tongue. He looked like some ridiculous snake. John let him take his time. He couldn't think of any games. He thought of long summer evenings with neighborhood kids on his block back home. But training pushed most of that part of his life to the back corners of his mind. Thinking about it again was like meeting an old friend one hadn't seen in a long while. Familiar, but uncomfortable.

"We can play a game if you can ask me in English," John said, hoping that would buy him some time to come up with something.

"Can we...*jugar*..."

"Play. *Jugar* is play."

Pablito scrunched up his face like a prune again. "Play. Let's play a...game."

That's what his SEAL instructor used to say. *"Let's play a game, boys. Hide and seek. Underwater. Ten...nine...eight..."*

"Good, Pablito. Okay. Um…"

The only thing coming to mind as John dredged up games he had played in the past involved Navy SEAL training. There was Basic Underwater Demolition Training. There was Hell Week — five days and five nights of training with an hour a night for sleep. A strange blend of childhood games and military life began to bubble to the surface.

John cleared his throat. "Okay. Stand like this." John spread his legs into a warrior's crouch. Knees bent, but still standing, core tight and perfectly balanced.

Pablito bent his knees in half and sat a foot off the ground, as if he were defecating in a shallow latrine.

John laughed, taken completely off guard. He blinked at the surprise from both these things.

He moved to the boy and pulled him up, slapping his knees and thighs lightly.

"Like this. Not locked, but not bent all the way." He patted Pablito's stomach. "Flex. Good. Strong."

Pablito made a tough-looking face. John shot one back. Pablito winked, which seemed to take half his facial muscles.

"Okay, now, when I point my gun at you-" John pointed his fingers at Pablito, miming a pistol. "You have to hit the ground as fast as you can. Like this." John threw himself to the ground at such a speed that the guard watching looked startled.

Pablito nodded, seriousness covering his face.

John got up slowly. "You can also try and shoot me, and I will have to dive. But if you dive and the other person doesn't shoot, the shooter wins. Let's see who can get who."

Pablito was fast. He pointed a pretend gun at John before he could get into his proper crouch. But he wasn't as fast as John. It became obvious after Pablito tried, twice, then three times. Then John drew and said "Bang" before Pablito realized what had happened.

"Okay, so, this game isn't about just shooting, Pablito. You have to think when it is time to shoot, and when it is time to dive. You have to guess what your opponent is going to do." John spoke in English to keep pushing the boy's language skills, but used big hand gestures to help indicate what he meant. Pablito nodded, even if John was sure the boy didn't understand everything perfectly.

They stood facing each other, hands hovering at their hips like they were in a Western movie, a high noon draw. John gave a low whistle. Pablito twitched his hand and John raised an eyebrow. The boy froze and focused again.

John pulled an imaginary gun from his hip and Pablito hit the ground. Maybe John had been moving a little slower than he needed to, but it was a victory through and through. John gave a whoop of delight, smiling as the boy looked up from the ground. He looked sheepish at first, then returned the smile when he saw the pride on John's face.

John helped him improve his stance and showed him a smoother and less painful way to hit the ground. It felt good to be moving and pushing his body. It made John feel purpose in his limbs and muscles; that they were meant to be used, that he was meant to be doing something. They kept playing the game until both had won and lost more times than they could count. They'd grown tired and sweaty from the physical toll of it all. And as much as John loved Antigua, the endless dust was starting to bother him. He could put up with it for a time but now it began to sting his eyes, and he took a moment to wipe them as he gazed at the slowly drooping afternoon sun. Pablito agreed when he suggested they return inside to studying. They looped around the other side of the house. Pablito wanted to show John his father's helicopter, going so far as to name some of the different parts. John was impressed, but could tell Pablito was putting off the inevitable.

"Maybe we can practice some of your new conversation skills. Remember the questions. What is your name? Where is this street? Questions help someone talk more. It's good to practice that."

Pablito nodded and yawned as he made his way to the kitchen. One of the servants had put out a plate of roasted broad beans. After some puppy-eyed begging, Pablito also managed to get half a kebab from one of the cooks preparing dinner. It had chicken and red pepper and pineapple grilled together. John ignored his stomach growling. Juice ran down Pablito's chin from the kebab and John stopped himself from reaching forward and wiping the boy's mouth. Pablito used his shirt. The boy caught John staring at him in disapproval and must have misinterpreted it as jealousy for the kebab. He looked for a moment at the stick of food then offered it to John.

Surprised, John quickly waved his hands away.

"*Graçias, señor* Pablito. But I am already a grown man. You need it so you can be strong. But you are very kind to offer."

Pablito wiggled his nose in delight, full of childish pride at performing a good deed and given recognition by an adult.

John pushed the comfort he was feeling aside for a moment. He couldn't get distracted. He still had a job to do.

"Maybe we could work somewhere else? You are always in the kitchen." As he was speaking John realized what the reason was. Pablito gave him the answer anyway.

"But that is where the food is!"

John gave a short laugh. "Okay. Well, let's try some other room." He wanted to try and inch around the compound as much as he could, observing anything out of the ordinary that might hint at the hidden location of the kill switch. It was most likely that the kill switch, whatever its form, would be hidden in some locked location, tucked away from plain sight. But moving about may help expose a weakness he could exploit later. Constant time spent in the kitchen was making him feel cooped up.

"Let's go to mine!"

Pablito took off down the hallways before John could voice a protest. The guard watching over them looked at John with a blank expression, then jogged off after Pablito.

John sighed. He had little interest in seeing the boy's room, but he took the opportunity to scan the halls, rooms, even get a glimpse of the art scattered shamelessly at every turn. It was obvious that Pablo had taste — expensive taste — and it was clear he enjoyed boasting about his wealth and reputation as *patrón* this way. Even while knowing the underlying reason, John couldn't help but appreciate the culture and artistic depth on display. John would never pretend to understand art in the same way a historian might, but it moved him nonetheless.

"*Profesor* Builder! Here! Come on!"

John tore his eyes away from an abstract painting depicting Guatemala's flag dripping onto a cornfield and turned the corner to find Pablito in his room. The boy beckoned John forward, and he jumped onto his king-sized bed as John approached. Two guards were posted at the doorway and watched John closely. He ignored them and passed them by.

"Welcome to my…*habitación!*"

"Room," John corrected, looking around.

"Roooom!" Pablito bounced on his bed, excitement bursting from his limbs.

If Pablito hadn't told John that the room belonged to him, he would have no way of knowing. Art hung on the walls like any other space in the estate. John noted a particularly mature nude painting of some beautiful figure, in a style that made him think of Classical or Renaissance periods. Apparently Pablo had little interest in treating his child like a child.

John's eye quickly found another gorgeous art piece dominating the wall near the door. He walked up to it immediately, drawn to it as naturally as a moth to a flame.

"A Mayan calendar," he remarked out loud, unable to conceal his fascination.

One of the guards had sneaked into the corner of the room, eyeing John with general disinterest, but Pablito bounced himself off the bed and ran to John like a puppy nipping at its owner's heels.

"Yes!" Pablito cried. "It's Mayan like me and my *papá*! *Papá* says it keeps the time!"

John thought about all the disappointed conspiracy theorists who had thought the Mayan calendar's dating meant the world would end in 2012. None of them had taken the time to simply appreciate its elegance. This Mayan calendar was particularly impressive. It was made of stone, hand carved, and painted a dozen different colors, resulting in a rainbow of ancient images.

"You like it?" Pablito asked.

"Yes, it's very nice."

"My favorite part is the little face in the middle!"

"The *Tonatiuh*."

Pablito stared at John then stuck out his tongue and furrowed his tiny little eyebrows. "The tanootooah?"

John smiled. "The *Tonatiuh*. It's the little face in the middle as you said, its tongue sticking out, like you. That's what it's called." Pablito seemed to be listening as John went on, recollecting what he'd learned and taught years ago. "It's the sun god of the Mayans."

"Like, God? *Cristo*? My *papá* went and met him tonight. And *Maximón*."

"No, um...that's different." John decided not to try and further explain the complexities between Christian and Mayan deities. Seeing that Pablito wasn't going to pursue that line of thought, John returned to marveling at the calendar. He was about to suggest they get on with their language lesson when he noticed Pablito shuffling at something on the floor and awkwardly pawing at the Mayan calendar. John turned to see Pablito standing on a little step stool so he could increase his reach.

John, perplexed, and concerned the boy might somehow knock the heavy stonework off the wall brought his hands to hold the boy's shoulders. "Pablito, what are you-"

And then Pablito pushed the centre face of the calendar. It pushed *in*, separating, and indenting from the rest of the stone before popping back out to its regular position.

John was taken aback. He'd never seen a Mayan calendar with a push-feature like that. He didn't know what purpose it might serve, even artistically. He began to ask Pablito when the boy interrupted him.

"My *papá* says to push it every day for good luck!"

John opened his mouth to reply, but not before hard realization kicked in.

John's pulse quickened as adrenaline poured into his system.

This was it.

This had to be the kill switch, if not something equally clandestine. It made sense. Pablo, insane and brash, and doting so much on his son that he'd give him the responsibility of guarding such a thing. Marcela hadn't been able to find it because she wasn't able to get into Pablito's room. But how did it work? What was the mechanism? And how would they disable it? His gaze snapped onto Pablito. The boy was full of excitement, trying to contain himself, but then he suddenly sunk back into himself. John realized his eyes must have gone cold. He blinked and tried to give the boy a disarming smile instead.

"He says to push it every day for good luck?"

"*Sí í.*"

"Oh, that's interesting. What happens if you don't push it?"

Pablito darkened. "I always push it. I have to. *Papá* says it is very important."

"Ah. And have you always done this?"

"I always push it. Every day."

"But have you done this all your life? For many years?"

The boy shook his head vigorously. "No. It is a new thing! But an important thing."

Pablito stepped off the stool and moved it back where he found it. It was as if the stool was set there specifically for the task of pushing the centre of the Mayan calendar. Following a hunch, John tilted the stone to the side and peered into the dark shadow of the calendar up against the wall. Sure enough, he saw a wire threading out from the centre of the calendar. But even more shocking was a square patch of metal along the wall, hidden entirely by the Mayan calendar.

It was the door to a safe.

"*Profesor!*"

John made it look like he was still admiring the artistic quality of the disc, as he slowly lowered it back in its flat hanging position.

"Yes, Pablito?"

Pablito moved close and beckoned John. John bent down to the boy. Pablito dramatically glanced over his shoulder at the guard, then cupped his hands and whispered in John's ear.

"Don't tell anyone. Pushing the calendar. It's a secret!"

John looked at the guard, who was staring out the bedroom window. He was distracted by a young gardener who had dropped some tools, bent over and picking them back up. John was about to tell Pablito that the guards had probably seen him push the button a hundred times. But then he thought that maybe that didn't matter. The guards might not know the location of the kill switch either.

John felt an itch, an urge to act on his discovery. Approach the guard from behind. Break his spine at the base of the neck. Lock Pablito in the closet. Eliminate the guards at the door.

But it wouldn't do any good to go prying into the safe now. Or to show he had any knowledge of the safe altogether. He needed to let Marcela know, then they could put together the last few pieces of their plan. If this was the kill switch, they could move on Pablo soon.

Soon.

'A secret,' Pablito mouthed to John.

John winked and pulled a chair out from a desk, facing Pablito, who had taken up residence on the too-large bed, finally getting to their proper language lesson. John began to ask the boy some basic conversational questions in English.

But Pablito, John wanted to say, *your father isn't supposed to have any secrets.*

***

John was more exhausted from his time spent with Pablito than he'd like to admit. But finding a hidden safe and probable location of the kill switch had given him a much-needed burst of motivation. He turned his renewed determination to the wig Marcela had given him, digging into the data over a cup of awful instant coffee in his hotel. He had decided to bring the safe house laptop with its decoding program to his hotel in order to limit their safe house traffic.

In most cases, John would send off the information to Esteban and his team to dig through and analyze. But because the wig proved such a useful tool, it had to have a failsafe in place — its data corrupted as soon as it was sent, even if through an encrypted email or private server. This meant users needed to be using the physical wig if they wanted to garner its stored information. The only way to get around such a limitation was to take a picture of the information one page at a time, and with so much data, it was impractical unless something was discovered and it wasn't a large quantity of content. In a world of regular leaks and hacking and other cyber-security nightmares, the CIA R&D folks made the wig an in-person and limited kind of gadget.

John took a sip, grimacing, and scrolled quickly through some land-ownership documentation that seemed promising, but ultimately yielded nothing of interest. He was trying to find anything to do with the safe or mention of something that would indicate what the kill switch entailed, when he found some intriguing legal documentation. He skimmed most of it, but paused when he reached mention of Sandor's death, and some saved files regarding his will. It looked like there had been some tampering, which was strange to say the least.

There were two copies. The first appeared to be the original, the second had been altered. The first indicated Juan would inherit much of his father's assets, including an exorbitant amount of funds and business resources. The 'business resources' were less than specific in the will, but must be referring to the sex trafficking Sandor was known to be heading. Yet here, in a second copy, Juan's inheritance had largely been siphoned off to Pablo. It seemed an obvious play by Pablo to take control of the cartel, usurping what Juan would have inherited and having to settle with answering to his nephew. But Pablo hadn't signed off on it.

Isabella had.

John's head spun for a moment as reasons collided with a variety of suspicions. John suspected Pablo wasn't able to sign off on the document to make it legally binding. But how had he convinced Isabella to hand over her son's inheritance — a large cut of the underground empire? Why would she want to rob her son of power and wealth? Did she simply favor her new husband over her son?

Moreover, why had Juan agreed to this? Had he? It could be something as simple as Pablo intimidating them both.

John leaned back in his chair and took another sip of his coffee, momentarily forgetting how terrible it was. He spat it back into the mug and promptly stood to dump it into the sink.

He decided to isolate the findings and send a few pictures off to Marcela. He'd see if she could leverage it. She was integrated into the Puentes family and would have a better chance using it to any advantage. John, on the other hand, was looking forward to getting the real operation underway. Every day they took increased their chances of being found out and the whole plan being botched.

The rest of the evening moved slowly as he dug intently through the wig, but he found little else of interest. That was fine. He had potentially found something, and his spirits remained high after finding the bizarre calendar and hidden safe. He eventually decided to call it a night, unplugging the wig, purging all the residual data from his laptop, and locking both devices in his hotel lockbox. As he brushed his teeth in the small washroom allotted for his room, he thought of the remaining piece of the puzzle: Pablo.

All he needed was an opportunity to get Pablo out of the compound and get him into the safe house for questioning. Esteban might be worried about the kill switch, but John was less concerned. If the hidden safe somehow didn't prove fruitful, he'd beat the answer out of Pablo. The kill switch was supposed to stay inactive as long as the man lived, so it shouldn't go off if the man wasn't dead. That, John could oblige him.

He laid down in his bed, ramrod straight on his back, using only a thin sheet to cover himself and foregoing the thicker blanket because of the stuffiness of the room. He turned out the lamp at the bedside night table and closed his eyes, forcing sleep to brush his consciousness. His mind managed to wander as he wrested to get it under control. He was back in Antigua. The place held good memories. It also held the worst memories. The place, he thought simply, was a lot of things. His last thoughts considered Pablito. An innocent boy in the middle of so much trouble, hopefully far enough removed from John's mission that he would be safe.

Antigua was considered safe for cartel families and kids like Pablito. Truthfully, John was happy for it. Innocent children like Pablito should never be hurt because their parents decided to profit through a life of crime and brutality. Hopefully, Antigua would always remain safe for the children.

But John would make sure it wasn't safe for men like Pablo.

CHAPTER 12

Pablo sat in the back of his Mercedes, comforted by air conditioning and greeted by a view of the countryside most didn't get to enjoy. His driver, Mateo, was winding his way past a mountain, carefully and methodically measuring his gas pedaling for a smooth but timely ride. Two of Pablo's best guards accompanied him — Vinicio riding in the front beside Mateo and Carlos next to him in the backseat. Both held Remington TAC-14's across their laps.

"It is nice weather, no?"

All three of Pablo's men nodded or voiced their agreement. Pablo smiled and looked out across the valley, seeing Antigua tucked between the mountains like a little egg in a bird's nest. It was a cozy sight that brought warmth to his heart. Shade bore over the valley for a moment as a fluffy cloud moved in front of the sun, then departed, leaving sunshine in its wake once again.

The mountains seemed to fold over themselves, forming ridges like the coils of a great snake. Roads circled around them and farmers carved their land and irrigation where the roads did not.

They were nearly at their destination, a church on the edge of Escuintla. It was one of the key players in Guatemala's power structure. Unsurprisingly, the Catholic Church had its fingers in the country's politics and socio-cultural values. They had supported the poor, many of whom opposed the *oligarcas familias* during the civil war, and continued to help the destitute today. The church helped morph what people thought and molded them to their leanings. They helped shape policy and were an important network for the country's underground to be rubbing elbows with. That was the reason Pablo was headed there.

Sandor Puentes had taught Pablo the importance of giving gifts to the right people and the right institutions. Sandor had been a man who worked with rather than against the powerful. He didn't carve his empire from his enemies — he assimilated them. Sandor's empire was built amongst the foundations of what was around him: mutual strengthening, partnerships, and symbiosis. 'Like a bee and a flower', Sandor would say.

For all their disagreements, Pablo recognized the importance of these actions. But to him this wasn't a partnership: it was clear cut bribery. Sandor was like a vulture picking at the leftovers. His philosophy lent too much power to his enemies. Pablo had no true desire to work with the elite as Sandor had. He was a man of the people. He fancied himself helping the poor like a modern day Hermano Pedro de San José Betancurt, Guatemala's first saint. But to help the people, he needed to placate the powerful, keep Sandor's 'symbiosis' alive. For now, at least.

The Mercedes pulled to a smooth stop on the gravel right in front of the church's front door, leaving little walking for Pablo to cover. Carlos and Vinicio opened their doors and left the car, moving to open the trunk. Mateo turned off the engine and slid out of his seat, moving beside Pablo's door in one swift motion, opening it obediently with a stiff little bow.

Pablo swung his legs over the seat and did up a button on his cream suit jacket as he stood. The guards that had gone to the trunk were beside him moments later, Vinicio carrying a large black duffle bag.

Pablo nodded. "Let us see our friends."

They entered the church without further comment, one of the men holding open the heavy wooden door for Pablo. It was an old church, built by Spaniards and meant for a Spanish faith, but now held a Mayan faith. It seemed some tensions would never abate. If one looked closely, they would notice the contempt in Pablo's eyes.

Not for the faith. He was Catholic, despite his enterprise, despite his heritage, despite himself. It was a paradox only the faithful, or the criminal, could understand. There were no true friends or enemies. Most of the time they were both. Pablo hated the wealthy corruption that infested the holy faith. The church was meant to be for the people, like he was.

Pablo and his men dipped their fingers into holy water and crossed themselves. The ceiling hung fifty feet above them, lights brought low, shadows flickering from candles lining the walls. A massive crucifix made completely of marble sat above an altar at the far end of the great hall.

"¿Señor?"

The voice carried like a whisper in a cave. It came from a young priest who was in the midst of lighting candles, surprised to see Pablo and his men stepping inside the holy sanctuary. The priest eyed the men cautiously. Even with their weapons left in the car, their uniforms and black berets made the men's presence imposing. Pablo wouldn't stand for them bringing shotguns onto holy ground.

Pablo eyed the priest in kind as he moved across the floor to meet them. He let the silence reach an uncomfortable level, then gestured to Vinicio. He handed the duffle bag over. The priest took it, an automatic gesture, not knowing what else to do.

"I hope it is enough."

He knew it was enough. Of course it was enough. Because it was more than anyone would pay and more than any priest would expect. Which was precisely why he did it.

The priest looked dumbfounded, staring at the duffle bag, then back at Pablo. Pablo's smile didn't waver.

"You can keep the bag."

Pablo reveled in these little moments. They brought him a special childlike joy.

"Ernesto, I said to tell me when the *patrón* arrived!" An older priest rushed from an open door in the back of the church. His voice was like a whip cracking against the silence of the church.

The young priest jumped a bit, trying to turn but struggling with the weight of the bag in his hands. By the time he managed to turn around, he was face to face with his superior.

"*Padre, lo siento,* I…*perdóneme.*" *Father, I'm sorry, I…forgive me.*

The older priest had a dark look about him, but Pablo didn't want young Ernesto getting into trouble. He hadn't done anything wrong by Pablo's account.

"*Padre* Eco, it is good to see you."

Father Eco's face brightened immediately, and he shooed Ernesto off into a corner of the church.

"And you as well! You look good!"

"I am, I am."

"Ernesto, place that bag in my office and return to your duties," Father Eco called in an even tone. "We don't want our lambs losing their way from the flock," he continued, speaking to Pablo.

"Yes, yes, of course."

The young priest darted off and Padre Eco smiled warmly, spreading his arms.

"Our church is yours. Perhaps a *café* for you? And your men?"

"A *cerveza*." Carlos grinned. Vinicio snickered.

Pablo whipped towards Carlos and snapped his fingers, poking the man hard in the chest. *Carlos,* Pablo thought. *A loyal man but talks too much. Likes to drink too much.* Carlos cast his eyes downward, ashamed. Pablo turned back slowly to *Padre* Eco, still smiling as if nothing had happened.

"We are okay. *Graçias.*"

"Or would you like to make a confession? My time is yours, *patrón,* it would be no trouble at all."

Pablo closed his eyes and gave a small sigh. He hated how this priest was always pushing him. One day he would bring the man something different than money. Perhaps a stick instead of the carrot.

"No. Thank you, *Padre,* but no. I have places to be. You know how it is. I just wanted to make sure I gave tithe to the church. The church that looks out for its people. The poor, the starving, the faithless. Bring them peace and comfort."

Pablo noticed the man looked a little sad at this answer, but then the priest looked over his shoulder where his underling had carried the duffle bag away and smiled all the same.

"Of course, *Patrón.* Thank you. Your help is much appreciated."

"I know it is." Pablo went so far to pat the priest on the shoulder. Eco frowned a bit, but then gave a stiff nod as Pablo and his men dipped their hands again in holy water and made their exit.

Once back in the car, Pablo made eye contact with Mateo in the rear-view mirror and closed them for a moment before opening them again. He curled his lips in a satisfactory gesture. The Mercedes came to life under Mateo's hands and Pablo's silent order, and they pulled away from the church.

They sped down the opposing side of the mountain road, roaring with haste and purpose. The driver knew Pablo had a certain amount of patience, but he also knew how important their real destination was. Mateo spared little time to slow on the winding road, though he took care not to throw his passengers around on the turns and bends. He eventually eased into a patterned smoothness only rural drivers knew well.

It wasn't until they were into the next valley and approaching Lake Atitlan that Pablo pursed his lips and said "Slow down, *amigo*."

Mateo complied with the immediacy that comes from someone used to following orders. They were on their way to Santiago, the largest community on the lake, and the source of Pablo's roots. It was the seat of his ancestral home and people, the Tz'utujil; one of the twenty-one Mayan ethnic groups in Guatemala.

Pablo's eyes lingered over the glistening blue waters of Lake Atitlan, reputed to be the most beautiful lake in the world. But Pablo saw more than its beauty. The lake was the site of much of the violence and bloodshed taking place during the Guatemalan Civil War. Pablo still remembered the tragedy of Father Stanley, an American Roman Catholic priest who was loved by his Tz'utujil parishioners. The priest was so passionate about the people that he translated the New Testament and celebrated Mass in Tz'utujil.

Right-wing death squads assassinated him on July 28th, 1981. In a fit of radical love, the Tz'utujil removed Father Stanley's heart and buried it under the altar of his church.

Though he was very young when it had happened, Pablo remembered. He crossed himself in silence, his men saying nothing. The car left the shore of Lake Atitlan behind as they pulled into the town of Santiago. They made their way past the first few streets, sporting middle-class buildings made of concrete and cinder blocks, moving further into town. At this point they had to slow down.

A crowd was beginning to form up ahead in the street. They were pulling in to one of the poorer districts of Santiago. The concrete buildings gave way to lean-tos, shacks, and haphazardly built shop stalls. A few more sturdy buildings stood between these ramshackle structures, but even they were old and unkempt: their clay and plaster walls chipped, tin roofs rusted, with holes eroded in the metal.

The Mercedes pushed onto the main strip of cobblestone road, which lead to the center of the village. The crowd clambered and pushed against the car, yelling incoherently, smiles and tears on a sea of faces. Vinicio and Carlos gripped their shotguns, stoically staring forward, faces hard but showing concern. Their master seemed to hardly notice them, pressing his face against the window like a little boy and smiling broadly.

Mateo gave a quiet snarl at the crowd as he struggled to continue moving forward. He raised a hand to honk the horn. He snapped to silence when Pablo gave the man's seat a hard kick.

"It is okay, we will move like the *tortuga*. It is no race."

Mateo gave a quick nod of compliance, carefully inching forward. The people were pushed away slowly, peeling off the car like a fruit's skin.

Pablo rolled down his window a couple inches and the cheers and cries from the crowd grew as they penetrated the car's interior.

"Puentes! Puentes!"

"*Patrón! Patrón!*"

"*Salvador divino!*"

Pablo grinned and waved a little hand like he was royalty. He reached into his suit pocket and pulled out a thick wad of American bills. He unslung the elastic, gave them a shake so they furled, then tossed them high out the window. The bills exploded like a green firework above the crowd, and people yelled and jumped, grabbing desperately at the spinning bills in the light breeze. Those who were clamoring at the front of the car ran to where the money was falling slowly, soon joining the mob of people snatching up money from the ground.

"There you are, *amigo*," Pablo said to Mateo. "Now let us find our way."

Less than a mile up the main road, a small group of villagers had gathered, waving their hands to flag the car down. Mateo parked and the other two escorted Pablo from the car, over to where the group waited.

They were dressed poorly, but didn't seem too underfed. Pablo made sure to take in these little details. These were his people, after all. Their features gave them away as Mayan.

"*Patrón*, it is an honor to have you back in our village," one of the women said as she took a small step forward. She was bigger and rounder than the others, reminding Pablo of his own hardworking mother, complete with apron and headscarf.

"I am Akna," she said, giving a little bow.

Pablo stopped her bow short, grabbing her gently by the shoulders. "No, no, none of that. We are family." He tapped his breast and pointed to her own, indicating her heart.

She smiled and received him in a great hug. She turned and spread an arm over the rest of the group in introduction. They waved shyly and Pablo nodded politely back at them. There was an awkward pause when it became clear the group had nothing more by way of fanfare.

"And who has our *Maximón* now?" Pablo asked, smiling, a note of seriousness seeping into his voice.

"Babajide, *Patrón*. Come, we will introduce you."

Pablo and his guards followed the group as they folded into an unorganized column and moved into the small low-ceilinged house behind them. Akna held the flap of cloth aside for Pablo and his men as they entered.

The house was made of small square rooms, filled with handmade artwork and old couches and other quaint furnishings. Dust and tobacco smoke moved visibly across beams of light that ventured into the house through the opened window flaps. But Pablo hardly took in the room and its décor. The only thing he had eyes for was who he had come to see.

And there he was. Sitting on the couch, politely waiting for him. *Maximón.*

He wore a black wide-brimmed hat on his brown oval head, thick lips open in an 'o' shape. His suit was mismatched: the jacket was pink with brown cross-hatching, the pants were navy blue. He must have had a dozen ties around his neck; finishing the look were cowboy boots, and dark black sunglasses over his eyes.

Strictly speaking, he wasn't alive or human. The figure sitting on the couch was crafted from wood and dressed by the contributions of this group. But the effigy could hardly be considered fake when *Maximón* was very real.

He was a powerful Mayan deity, and was the product of the combined Catholicism of the Spanish and the native Mayans in Guatemala. *Maximón*, also known as *San Simón*, was revered by Pablo and so many of the people he cared for. He liked *Maximón* because he was a bit of a trickster. One legend said that *Maximón* had been asked to watch over some fishermen's wives because the men were afraid they would sleep around while they were out in their boats. *Maximón* agreed, but when the men came back they had found that their wives had all slept with the deity. But aside from old legends, everyone today had a story about *Maximón*. So many had been healed by him, or come into prosperity, or otherwise had their prayers answered in the hardest of times. Some had powerful visions. Pablo felt a strong connection to the deity and his patronage. The Catholic Church might reject *Maximón*, but the church hadn't answered Pablo's prayers. *Maximón* had.

"*Patrón*, I hope you like him. I made him myself."

A wiry middle-aged man had a hand on *Maximón's* shoulder, brushing it with pride and moving to fuss over the effigy's ties.

"Ah, you are Babajide?"

"*Si, Patrón,*" the man said shyly. He took off his hat. It was similar to *Maximón's* wide brimmed one and he held it nervously with his eyes downcast.

"Akna said you were the man of the hour! Now, is this where we will have our prayers answered?" The slightest disdain entered into Pablo's voice.

Babajide's eyes shot up and he put his hat back on in an instant. "Oh no, *Patrón*! We were only waiting for you!"

"Good, good, let's go then."

Babajide waved another man over and the two carefully picked up *Maximón* and moved through a flap of cloth into another room. Akna smiled at Pablo and led him and his men on, with the rest of the group following on their heels.

Different villages and towns had different *Maximóns.* Occasionally, new ones were created and they would travel around, be kept in different houses and placed on different altars. Pablo made an effort to visit as many new ones as he could, even if it meant leaving Antigua. It also meant he could spread his wealth a little farther as well, and meet new people who would come to love him.

They moved through a cramped kitchen then turned toward the back, leading to a room normally used for storage. The late afternoon sun shone through cracks and holes in the tin roof overhead. The dirt floor was hard under his feet and he kicked up dust as he pushed past a cloth curtain covering the entrance. He quickly saw how the storage room had been converted into an altar and worship space. Candles lined shelves along with jars of preserves, and large potted flowers crowded around a massive chair at the far end of the dark room. The men were placing *Maximón* in his seat, making sure he was presentable and in good shape.

Pablo pulled a cigar from his suit jacket then removed the jacket altogether, handing it over to one of his men. He retrieved a small box of matches from his pants pocket, lit a match, and held the flame delicately to the end of the cigar. He puffed a few times to get it going, then waved out the match and flicked it away. He approached *Maximón*, sucked on the cigar a bit more, then removed it, eyeing it for a moment, before putting the cigar in *Maximón's* mouth.

"Enjoy, *amigo*," Pablo said softly, smiling as he turned to look over his shoulder.

One of his men held out a bottle of *Quetzalteca*, a sharp raw cane liquor. He took it, twisted open the cap and gave the liquor a sniff.

"Only the good stuff for my *Maximón*."

He raised the bottle in a toast, took a swig, then turned to find Akna at his side. He offered the bottle and she took it, toasted the effigy, then took a drink as well. She closed her eyes and smiled as the liquor warmed her throat. After a moment she leaned closer to Pablo than he'd normally find comfortable.

"And what does the *Patrón* ask of our beloved *San Simón*?"

Pablo didn't turn to look at her, though he could smell the liquor on her breath. He stared at *Maximón* a moment longer, closed his eyes and took in the dank air, then looked up to the ceiling, focusing there for a time.

"I want what anyone wants," Pablo finally said, slowly, choosing his words with care. "But I come to ask for *Maximón's* approval." He was suddenly very aware of the group of people behind him, his own men among them, hearing his words. He didn't want them to leave. This ritual was not just for him. But he did not want everything he had to say be heard either.

He lowered his voice. "It has been a trying month. A good month. Yet…with my brother's death, and taking everything over, and doing things…right."

Akna bristled. She opened her mouth to speak, then closed it. Pablo brushed her hand with his, gesturing for her to tell him what was bothering her.

"We had…many missing girls and women here, *Patrón*. It is no secret where they went."

"I do not like secrets," Pablo replied softly, trying to contain his rage. "And I am not my brother. I will not have such practices continue. Things will be different now. The way they should be. The way they should've been. For poor Isabella's sake, and for my people's."

Akna was on the verge of tears as relief flooded her face. "Thank you, *Patrón*."

Pablo raised a finger. "I want *Maximón's* blessing, and him to let me know if things are wrong. And protection. For my little *hijo*. If I do wrong, have him tell me. If Pablito is in danger, I need to know. With these prayers, I shall be at peace."

She nodded slowly, and took a small sip of *Quetzalteca*. "You will have his blessing. Do not fear for your son. He shall be safe. *Maximón* hears you, and will say if he is angry with you. When he wants to get your attention, *Patrón*, he can make the very mountains shake if he wanted to."

"I didn't think *Maximón* was an angry god."

She shrugged and her eyes twinkled. "He is a trickster. He would sooner toy with you."

Pablo couldn't help but let a laugh loose. Then Akna turned back to business and Pablo followed suit. She took a large gulp this time, and Pablo raised his arms and tightened his face in affirmation.

She sprayed the *Quetzalteca* from her mouth in a short burst.

He turned slowly, taking in the ritual, trying to soak in the spiritual connection as his shirt soaked up the alcohol. She sprayed again as he turned, again and again.

"*Maximón…*" Pablo said soft enough that only Akna could hear, and in a way that one would only say to a lover or trusted friend.

And for a moment, Pablo thought he heard *Maximón* reply.

***

Pablo and his men had stayed longer than intended, but this was common whenever a visit to *Maximón* took them out of town. They had feasted with their hosts and swapped stories, and Pablo had gotten a little drunk while he was at it. It had been a good night. It was customary to give tobacco, alcohol, or money as an offering to *Maximón*, and seeing as how he'd done the first two he'd been sure to hand over a duffle bag of money. Pablo enjoyed watching dreams come true before his eyes. Many prayed for wealth and prosperity from *Maximón*. Some saw this as an answer to their prayers. Perhaps *Maximón* worked through the *patrón*. There had been many tears before Pablo and his escort had gotten back into the Mercedes.

"Okay. Let's go," Pablo said, stifling a small yawn.

"Home, *patrón*?" Mateo asked. He at least had stayed mostly sober.

"Oh, no, no, we will go to the summer house. Have a little rest there."

It was another customary move by Pablo. After seeing *Maximón* and returning late from out of town, he loved to spend the night at one of his favorite properties in Jocotenango, north of Antigua. It was as much a part of the ritual as praying to *Maximón*. The men usually enjoyed it too, although the stretched security made them anxious and they'd have to pull longer shifts. But such was the cost of luxury.

Mateo started the car and they pulled away, off into the mountains once more.

"And how was your praying, *amigo*?" Pablo asked of no one in particular, drunk and more loose-lipped than usual.

Mateo said he had asked for wealth and Pablo laughed, telling him he didn't need *Maximón* for such things. Vinicio said something quiet about a long lost lover from Escuintla. When Carlos, who sat beside Pablo, didn't respond right away, Pablo grew irritated and prodded the man.

"Yes, *Patrón*, you know I always pray, but…"

"But what?"

"But, you know, *Maximón* is a trickster, and I am always more afraid to get what I pray for than not."

Pablo was silent for a moment, scrunching up his nose and brow in a thoroughly concentrated expression. Then he let out a harsh laugh, and the other two men joined him, and eventually Carlos laughed as well.

I'll take my chances, Pablo thought, as he wiped away a couple tears from laughing so hard. *As long as my Maximón doesn't sleep with Isabella!*

CHAPTER 13

─────────

John slept soundly in his hotel bed. The mattress was softer than he'd expected and the sheets were thin but warm. He lay peacefully resting, enjoying a piece of tranquility almost foreign to his being. If he were able to see the small smile spread across his lips, he'd sheepishly think it looked stupid.

It had been a successful operation so far. After the hiccup of almost being killed by the taxi driver, things had more or less gone smoothly. There were other worries, to be sure. The kill switch was still active, and John would have to make sure he continued to tread lightly as he investigated the safe behind the Mayan calendar. He still had to smuggle Pablo out to the safe house for an interrogation, and not get himself or Marcela killed in the process. But those were just regular work problems. Everything else made him feel rather spoiled.

It had been a few days since arriving in Antigua, but he was already settling into a sense of routine. He was able to go for morning runs in the city. Running in Antigua was a unique experience. There were no traffic lights and no honking of horns allowed in the city. The sidewalks were narrow and often had telephone poles planted in the middle of them. The cobblestone roads were a challenge on the feet when running.

In the early mornings, he could see pickup trucks filled with produce and Mayan vendors heading to the Antigua *mercado*. He loved the cool morning mountain air and views of the three volcanoes surrounding him. They made him feel alive. And that was the feeling he wanted when he sat down to enjoy his black coffee at his favorite cafe, *Gato Gordo*, and continuing to gaze at the volcanoes, people, and architecture around him.

As for work, he was an undercover tutor for Pablito. He was teaching in the afternoon and poured over the wig in the evenings. He continued to plan the op, and would briefly message Marcela updates. She had been ecstatic when he shared the discovery of the possible kill switch location. He managed to squeeze in some reading — fiction, of all things — when he wasn't going over wig work or op research. He could even enjoy wandering before the streets closed down. There was no official curfew, but there was an unspoken rule in Antigua and in most of Latin America: when it gets dark, go home.

It had become strange, thinking of fieldwork as tutoring Pablito. John's guard hadn't dropped (it hardly ever lowered), but he had enjoyed what time he had working for Pablo. This undeniable fact was a little hard to swallow at first — the straight-laced John Carpenter enjoyed working under a man who committed heinous crimes. But the work John was doing was what he loved. He was teaching, he was soaking in the spirit of Antigua, and the kid wasn't so bad. A bit too needy and pampered in John's eyes, but he was only his language tutor. He would never admit to himself how much he loved the boy. The mission was coming together and things seemed to be falling into place. He slept soundly with little to worry about.

A drill sergeant had once told him there was nothing better in life than a routine. And there was nothing more that John felt like he needed.

But it was time for his routine to be broken. His job demanded it.

***

While John slept contentedly in his bed, over a thousand miles away in the United States of America, the man John knew as Esteban stirred to the sound of a phone call. The time difference was two hours, but he had been enjoying the night just the same as John. It didn't wake him because Mike never really slept, but he stared at the phone just the same, filled with dread.

A phone ringing in the middle of the night is rarely a good thing.

Ever the night owl, Mike had been working on his desktop, reviewing sensitive files in pajamas while picking over a half-empty bowl of candy. The late night phone call darkened his mood quickly and spurred him into his car within the minute. He managed to find a spare shirt and pants in the car, doing up buttons and finished pulling his pants up at a red light. He arrived at an office building on the outskirts of downtown (the sign boasted a bogus company that had something to do with marketing), parked underground, and rode an elevator to the top.

As he stepped off the elevator, Mike entered a room in chaos.

Men and women set to various tasks tumbled over one another as they milled frantically about. File clerks pushed carts and found desks, got yelled at, bumped into one another. Agents scoured files, dialed phones, yelled at others on the phone, yelled at each other. He made his way to the darkly lit command room. A large wall screen dominated over the cubicle desks, split between data crunching, several maps overlaying one another in increasing satellite zoom qualities, and an email thread that was probably too high clearance for half the people in the office to be privy to.

It seemed there was a crisis every month. But this was what Mike did. Here he commanded an air of respect that made others follow willingly and enthusiastically. This was his palace. These were his subjects. Mike didn't revel in his power. He was simply very good at his job, and people liked working for him. Especially because he had the tendency to fix their problems.

Two aides met him with tablets, headsets, and smartphones in tow. Some of the tech was unfamiliar, even to Mike. Half of it wouldn't be released to the general populace for another five years.

"Talk to me."

"Sir. We got a call from our Latin American desk," one of the aides said as the other fitted him with a headset. That meant Locklee. That was enough to make Mike worried. A brief pop of static and chatter began to claw its way into his ear as the headset activated, and he mentally began filtering the conversations and bits of keywords he needed to latch onto. "They tipped us off to an inbound kill-team. Orders to eliminate Pablo Puentes."

Mike's expression grew grim. He waved off the aides before they could say more.

"Barker," Mike called. His head assistant looked up from the chaos of people milling about, amongst computers and files being scanned by analysts. The constant sound of computer keys rapidly processing sounded like a steady river moving over rocks, threatening to drown out any words.

"Sir." Barker was a young man and although he was Mike's head assistant, he may as well have been his steward. He passed a cup of coffee in a Styrofoam cup to his boss and spoke quickly after Mike gave an approving sip. "We briefly managed to listen in on their communications. They are going after Pablo."

"Civil National Police? Or are the Russians stepping on our toes again?" Mike didn't

want to get into another pissing match with the Russians. They were already stomping around Venezuela as of late, but Guatemala was a whole other ball game. He'd given them a good licking the last time around.

Barker's face was twitching with impatience. "No, sir, neither. Americans."

"What the-"

"I know, sir, it makes no sense."

Mike would normally reprimand his underling for interrupting him, but now was not the

time. He just wished Barker wasn't so damned excited about serious matters. "Who are these guys?"

"Not our department, but they're using Special Activities encryptions. So it's us…"

"But not us. Got it. Damn it. We need to shut this down now. Get me Linda."

Barker grinned, which was a disturbing thing, especially in light of their current crisis. He seemed almost to be getting sexually aroused by all the chaos. "Already on it, sir."

"Any other communications?" Mike asked.

"No, sir." Barker was wringing his hands and his face twitched again.

"They're on the move again!" Someone yelled.

The giant wall-screen had input coming and going, but Mike gauged anything useful would be tentative guesswork agents were pulling and dismissing. They still hadn't managed to get a proper video feed going.

"Where's my visual?" Mike yelled back, disappointed. "Damn it, I asked for Linda-"

"Chief! I have her." An agent shrugged apologetically at the interruption and patched the line over to Mike's headset.

Mike accepted the call immediately. "Morrandon."

"*God damn it*, Mike, what the hell is going on down there?"

"I could ask you the same. We intercepted a call on a kill-team. Special Activities. They're after Puentes."

Silence filled his headset for a good ten seconds. In all the time Mike knew and loathed Linda, she was never known for having nothing to say.

"Boss? What am I missing here?"

"Nothing, Mike. This isn't on our end."

"Whose end is this?"

"I don't know."

Linda, the head of the Special Operations Group, didn't know of a strike team within Special Activities overlapping the Latin American desk.

"Chief!" Barker had been talking to some jockeys but now snapped his head over his shoulder, having the expression of a gleefully deranged owl. "We managed to get a trace on one of the calls, but it's indirect…we can patch you through if you like."

Mike's stomach flipped.

"Linda, did you get that?"

"Yes. Do it."

Mike nodded curtly to Barker, ignoring the man's disturbing demeanor while patting the bead of sweat rolling down his brow. A second later, his headset beeped with a new call. Mike took a few steps away from the commotion of his officers.

The gentle hum and echo of radio silence greeted him.

"Who is this?" Mike asked.

A shuffling sound. No reply.

"Inbound kill-team to target Pablo Puentes, stand down immediately. I repeat, stand down."

Another bit of shuffling, then the distinct sound of someone breathing. Still no reply, so Mike tried again.

"This is a division of the Special Operations Group, we have intercepted your communications. We know your orders. I have authorization from our director. Do not engage Puentes, I repeat do not enga-"

"My team has its orders." The man's voice came through the headset like ice.

Mike clenched his teeth. "Understood, but I have authorization from-"

"Puentes is our target. Do not interfere."

"Negative. Puentes is a person of interest for SOG and elimination is not acceptable at this time."

A pause. Mike was starting to think he was getting somewhere. He sure hoped so, or everything was about to go belly-up.

"Do you require authorization codes for identity confirmation?" Mike asked. "Who am I speaking to?"

"For your sake…I hope you never find out."

The line cut out.

Mike's blood ran cold. The visual was up. GPS trackers were laid over a digital map of Antigua's streets. It wasn't the thermal-displaying face-recognition equipped program they were spoiled with in North America, but it gave him what he needed to know. The kill-team was on the move, and fast. One target was in a hotel; probably to cover tracks. A man to mind the communications. It was an unenviable position.

Mike noticed Barker's grin was fading into a concerned expression as he thought about the situation and all its variables.

"Chief?" He was barely audible over the commotion.

Mike waved him off. "Linda, did you get that?"

"Yes." Her voice was crisp over the headset. "I don't have a good reply for you, Mike. I won't let that blackmail get out. This kill-team isn't ours. It can't be."

"But the encryption-"

"I know. But as far as we're concerned, this team should be considered hostile. I'll do some digging. In the meantime…you know what you have to do."

Mike nodded, even though he knew she couldn't see him. He ended the call.

If they killed Pablo now, the mission would be a failure. He needed options. Failure was not one of those options.

"Shit." He stood there stupidly, staring at the screen. Little red GPS tracking dots flew across the map of town. He slammed the desk with both his hands. "*Shit!*" Some Blackthorne agents turned to see his face trembling with rage, but most were still tied up trying to establish communications or performing what damage control measures remained. He flew through every conceivable option, all the courses that could be taken, but he knew what the answer would be even before he began.

He pointed to Barker, considered for a brief moment how disturbing he looked, and then pointed at a phone on a nearby desk. His voice was harsh, but commanded assurance all the same.

"Get me Carpenter."

***

John awoke to the sound of his Firm cell phone ringing. It was always on his person or sitting on the bedside table at night. If it rang it meant Esteban; although it wasn't necessarily a bad thing, at this time of night and unaccounted for, it meant an emergency.

In the throes of sleep the sound immediately made John smell smoke and taste sand, and hear the rattle of an AK-47 unload its magazine. He heard gravel crunch and smelled sweat and tasted blood.

The sensation happened so fast he hardly recognized it. He was up out of bed and moving before he was fully awake. By the time his senses were fully alert, he felt no grogginess or disorientation. Other than an underlying subconscious dread, he was ready.

He made his way quickly to the bathroom. There were no windows there and it gave him vision of the hotel's front door. He was careful to avoid the balcony window, but took a moment to see if he could spot anything as he padded his way barefoot across the floor. His Glock was cocked and in his hand. He hardly remembered how it had gotten there. His eyes were adjusting to the dark slowly so he couldn't see it, but the metal felt good in his hands again. The phone was in his other hand. He accepted the call.

"Carpenter?"

It was Esteban, which for some reason was a relief to John. It shouldn't be anyone else on the other end, but stranger things had happened. The voice was low, whipcord and sharp. If a call in the dead of night didn't give reason for alert, his tone confirmed it.

"I'm here," John said. "What is it?"

"A situation. I need you moving."

John eyed the door and then the balcony in two quick movements. "Is my location compromised?"

"No. But the mission may well be. I need you moving."

John retrieved a pair of earbuds and plugged them into the phone. He threw on a pair of black pants laying on the edge of his bed and slipped on his shoes. He was already wearing a black shirt. His gun went into his waistband as he unlocked the hotel room lockbox. He pulled his small black backpack from inside and slung it over his shoulder.

"Carpenter?"

"Where am I going?"

He was out the door even as he replied. He made his way to the hotel steps.

The voice came clearly over the earbuds. "A hotel. *Doña Maria*. Address is *5a Calle Poniente* 25. First floor, room three. You're at your own hotel?"

"I'm outside it now." The brisk night air met him as he felt the shadows engulf him. There were no street lamps. He picked up into a jog.

"There should be one hostile there," Esteban was saying before he could ask. "The others are on the move."

"Got it."

No one roamed the streets of Antigua at night. No one who wasn't suspect, that is. At one point he ran past two men carrying shotguns and reached for his pistol. They made no move to stop him, so he kept moving.

"They don't know you're coming. We need them eliminated. Fast."

"Got it."

He counted the building numbers, but the street wasn't altogether strange to him. It wasn't far from where he was staying and he knew this side of town. It was lower end and poor, but no more so than most of Antigua.

"Here," John whispered. Esteban was silent but he could hear him suck in his breath.

John eyed the building. He unslung his backpack and rooted through for his mask. While a balaclava would do, he had spent so much time in wetsuits that when it came to a facemask he could think of nothing more he preferred. Wetsuit masks were tight, so this particular piece of gear was a little looser. It sucked up sweat like a sponge too, which always helped. He pulled it over his head and proceeded onto the front door. There were a million ways to approach the task at hand. He opted for the front door.

The door opened to a lobby, which sported a locked glass door. He kicked at the glass, which shattered under the force of his foot. He expected an alarm but none sounded. Antiguan hotels were poor and often couldn't afford to sport such measures. He moved past the metal frame of the door and crunched through the glass fragments on the floor. His gun was in hand again. He swung the barrel left and right as he moved, but no one was there.

He entered the door to the hall.

He made his way past the first row of rooms, padding softly on the dirty floor.

"Carpenter. We need this done quick."

He blew out air, filling the earbud's receiver with static. An unspoken acknowledgement and one that also helpfully expressed irritation. He hoped that would keep Esteban at ease for a minute.

John quickly located room three. Again, he found himself with a number of options to proceed.

He kicked as hard as he could, as he had a thousand times in both training and in the field. The door collapsed on its hinges and splinters flew at the edges where they met the frame. The chain-lock clung desperately to its wooden master, but split after a second kick. John grunted and leapt inside.

A sitting figure was illuminated by the faint light of the window and a computer screen's haunting glow. It jerked in a surprised attempt to face John, reaching for a gun on the desk.

John's finger squeezed and his gun rocked. Two silenced rounds pumped into the man's chest. John swept the room and adjoining bathroom before moving over to the figure and put a third bullet between the man's eyes. No sound came from his mouth. Only the slumping of his body in the chair threatened the night's silence.

He spent no time taking in his surroundings, but he surveyed his mind's eye as he left the way he came. An expensive laptop, a gun on the table. Two beds. An open file folder with a photo printout of a man's face.

Pablo Puentes.

Once he was heading down the stairs, he spoke and told Esteban what he'd seen.

"Good. Cleanup is inbound. Not your focus."

What was this?

John knew not to ask. He didn't ask questions that weren't pertinent to the mission. He only needed a direction and an objective.

"Where?"

John felt Esteban tense as he spoke. "Not where. Who." A pause. Then he spoke again. "Puentes."

It was John's turn to tense. *Had someone disabled the kill switch or decided it was dormant? Was it time to go for the kill already?* He was on the road now, jogging hard but trying to reserve his stamina. No one met him as he made his way.

"Is Puentes my target?"

"No," Esteban said at once. "You need to protect him."

CHAPTER 14

It was well after midnight when John had answered the call from Esteban and left his hotel. The sky wouldn't threaten the sun's rise for some time. That was good. John always preferred the cover of dark for missions such as these. People were tired and clumsy at night. The senses were impaired.

"Carpenter."

He grunted in response. His breathing rose and fell, heavy but even, as his heartbeat and footfalls pounded down the streets of Antigua.

"There should be seven more of them." Esteban was sounding calmer now, as if the mission was already successful. The tone bothered John. Seven was a fairly large group of men. Trained men, based on the setup in the hotel room. Mike wasn't telling him something. "We're hoping Pablo's guards can take care of the enemy if they're given a warning by you. Raise an alarm and make sure they win. You won't need to break cover."

"Puentes is not at the compound."

"What? Carpenter, don't fuck with me."

John was taken aback for a moment, but didn't let it affect his tone. "Puentes is not at the compound."

There was a short pause. John could picture the man's panic rising. He didn't blame him. "He's at his summer home in Jocotenango," John said. "Pablito said he goes there after visiting *Maximón* out of town."

There was chatter in the background of the call as Esteban verbally assaulted someone on his end, then confirm something with someone else. Then he was back and talking to John.

"Shut up. Not you. Shit. It looks like you're right. How well protected is this place?"

John turned a street corner and cursed as he saw a light poke through the trees. It abruptly went off. He moved to the other side of the street without breaking stride. "He'll have guards, but not as many."

"Shit."

John turned another corner, feeling his breathing begin to grow harder, his lungs raw. He was coming up upon Antigua's gated compounds and its expensive properties.

"Have you found and disabled the kill switch?"

John's irritation flared briefly, then died as it passed his filter of cool and collected focus. Nothing could distract him now. He couldn't afford that.

"We have a lead."

John could hear his handler bite back his own irritation. If the kill switch had been disabled, this conflict could prove an opportunity to extract information and eliminate Pablo. But with the kill switch active, it gave John and the Firm no choice.

"Protect Puentes," Esteban said tightly. "And Carpenter. They're trained men. Not thugs."

He had a feeling. Something was dangerously amiss. But the only thing he could do now was find these targets and kill them. Esteban wouldn't tell him more than he needed to know. And he'd fill in the details later, but only if he needed to know.

I don't need to know and I don't want to know.

That was the last coherent thought John had of his own before he came up upon Puentes' summer house. Everything else was automatic, playing out before him like a reel of film. As if some other being had taken control of his body.

The building was fairly standard for a luxury summer house. Cream plaster walls met orange clay tiles, overlooking a pool and surrounded by a gated courtyard brimming with patches of ivy. There were no lights to be seen, but as he drew closer he spotted a guard yawning, holding his shouldered shotgun lazily. Pablo would probably have the man beaten for such a display.

John removed his mask and moved as non-threateningly as he could, with slow and casual steps. He crept remarkably close before the guard finally noticed him. John waved at the man and put a finger to his lips, but the guard's eyes grew wide and began to shout anyway. He fumbled to ready his shotgun and only slowed as he seemed to recognize John.

"*Eres uno de los hombres de Patrón* Pablo," the guard said. *You are one of Patrón Pablo's men.* He pointed the gun at John anyway, though he was more confused than hostile.

"*Sí, sí,*" John said, arms raised in the universal gesture of submission. "*Pablo está en peligro.*" *Pablo is in danger.* The man's eyes widened and raised his shotgun a little higher, but John pressed. "*Los hombres han venido a matarlo.*" *Men have come to kill him.*

The man gave John a hard look then, as if to test his trust, so John pointed at the front of the house and hissed, "*¿Quieres que tu patrón sea asesinado?*" *Do you want your patrón killed?*

That seemed to spur him. The guard bolted to the front. That would buy Pablo time and alarm the others. Perhaps that was all that was needed. But even without this poor display, John had seen some of Pablo's guards. They were very good at showing their muscles and holding guns, but he wasn't so sure how they'd fair in a fight.

He wouldn't leave it up to chance.

John took a moment to slip his mask back on, then ran hard and straight at the wall of the house. He managed to get enough elevation to grip the top edge of the courtyard wall. He hoisted himself up and brought his legs into a crouch. He pulled his mask back on and quickly took in what his senses could lend him. Off to his left, where the entrance was, he heard a shotgun blast. The sound of metal hitting plaster and rock. Then the unmistakable sound of silenced pistol fire.

The guard I spoke to is dead.

He had known the guard would die as soon as he convinced him to move. There was nothing to be done about it. If he needed to, he could feel remorseful after. But the shotgun blast would rouse the other guards and give warning to Pablo, he hoped. It also gave him an opportunity to get into a better position.

He sprang from the wall and onto the roof, taking a moment to find his footing on the tiles. Slipping and falling would probably mean only minor injury, but then the enemy would be alerted to his presence and would kill him. It was more important to catch his balance before pressing on.

Once surefooted, he flew across the roof, tiles clicking no louder than a bat's wings. His Glock was out of his waistband again, cocked and safety disabled with one swift motion. The weapon was an extension of his hands. It pointed slowly down into the courtyard as he crept to the edge, above the building's entrance. He held his breath as soft shadows crept toward him below. John heard the muted creak of the courtyard gate.

They're inside.

Somewhere he heard breathing in his ears and it took him a moment to realize it was only Esteban. The man had remained silent to let John focus on his bloody work. John could thank him for that much.

Three of Pablo's guards emerged from the house under John's's feet, guns raised and moving cautiously against the blast that must have alerted them. John sensed the carnage about to take place a breath before the first gunshot.

Muzzles flashed in the courtyard as the attackers saw the guards enter the fray. Their outlines remained nearly invisible, only betrayed by their quick movements and shots, like fireflies dancing amidst a grove. To the guards' credit, they took up defensive positions immediately, one crouching beneath the edge of the porch, the other pressing against a pillar. The cruel sound of shotguns blew the silence of the night away as they tried to weave in and out of cover, firing into the night. But one guard rushed the steps.

"*Puta madre!*" *Mother fucker!*

The guard pumped and fired, pumped and fired, lighting up the night. Then his face exploded, then his chest, and he slumped over sideways, dragging a red mess with him as he bounced down the rest of the stairs.

John took a meditative breath, spent a millisecond visualizing his task, then got to work.

It wasn't quite like shooting fish in a barrel. The courtyard was bigger than a barrel, and the fish were masked by darkness and their own scavenged covers. But John placed two bullets in the head and neck of a shadow poking out from the stairs' ridge, and another two in the crotch and torso of a man trying to flank the guard at the pillar. One other shot sounded like it connected with meat, but others went into bushes and sparked off the gate. With their surprise advantage compromised and up against shotguns, the men had done the sensible thing and scattered, drawing their opponents into a back-and-forth firefight, playing on their advantage of numbers and precision. But the shotgun blasts had the advantage of a heavy spread.

John wasn't sure if he had seen another of Pablo's men enter the courtyard or not. He was forced to duck even as he began to reload. A bullet whizzed past his head while a tile exploded next to him. They knew where he was then. And all they had to do was flank or force their way inside to Pablo and they'd win…

By the time he slapped a new magazine in place and was able to peek over the edge, the enemy seemed to be mobilizing. One guard was dead for sure, the other behind the pillar looked injured or simply pinned, and some of the men in black were moving up the steps.

Somewhere in the back of his head, an instructor in a class on tactics had said something about not taking the enemy by surprise. Instead, *make* a surprise. Without a second thought or even a pang of anxiety, John jumped off the roof. Whether it was stupid John couldn't say, but he might later admit to himself that the move was rash.

It certainly didn't matter to the man whose back he'd just broken. John's impact landed on a chest that absorbed the shock to both of John's legs. As John felt the spine crunch under his feet, he rode the momentum and somersaulted forward, breaking up the group of men. He immediately groped for the nearest opponent and braced for a hostile reaction, but they were distracted and staring at the entrance. John spun behind a man and put him in a harsh chokehold, so he was able to see what the others were looking at.

Pablo Puentes had burst from the front entrance, double doors flying open and glass shattering as they slammed against the walls. Pablo Puentes, the very target these men had come to kill. The white of his clothing seemed to make him glow in the dark, a vengeful ghost come to attack the group of shadows. John noticed he was wearing pajamas, but he was fearsome even still. That, coupled with the AK-47 he held in his hands. The courtyard seemed to draw in its breath. Pablo's AK-47 roared his answer.

He sprayed his fire in a wide arc, the cutting scythe of bullets coming straight for John and his choking opponent. The recoil made Pablo's fire erratic but he simply kept spraying, rotating to focus on a nearby assailant, causing their own attempted shot to go wild.

John tightened his feet and drew himself thin as a rod as bullets impacted the man he held in front of him. They thudded into armor and flesh, reminding John of hail against a window.

Pablo polished off his magazine, reloaded with practiced ease, and turned his head to another enemy on his other flank, aiming with a deadly calm. The rapid-fire sound of the assault rifle rocked the courtyard a second time, and John was certain now the cartel leader could handle himself better than any bodyguard. Pablo had a true warrior's ferocity, and John nearly cringed as Pablo unloaded on the agent not twenty feet away from him. It had been a while since John had seen a live target shredded with assault weapon fire. The rounds tore through the enemy's chest and launched a dark splash against the courtyard wall. The man dropped to his knees as if kneeling in submission. He was dead. It didn't matter. Pablo continued his attack, firing again and again as the body jerked like a crazed marionette. He didn't stop. Pablo kept going and going until his ammunition was spent and another magazine clattered to the floor.

His guards were moving to protect him now, blocking any retaliating fire and bringing their own shotguns up. They shot at a man that had taken to the bushes, oblivious to John's position behind his corpse amidst the confusion. The courtyard should be clear by his count, and it was dark enough and he was close enough to the gate now that he could slip away into the night.

There was movement behind.

First he thought them cowards, but soon realized there must have been a rear-guard, meant to provide cover or support from out of the action. They probably never expected a direct confrontation.

John was happy to provide it for them. Two men not twenty feet away, taking pot shots at the bodyguards and still presenting a threat to Pablo.

John rushed the man closest to him. The attacker must have been surprised to see John running to attack so wide in the open; the man had his gun out in front of him ready to fire. With John's break from the courtyard confusion, he was giving the man a clear shot. He took it. The suppressor must have been removed or damaged, because nothing smothered the sharp sound of the pistol. Death came for him.

John had his old trick up his sleeve. He had spun the backpack he wore to face his front, protecting his chest. He ducked his head and felt the *whump* of a bullet slamming into the armor insert in his bag, the ceramic plate absorbing the bullet. The blow knocked the wind out of him and would leave a nasty bruise, but John was still sprinting to meet the enemy. Some mercenary had, quite literally, stabbed him in the back in Panama City years ago, nearly crippling him. He'd always wanted to make the backpack work, and finally he could cash in the age-old bet he had with Brian. He idly remembered Brian was dead, and swung the pack off him and at the second man. It wouldn't hurt him, but was enough distraction that he also got a free shot off, forcing the man to dive to the ground and scramble for the gun that had fallen from his hands. More importantly, it allowed John to deal with the other threat directly in front of him.

He saw the man's eyes grow wide as he realized John had escaped death from his gunfire. He was about to squeeze off a second shot, but John was too close and he weaved sideways. By the time the gun spat, John had kicked the man squarely in the crotch and the shot was going wild.

The roar of the gun struck John's right ear and sent him reeling momentarily, reaching up to clutch at the nauseating ache ringing the inside of his eardrum. It was enough of a chance for his opponent to begin to lift himself up from the feeling of crushed testicles, swipe John's 's gun away, and start to point his own pistol again.

But John had snapped back to the fight as well, even if feeling lopsided with a temporarily deaf ear. He kneed the man hard in the face before he could fully stand, swiped a combat knife from his leg as crushed cartilage and blood leaked from the blow, and resisted the man's pushing hands as he tried to peel his broken face away. John held his knife with his thumb on the end of the handle's grip and stabbed for the neck. The man choked on the blood that began to flow from his mouth and nose. John bounced him off his knee like he might a toddler, cradled the back of the head, then slammed the man's face back into his knee again. The man slopped off his knee with the sound of wet meat, the knife sticking out like a pin in a cushion. He had no time to retrieve it.

The fight had only been a couple seconds, and John was turning to face the second attacker. The other man had found his pistol and had it raised, but John was too quick for him to get a shot off. He chopped at the man's wrist, focusing the blunt power of his hand's edge on the soft tissue in between forearm and hand. The man stifled a cry and dropped his gun, but responded in kind with a heel to John's nose. John leaned back, stopping a probably fatal blow, but it still clipped his chin, slamming painfully into his nose — thankfully not as hard as it needed to be for a killing blow, but hard enough. Disoriented, the man took advantage of his attack and placed a foot behind John's leg. He pivoted and shouldered John hard in the chest.

John was down then, tumbling to the ground, hitting his tailbone hard but saving his head from a concussion. A boot was coming for his head — another devastating kill-move. He tucked his arms in tight, log-rolled to the side, and narrowly avoided the crushing foot. But although he had escaped the attack, John's roll left him open to the second. A fist drove into his solar plexus and he arched forward against his will. Stars flashed as he gasped for air. He fell back hard onto the dirt, this time hitting his head, and the onset of a headache flew over his skull from back to front like a wave. The man brought his boot down again to finish John off.

"Are you a pussy or a SEAL?" a drill instructor's voice somewhere far off crept up from his subconscious. *"Are you a pussy? Or a SEAL!"*

"I'm a SEAL."

"Then get up and show me."

John had taken all the punishment he would allow himself to suffer. In the depths of his being, he remembered his training and summoned an impossible reserve of strength. Without a gun and briefly lamenting his knife, John made do with the ancient killing tools God had given him. His arms moved as quick as a rabbit, latched onto the foot and leg of his opponent even as they were rushing toward him, and was presented with a hundred options for the follow-through.

John opted for efficiency, as was his habit.

He twisted the foot savagely, around and up, with all the force he could muster. The boot was hardened leather, allowing for some flexibility but locked the foot in place when up against such ferocity. A well-trained man could have spun his entire body to escape the twist — which the man had begun, to his credit — but John's combined upward jerk took his enemy off guard. The result saw the toe of the boot crammed against calf.

The ensuing *snap* of bone, cartilage, and tendons greeted the night air as a gloomy precursor to the scream that followed. It was bloodcurdling and animalistic, more a dog's howl than a human cry.

John ignored the feeble grappling hands at his head and drew a leg up to his chest while remaining prone on the ground. He pointed it at the enemy's knee and rammed it forward with all the force he had kicked in the hotel door earlier that night. The leg reversed itself against its designed purpose, finding itself in an unnatural, contorted position, and looking distinctly wrong.

This time the night only heard a whimper. The man's throat would be raw and his pain must be moving to the numbness of shock. He collapsed onto his good knee and looked up at John, searching to see if there remained anything left to challenge his opponent with.

John stood, wearily but without swaying, and retrieved his gun. He met the man's eyes, speaking the silent acknowledgement that was the end of a life. The man's eyes hovered over John's shoulder for a moment, and he noticed his sleeve had ridden up during the fight. He saw the tattoo on his shoulder. A frog's skeleton holding a trident. For those who knew, it was easy to identify.

"Navy SEAL?" The man rasped, looking at John in bewilderment and defeat. "American." He pointed feebly at his own chest. "I'm… American." The sound from the man's lips already seemed like they came from a dying man. "What are you…doing here…?"

John didn't have to answer. But he hoped some words would give him an inkling of peace. Him and the man about to die.

"Following orders."

He put two bullets in the man's chest and immediately placed a third between his eyes. The body slumped over its side, collapsing on its ribs then wobbling at the waist. The sound of a heavy wind drowned out the shouts of Pablo's men and whipped against the foliage as the man fell with a soft thump on the earth. The sound begged finality. John's ear still rang painfully, and his nose, chest, and head ached, but he registered the empty-sounding static and breathing of Esteban in his remaining good ear. It was as empty as the bodies left behind, as empty as John felt. Blood and dirt mixed as the moon shone through the clouds, lighting an otherwise beautiful scene. Tourists and Antiguans would flock here soon to admire and wonder at the inhabitants behind its walls. They would never know the carnage that had taken place.

John pulled off his mask, folded it slowly and stuffed it in his backpack. Then he stuck his Glock in the back of his waistband, tucked his shirt sleeve back down, and walked away without a second glance.

CHAPTER 15

———

Mike was a man who became more engrossed in his work the worse it got. He wasn't just a workaholic, but a fix-aholic. He worked to find problems so he could fix them, usually finding more problems in the way things were fixed. Usually this buzzed playfully in the back of his head as he worked, healthy doses of cynicism accompanying him along the way.

Today the buzz wasn't there. The gears in his head were silent. He was numb.

He sat in his office pretending to do work. Barker — who reminded him increasingly of something he would find in a swamp — kept darting in excitedly, putting files on his desk to review and making passive remarks about local office intrigue. The current flavor had to do with Sharon's new navy dress. Mike wasn't entirely certain who Sharon was.

"She usually wears pants, sir. At first I thought she was just gaining weight, but that can't be the case. She eats a lot of salad. Almonds are her main source of protein, at least what I see her eating here."

Mike looked at Barker for a long moment. The young man looked poised and swayed slightly, like a cobra waiting to strike. Only in this case, he was waiting for his boss to say something profound in answer.

"Barker?"

"Yes, sir?" His eyes shone eagerly.

"Get out of my office."

Barker's shoulders slumped. "Yes, sir."

He slunk off and left Mike with his empty thoughts again. He opened files, read them, forgot what he read, reread them, closed them, then opened them again. He went to take a sip of coffee and found his mug empty. It pained him. He wiped his face with his hands in exasperation.

Everything is shit.

Marcela and John should be moving in on Pablo by now, but instead they were still working the area, and in the meantime some CIA kill-team had moved against their target. The good news was that John had managed to wipe them. It was a goddamn mess.

After sulking for most of the day, Mike decided to get up and stretch his legs.

He got up out of his comfy office chair and opened the glass door separating his windowed

office from the dark command room, where any kind of operation was led from. Right now it was being used passively: intelligence officers were monitoring threats all across Latin America, talking in hushed tones on phone calls to follow up leads, sifting through emails flagged with suggestive keywords, while data sent by agents was interpreted and persons of interest profiles were updated. The officers looked like phantoms by the lights of the computer screen glowing all about.

Mike sighed. They did good work. He liked to think he did too. But there was something else

in the air today. The hesitancy that something was missing. The feeling of failure. The reluctance to keep pushing on. He couldn't blame them.

The unit attacking Pablo from an internal source had rocked Blackthorne at its core. Worse,

there wasn't much Mike's team could do about it. He had made the phone calls, he'd gone to an emergency debriefing meeting, and he'd been told that everything was a miscommunication. The kill-team had been nothing more than hired guns from another cartel. When Mike had raised the question of the team using CIA encryptions, he had been told he was flat-out wrong. After that, he'd been quietly benched. But if there was anything Mike had been taught about working in the CIA, there was always more to uncover. There was always work to be done.

Mike turned to his assistant.

"Barker, close the door."

The assistant moved to the door separating the command room from the menial paper-shoving, lower security clearance work. The light from the outer office was snatched away as the door closed. Mike turned his attention to the intel gatherers and keyboard jockeys scattered about the dark room. Noticing him standing there looming, they ended phone calls, finished writing down information in tiny notebooks, and stopped the pattering of keys until they were all looking at him. Waiting.

"What I'm about to ask of you all is outside of my comfort zone, so I imagine it'll be out of yours. After last night's tango, I've come to suspect some unfair play. We're going to investigate one of our own."

One of the agents spoke timidly. "Sir, that's-"

"Not what our unit is for, no. But we do damage control."

The woman who had spoken looked disgruntled, but wasn't about to speak out again. For all he knew, she wasn't going to object to using Blackthorne in this fashion. She might have been asking a legitimate question to better understand the task at hand. But he wasn't in the mood for questions and couldn't risk his people reconsidering what they had to do. He wanted to nip that in the bud.

"And we just experienced internal damage," he continued. "*Colossal fucking internal damage.* We're going to patch her up and make sure that doesn't happen again." He pointed to the main screen. "Paul Locklee." In seconds, his image was on the screen. "I want everything we have on him. All the dirt, all the secrets, anything remotely similar to leverage. Find it, people."

They hesitated. Some of them probably knew the man personally. "*Go.*"

The room suddenly sprang to life as his people pounded on keys and began to prowl the underbelly of internal intelligence gathering. Barker licked his lips over a grin and glanced over at Mike. He scowled back and the young man looked away, the disturbing gleam in his eye jumping across the jockeys. Mike saw a couple of them glance up at Barker nervously before returning to their work, but most were too engrossed to break concentration.

Then the goods began rolling in.

"Sir, I have an unpaid parking ticket...looks like the car was parked outside a bar."

"Any drunk driving?" Mike asked.

"Going through police archives now...no. I don't think so."

"Stay on it."

Another woman jumped in. "Sir, I have a hotel bill in Florida, looks like...two nights."

"What was he doing there?"

"Checking now..." The woman didn't reply after that.

"Sir! Couples therapy meeting, office just out of town. Looks like marital trouble."

Mike clenched his teeth. "God damn it, all our marital statuses are in jeopardy," he growled.

Was this the best they could do? There was a lull in their feedback and it irked him.

"Come on, people! I don't want petty shit here, give me some meat I can chew on! I'm talking internal, agency, departmental, let's go!"

Sweat began to bead a few foreheads. He sure as hell couldn't fault them for not trying. But it was a long moment before someone said those sweet words: "Sir. I think I have something."

Mike moved to the computer jockey's terminal and looked intently at the screen. It was a moment before he put his hand on the man's shoulder and gave it a quick squeeze.

"Good work."

He made for the door and passed close to his assistant.

"Barker, have them follow that lead as far as it goes."

The young man's eyes twitched and he moved greasy hair out of his face. He grinned a smile full of saliva.

"Yes, sir. Where are you going?"

Mike smiled grimly. "I'm going for a walk." He opened the door and turned his shoulder. "Oh, and Barker?"

"Yes, sir?"

"Send me a couple of the Boys, would you?"

For the first time that day, Mike's assistant looked distinctly nervous rather than excited. It was a small difference not many would notice, but there it was.

"Yes, sir."

Mike walked out the door and left the dark room, making for the elevator.

***

Paul Locklee sat in his comfortable computer chair behind his large desk, in an office that was also unnecessarily large. The head of SOG's Latin American Affairs had done well for himself. Even so, he was disgruntled. It was true that some things even money couldn't buy.

"Mr. Locklee?"

He jumped in his seat a bit, exiting the website browser that was displaying information for divorce lawyers, and looked up from his computer.

Two men were standing by the doorway. The one who had already spoken knocked on the door, a cocky disregard for courtesy seeping from him.

Locklee's first thought was anger at his secretary; why hadn't she stopped anyone from barging into his office? But this was quickly answered by seeing her moving quickly behind the two men and waving to him, as if they had strode right past and she were trying to catch up.

The second thought was a mix of fear and wonder, trying to figure out why the men were here and what they wanted with him. What secret had leaked? Was he a loose end?

The third thought was to reach for his gun. It sat cold and ready in a side drawer under his desk.

But that'd be downright stupid. If these men wanted him dead, he'd already have a bullet in his skull.

He'd know. He used to be one of them.

They were a sort of secret service bodyguard, escort, and general foot-soldier of the

intelligence community, at least within Special Activities. He didn't know what they had in other divisions. They were officially called the Special Activities Division Escort Group, but most just called them the Boys. The history of the Boys crept all the way back to the Cold War days, where tensions in different offices spun people so tight it was determined a small chunk of change could be spent on security detail. It placated many nervous intelligence workers on the lower end of the chain, but most up top knew the security detail was nothing more than extra eyes on its own people. The Boys managed to hold onto its budgets and personnel, becoming a personal but neutral attaché for general use by all sanctioned offices. Locklee had to admit that they delivered. It was always a bit more of a show to have men in suits, shades, and earpieces around. It was no wonder so many rumors and conspiracy theories about them had cropped up among the American public.

He eyed the two men carefully. These guys weren't any more dangerous than the average bodyguard. Inherently, anyway. Show of force, plain and simple. What made them dangerous were the folks who ordered them around. The list was narrowed to someone from inside Special Activities, but he didn't know who it was. Though he had an idea.

Locklee looked at his wristwatch. He would've been done work in ten minutes. Whoever had sent the Boys was a proper bastard.

He gave a long sigh.

"Don't worry, you won't have to drag me. Let me get my jacket."

They didn't reply. They only watched him carefully through their shades as he gathered

himself and began to follow them out the door. They patted him down before they led him out.

***

Mike watched the black Sedan pull up to the curb. They were on a quiet side street from downtown, outside a pawn shop that had closed half an hour ago and a gravel parking lot that charged too much for anyone on this side of town to be using. Three blocks over, a small park sported a broken fountain and a long-abandoned jungle gym. The empty church across the street chimed the quarter hour.

The Boys he'd sent got out of the car and parted ways, taking off their shades and jackets, promptly beginning to loiter, looking like businessmen just getting off work. One answered a phone call. The other pulled out a pack of cigarettes.

Mike walked over to the car, popped the front door, and slid inside. He looked in the rear-view mirror to meet Locklee's surprised eyes head on.

"Hey, Paul. What are you doing here?"

The man scowled.

"Surprised to see me?" Mike didn't get to catch others off guard like this often. Usually he was stuck in the cage they kept him in. He could get used to this kind of power.

"Yes, actually," Locklee said slowly. "Pleasant surprise seeing you, Michael. You weren't even my second guess."

Mike grunted. "Don't call me that."

"What?"

"Michael. It was always too biblical for me."

Locklee's eyes fell to half lids as his expression seemed to say, *really?* He smiled despite

himself, ran a hand over his hair and touched his ponytail as if to make sure it was still there.

"What can I do for you, Mike?"

Mike's expression grew hard. "You can start by telling me what happened yesterday night."

"You were at the debrief. Rival cartel. They're getting quite sophisticated these days."

Mike almost snorted. "Oh, please. I was fed so much shit I could've sworn we were in a pigsty. I want the real answer. I think you know. I think you're hiding it."

Locklee looked out the window, disinterest creeping over his face. "Sorry, Mike. Blackthorne is an asset for authorized Special Operations Group divisions to utilize, without provisions to further information if deemed unnecessary for the requested operation to proceed. If we want you in the dark, you don't get to turn on the light."

"So you admit you're keeping us in the dark."

Locklee laughed, the sound of some vicious thing let loose from a cage.

"Sure, Mike, sure. We're keeping you in the dark. For the trouble you went through to pull the Boys and surprise me in a car, I'll tell you that. We don't want you knowing some things. There you go."

He moved to open the door. Mike hit a button on his car door and the brief sound of clicking locks surrounded them. Locklee sighed.

"Mike. Come on. Let's be professional."

"Professionalism," Mike said slowly as he reached into his jacket pocket. "Is something I pride myself on. That's why those Boys made sure you weren't carrying anything. That's why we're across from a nondescript parking lot that no one uses."

Locklee's face started to go pale as his imagination started to take hold. He was slowly realizing that Mike was a capable man. Mike continued to talk in a hard, flat tone.

"And that's why I can kill you now and no one will hear a thing. People ask me how I sleep at night. Well, Locklee–" Mike moved his hand to his jacket pocket. "I don't sleep at all."

Locklee's eyes were clenched shut, waiting for the sound of a gunshot to be the last thing he heard. There was nothing. He slowly opened his eyes.

Mike was holding a phone over his shoulder, the screen displayed for Paul to see.

"I don't need to kill you, Locklee. But your career may as well be dead."

Locklee stared at the screen. At first he didn't show any recognition. Then his eyes widened as he recognized his personal bank account information on Mike's phone. Mike watched him move through the stinging motions of recognition, shock, fury, then resignation.

"Now I know how my wife must've felt," Locklee finally muttered softly, after a long pause. He looked at Mike in the rear-view mirror. "This isn't what it looks like."

"Oh?" He tried not to let the satisfaction overtake him. "Because to me it looks like six hundred and fifty thousand American dollars landed in your personal account from a mysterious donor. Well, not so mysterious once you do a bit of work. Sandor Puentes didn't try too hard to hide the fact he wired it."

"Using Blackthorne jockeys to dig into internal affairs. I didn't know you were one to break rules, Mike. A biggie, too."

I don't break rules. Not usually. Not the big ones. But maybe I should do it more often. Maybe I should've done this a long time ago.

John and Marcela wouldn't end up like Brian. He'd go to war before letting that happen.

"Damn." Locklee made a fist and brought it down on his leg. "Damn," he said again, with more conviction. "I thought I could... well, it doesn't matter."

Mike lingered with the phone, but Locklee was looking out the window now. It had started to rain. The phone's use seemed to have been completed. Mike pocketed the device and waited. He thought he'd have to prompt the man, but Locklee finally spoke up, not quite bringing his eyes to meet Mike's in the rear-view mirror.

"I'm assuming you'll bring that before judicial scrutiny if I don't fill you in. String me up on half a dozen charges.

"At least," Mike said sharply.

"Will you let me explain what the money is doing in my account?"

"Eventually." Mike shrugged. "I'll give you the opportunity if you do well."

"Then I'll ask again. What can I do for you?"

This time the words were genuine, tighter. The sort of tone that would suggest to an experienced interrogator that the subject was about to squeal. Mike ran his tongue across his teeth. He hadn't been sure he was going to get this far. And now came the tricky part. The delicate dance of information extraction.

"Let's start with the kill switch. Are you bullshitting that, or is it clean?"

"Right." Locklee nodded slowly, thinking hard. "Right, it makes sense you'd be concerned about that. Okay. It's clean. There is a kill switch, as far as we know. It is a problem."

"But…"

Locklee gave a tiny sigh. "But the blackmail isn't regarding our hit on Sandor."

"That was the bullshit."

Locklee nodded.

"So the kill switch…"

"It's not a bomb or hostage situation, or anything like that. It's still blackmail, plain and simple."

Mike would return to that. But first he wanted something else.

"How does it activate?"

"If Pablo dies, or so he's informed us, journalists across the country get a simple email detailing some highly sensitive agency information. We don't know how it's rigged. We don't even know if he's bluffing about having a kill switch. But we do know he's not bluffing about the information. We know that for sure."

Mike knew that something was awry. He had a small piece of a puzzle. Mike could feel the information pushing up against Locklee like a torrent of liquid down a funnel. He needed to make that hole wider.

"How did he get this information? Against who? What does it entail?"

"Slow down." Locklee bit his lip.

"Answer."

Locklee's lip drew blood. He whispered something under his breath.

"Answer!"

"It's against me," Locklee said, a little too loudly.

"I knew it. You bastard. This whole op is about covering up your shit."

Locklee winced as the words hit him. Mike was mildly surprised himself, the venom unfamiliar on his tongue, but he was in the power seat. He wanted to make Locklee squirm. How dare he use Blackthorne assets to settle some back-channel corruption?

"Mike, please, slow down. I want to do this right."

"I wish I'd pulled a gun instead of a phone. Maybe it's not too late." He moved a hand to the back of his waist.

"Damn it, Mike listen to me! I don't know exactly how Pablo got the information. I assume it was from Sandor. Maybe Sandor shared it before he…or maybe Pablo dug it up?"

"Figured out what? Why would Sandor Puentes have agency secrets?"

"Look, you don't get it. That *is* the secret. That's the information."

Mike was silent for a moment. He moved his hand away from his waistband. There was nothing there anyway.

Locklee seized the moment to take a deep breath and let it out, composing himself somewhat, before speaking levelly again.

"What's the textbook way to hide a secret, hm?"

"Don't tell anyone."

Locklee smiled grimly. "Right."

"Pablo does the opposite. Everyone knows everything."

"I'm not talking about Pablo. No one actually gives a shit about Pablo, Mike."

Now Mike was properly irked. "He declared an attack on the agency."

"Through blackmail. He's blackmailing the agency with information. Do you realize how insulting that is? That's what we're supposed to be doing. And now some cartel leader is beating us at our own game."

"And so you want him dead. Make it seem like you're saving the CIA's rep. But really you're covering up your tracks."

"Sure, Mike. Honestly, if that's how you want to buy it, sure. I can leave now and we can leave it at that. It'd be a lot simpler that way."

"But there's more."

Locklee closed his mouth abruptly. The rain continued to patter against the car's roof and window.

Mike wasn't about to stop now. "I need to know what the blackmail entails. What that information is. You're going to tell me."

Locklee scratched his forehead, and an ugly little laugh escaped his mouth.

"Oh, Jesus, Mike. Mike, you have no idea what you're here for."

Something had changed. He didn't know what had been said, or what exactly turned the tables so suddenly, but Mike was no longer interrogating a corrupt colleague.

"Tell me anyway."

Without even realizing, Mike had suddenly become trapped as an unwitting confident.

"Okay. Fine. Well, to understand all this…fuck it. Let's start with Sandor. Sandor Puentes. When he was still alive. How much do you know about him?"

"Enough. He was a player, but on the rise. Knew how to cut deals instead of cut out opponents."

"He was an assimilator, a conqueror through diplomacy."

"Right," Mike said. "A regular Bismark. Analysts had suggested he was going to form a unified cartel. Your desk had pegged him as a person of interest because of this. And we were going to take him down if he got too big." Mike was fairly proud of how quickly he could jump into situation analysis and prior involvement. This was what he did best. "And then the order came down, and we did. But then somehow our agent got killed." His temper flared. "And I have a feeling you know a little something about that. About how Sandor could know he was coming. About getting paid to-"

"Damn it, Mike, shut the fuck up for a second. Yes, this has to do with that. No, I wasn't involved. Not the way you think."

"You gave the order to-"

"Oh, I know. But this dirty shit isn't on our end."

Mike froze. He didn't like where this was going.

"There's an off-the-records op, isn't there?" Of course there was. There were dozens of them. The difference was that this one sounded like it was interfering with directives. And if they overlapped, someone was supposed to make things work. He amended his previous question. "An op that shouldn't be going down."

Locklee raised his eyebrows in acknowledgement and tapped the window with his fingernail. A raindrop dripped down the window from where he touched.

"Yes. But it's complicated. Let's get back to our buddy Sandor Puentes."

Mike raised his own eyebrows at the words 'buddy' and 'Sandor Puentes' being in the same sentence. He gestured for Locklee to continue.

"Certain informants in Guatemala tipped us off years ago that Sandor Puentes was a major player in the drug and sex trade. A few interested units, yours included, were sharing information to make sure we were all on the same page. What we didn't share was that my team has suspected for years that Sandor was backed by foreign money. It was an early lead and we weren't about to bring anyone else up to speed until we were sure. We used to do things by the book. So we figured Russian, maybe even Chinese influence. Maybe government sanctioned, maybe not. We monitored the regular channels. I think you guys did a quick favor for us a while back. Piecemeal.

"We figured it's got to be linked to something foreign, or maybe some shady American character. Wrong again. We got a lead. We tracked it. Tailed it. Maybe half a year of work. Turns out money's coming out of Langley."

Mike sucked in a breath of surprise.

"And then we finally found out who it was."

Paul paused for dramatic effect. Mike gave him the benefit of an enticed audience.

"PAG."

Mike blinked. "The Political Action Group?"

"That's the one. We happened upon a PAG member cutting a deal with Puentes."

Mike's head was spinning.

"But-"

And then he remembered Sara. That attractive PAG officer he and Locklee had met.

Locklee gave him a look that confirmed he was thinking the same thing. "Yeah. Sara Burnes from the PAG was sitting in our initial meeting. I mean, why would she be there?"

"Because…" Mike didn't have a good answer, and was secretly thankful, if not a bit irritated, to be interrupted again.

"Because this isn't an SOG op. The PAG is pulling the strings here. And look, PAG hates oversight. They like working in the dark."

"That's a broad brushstroke."

"It's a fair one."

Mike's mind was no longer spinning. It was becoming still. He felt dense, stupid almost. He was an *intelligence* officer, damn it.

"Fine. Less oversight. Are they conducting more controversial activities?"

He expected Locklee to scoff at him, but he only shook his head.

"Yes and no. Maybe. I wouldn't know. I'm not PAG."

"But you have a hunch."

"Oh, absolutely.

"What does it say?"

"That the PAG is running something alongside an off-the-records op that's even worse. The nature of the op hides whatever else the other thing is. No, I don't know that for sure. But they were involved with Sandor, and Sandor was as bad as they come. I mean, sex trafficking, Mike? The man made it an art. What's worse than someone like that, really?"

Locklee let that sink in for a moment, but he was on a roll now. Like he was letting something off his chest. Like he was having a beer with the guys after work. The rain continued to fall.

"Mike, I don't have to tell you that things used to be different. More hands-on. Common

goals. And look, I can respect you. You and I are cut from similar cloth. We're both spooks and we hate each other, but in the Special Operations Group we're still one team. And we do bad stuff, but we're still the good guys. I've spent enough restless nights and a rocky marriage to decide on that, at least. PAG, on the other hand…" He let out some air as if to make his point.

Mike didn't really think of himself as a 'spook', but maybe that was a more apt description of what he was. Regardless, his urge for disarming humor was starting to bubble.

"Locklee, are you saying all of this is just one big feud between you and a department you don't like?"

Locklee shot him a look as if Mike had insisted insects were people too.

"Mike, what kind of people go into politics? No, let me just answer that for you. A few really good people, but mostly every power-hungry cockroach and slug you can find. Now, ask yourself what kind of people end up in the PAG? The *Political* Action Group. I'll answer that for you, too: a group of people playing politics, but instead of approving bridges or hedging corporate bailouts, they're running a powerful branch of the CIA's Special Activities Division. We know how vicious politicians can get. Don't cut these guys short. I mean, remember, these are the people who were overthrowing governments once a week in Latin America. Installing capitalist puppet dictators. Think of Chile."

"I know my history, Locklee."

"Alright. Great. So you know who we're dealing with, then." He pinched the bridge of his nose. "It's like, the Cold War was a shitshow and everything, but at least we had a goal, y'know? Drive those commies into the dust. It was winnable. We won. But the War on Drugs and the War on Terrorism has scattered us so thin. It's a reproducing problem that *we* engineered, for Christ's sake! It was fine for a while, but now we've gotten careless and petty. Not just with procedure but with…with our morals."

Mike thought the man was going to cry for a moment, but then he seemed to collect himself.

"Anyway."

The rain continued to pick up. It was loud enough that they'd had to speak up to make themselves heard. There was something unnatural about yelling secrets.

"Locklee, if the PAG was talking to Sandor, I'd think they were trying to work him. Manipulate him. I wouldn't think it was dirty, maybe they were eventually going to take him down. Or take something even bigger with him."

Locklee grimaced. "That's what I thought too, Mike. Honestly. But the more we worked that angle, the less it made sense. Sandor was doing a little too well at that point. He told our contact that he was thinking of growing his enterprise. He planned to unite the cartels under his banner and join the other oligarchs. He didn't want to back the right *oligarcas familias* anymore; he wanted to *be* an *oligarcas familias*."

"Okay, fine," Mike said after Locklee paused. "But the *oligarcas familias* doesn't like this new money. It's *dinero nuevo.* I mean, extortion is one thing, but drugs and sex trafficking? These were landowners who got fat the traditional way and crushed a rebellion. They're not making room for a fucking Mayan dealer." Locklee raised an eyebrow.

"Would the PAG work a guy in this position?" He asked. "Do they back a single ambitious Mayan who's probably smuggling young girls into America for all we know, or do they please the fifty-odd families that not only control Guatemala, but have already received our support in the Cold War? That now make their American partners economically happy and swear to uphold the democratic, capitalist way?" Locklee stopped talking. Mike realized that he was waiting for an answer. He thought hard.

"What if the PAG were trying to disrupt things? What if they wanted someone they could count on? A seemingly rogue maverick in the establishment to break up some too-strong alliances, or…"

"Sure," Locklee said, sounding as if he'd already considered every possibility. "But look at the rabbit hole. The CIA is now working with a brutal cartel leader for political gain. I think you're right, but I also think they realized they made a mistake. But they were stuck. Maybe one office backs him and another wants him out. Who says the PAG is unified on the issue? I wouldn't be surprised if those bastards are actively working against each other. Anyway, Sandor was becoming a problem on our end, as you pointed out, and at the time I'm still naïve to us being a big happy CIA family. So I do what I think is the sensible thing. I go to you and Blackthorne and ask to eliminate him. But…" Locklee sucked on his teeth for a moment.

"What?" Mike asked, after waiting too long.

"I took my own precautions. I called our agent before the mission, and asked him to snatch some information."

Mike could hardly contain his rage. He felt his face burning and turning red as Locklee spoke. His words came out as an ugly hiss. "You did what?"

"I needed to find out for certain if my hunch was right! I had to follow up-"

"Do you realize what you've done?"

"Yes. I went behind your back. I asked your agent to do something that you hadn't authorized. And I'd do it again."

Mike seethed. "You got him killed."

Locklee held firm, eyes and jaw sharp against Mike's verbal blows. "No, I didn't.. Sandor was tipped off."

"Then Brian betrayed me. He should've reported it to me."

"I used my clearance. And I said I didn't want anyone else involved. I wanted this kept tight. Your agent was good. He pushed me. I had to tell him what I was piecing together. I told him he could have a look at any of the information he gathered if he doubted what I was saying. I wasn't going to withhold it from you. But I needed him to get it first."

Mike slowly unclenched his fists. He was here to make Locklee talk. He didn't have to like it. He took a deep breath. "Continue."

"I wanted to send in our guy and wrap this up with a big fat bow. That way we'd get the information, but we'd also take out Sandor so there'd no blowback. The asset — Brian — went in and got killed, and we had no idea how."

"Sandor was tipped off."

"Yeah, but maybe not because he was in the crosshairs. They may have feared us learning something while we were down there. I can't be sure."

"Which we would have, if Brian had been able to gather anything."

"Exactly. The mission was doomed from the start. And I got six hundred and fifty G's landing in my personal account from Sandor beforehand, looking like I was paid off to botch the op. But Sandor's dead too, so there's no way to prove or disprove anything."

"And then Pablo starts sending threats that he'll blow the lid wide open. How was he able to contact you?"

"I'm guessing the PAG fed Sandor my information, and Pablo dug it up. Or gave it to him directly."

Mike looked sceptical. Locklee didn't offer anything more, so Mike moved on.

"What exactly did he threaten you with?"

"He has the information that Sandor was working with American officials in the CIA's Special Activities Division, but it's all off the record stuff. The only real damning piece is what you found. It links everything to me and seems to prove it."

"The deposit."

Paul nodded. "It's all laid out for the journalists: 'Drug and sex trafficker found working with Paul Locklee, CIA official'; 'Assassination attempt foiled for blood money'; 'Cartel leader supported for political gain in Latin America.'" Locklee looked as if he was going to spit. "The worst part is no matter what happens, they win. The only way I get out of this is if we manage to kill Pablo and stop the leak. You made things difficult by requesting the interrogation because SOG's going to find out about the deposit, but fine, I'll suffer damnation as long as it's internal."

"You think PAG will let you talk?"

"They won't have a choice. At least if I'm implicated, I get to tell my side before judiciary and try to take down these PAG fuckers with me. We both know Linda wouldn't let it reach the public."

"But if the lid simply blows off..."

"Then it's just me going down. PAG will get off scot free. And we still won't know what they were up to."

"Which would have happened if last night had gone differently."

For a moment, Mike could see everything clearly. The attempt on Pablo's life at his summer home was nothing more than PAG pulling strings. Pablo dies, and the journalists get their info with Locklee's name attached. Doing it through some anonymous kill-squad, an entire team dead for the opportunity to cover up some dirt and pawning the blame. Mike could hardly contain his disgust.

"You know, it kills me," Locklee continued, not noticing Mike was lost in thought. "Picturing that people might think I'm the bad guy." He scoffed. "You ever been on tour, Mike?"

He didn't like the casual tone Locklee had now. It meant he'd lost his power over the man.

"I wasn't military," Mike said slowly. "I was a detective in New York before Special Activities. Worked intel gathering, mostly. Liked being in the field so moved to Special Operations, even if I became the equivalent of a beat-cop. Got too good at the job, so they put me in charge of the unit. I climbed the ladder."

"You didn't climb the ladder. You hopped the rungs. We both know that."

Mike didn't reply. He didn't like giving so much information. Besides, Locklee was supposed to be the one in the hot seat.

"You were good, so they put you behind a desk. Thankfully, the right people gave you Blackthorne because you have a conscience."

"Huh?"

"Your unit can't just have anyone in charge. It needs someone totally incorruptible."

"I know that," Mike snapped.

But Locklee just ignored him. "Someone who isn't eager to use the unit, someone who calls on his boss to approve action when his colleagues are making requests." He tilted his head back, thinking for a moment, then brought his head forward again and looked straight at Mike. "We have to make sure Blackthorne stays in good hands. I shudder to think what might happen if the PAG were able to access it or your agents."

"Yeah, well, I'll make sure that doesn't happen."

"Again, Mike, this is why you're in charge. Others would see that as an opportunity."

Mike's eyes narrowed. "Let me ask you this, Locklee. Who's to say you're not making all this up? Maybe this is an opportunity for you."

Locklee raised his hand again. "I can't prove any of this. All the PAG business was done in back channels, in-person meets. Like I said, no oversight."

"Just like we're doing now."

"Right. But really, Mike, do you think I'm lying?"

Mike ignored him. "So if I had done this in my office?"

"I would have said we should go for a walk."

"You're no better than PAG, then."

Locklee looked like he would lose his temper, but visibly held himself back. He gave a quick roll of the eyes instead. "It's a catch-22, Mike: damned if you do, damned if you don't. The bottom line is that we've grown so clandestine we can't even keep track of it anymore. And that's a huge boon to ambitious individuals who aren't afraid to play a little dirty. After all, we're the most ambitious dirty organization in the world."

"Except for maybe the church," Mike said harshly.

Locklee chuckled at that. "Except for maybe the church." He shifted in his seat a bit, trying to get more comfortable. "So. Ball's in your court, my friend. I'm not asking you to rescind your interrogation efforts. But I am asking you to help me see this thing through. Not just this mission."

He held out his hand.

The hot air in the car from two sweaty people was giving Mike a headache. The rain still fell but had begun to quiet. Mike thought for a long hard moment and eyed Locklee's outstretched palm. The vulnerable look in his eyes. Mike looked away.

He popped the door and felt wet raindrops pepper his shoes and pants.

"I'm not your friend," he said before getting up. "The Boys will take you home."

He shut the car door and was about to call a cab. but decided to walk home despite the rain. He felt like he needed a shower anyway.

CHAPTER 16

———

John was a firm believer that no mission should have calm. Just as a weight lifter continually upped the weights they lifted, nothing should plateau. Natural slow-down points happened all the time. Sometimes John found himself undercover, blending into a community and observing a target for weeks or even months before being ordered to move in. There were lulls. But when something remained calm and comfortable, that was always a warning sign.

The action last night had spurred him. John was certain that if he and Marcela didn't execute their mission soon, Esteban would prod them anxiously. He didn't know what fallout was happening on the Firm's side of things, but he didn't need to waste any time to consider it. All he had to know was that shit rolled downhill. He'd be hit soon enough.

And Marcela, too. She must be anxious to put a plan in action. She had been undercover for two weeks, and her time had been taxing, her position much more compromising. Her freedom, he knew, rested on his ability to complete the mission successfully alongside her.

John was cautious and calculating by nature. But he John saw a potential opportunity present itself when he went in to tutor Pablito that morning, he knew he had to take it.

"*Señor* Carpenter!" A guard said as John entered a sitting room on the way to the kitchen.

John tensed, but quickly overrode his defensive reflexes when he heard that the tone was friendly.

"*Buenos días.*" *Good morning.* John was trying to take stock of the guard.

"*¿Cómo estás?*" *How are you?*

"*Estoy muy bien. Graçias, señor. ¿Dónde está Pablito?*" *I'm fine. Thank you, sir. Where is Pablito?*

The guard shrugged. "*Él viene.*" *He's coming.*

The guards didn't usually speak, at least not to him, and not without reason. Small talk was frowned upon. Then John noticed that the man was familiar. He was the one at Pablo's summer house, the one he had warned when he first got there during the attack. John blinked, taken aback. He'd been sure that the man had been shot. The guard grinned.

"You remember me," the guard said.

"*Sí.*" *Be very careful*, John warned himself. This had the potential to ruin the entire mission.

"*Gracias* for the warning last night, *Señor. Patrón* Puentes is safe, because of you." The guard shook his head ruefully. "Didn't stop me from getting shot, though. But the Lady was with me." ." He was grinning stupidly as he pulled out a silver chain necklace from beneath his uniform. It had a thick disk on the end. "*Nuestra Señora de Guadalupe.*" *Our Lady of Guadalupe.* He gave his fist a kiss as he held the disk then tucked it back in his shirt. "She saved me."

An absolute fluke, thought John. He had seen stranger things, but they were rare. This was the man who had seen him. John's face tightened. He would probably have to kill this man.

But if he had already returned to guard duty, he must have said something to Pablo about John being at the summer house last night.

Mild-mannered tutor John Carpenter shouldn't have been there. Not at that time. And it was strange enough that he had warned a guard about the attack. No, if the guard had reported John, something didn't make sense. No one had come asking questions of him. Sure, John would come up with a cover story if he had needed it, but that could have stretched the imaginations of Pablo Puentes. The problem had been solved with this guard's death. Until now.

John unslung his shoulder bag and pulled out notebooks, pencils, and his lesson plan. From the corner of his eye, he noticed the guard shift uncomfortably on his feet. He opened his mouth to say something, but when John turned to face him again he stopped.

"¿Señor?" John asked. He raised his eyebrows and stooped his head, gesturing the man to say what seemed to be on his mind.

"Yes…sorry, Señor Carpenter. I…last night at the summer house, I…"

Here it was. John braced himself. What this man said next would determine if the mission were blown, and who would have to die. His hand closed around the grip of his gun at the bottom of his bag.

"I did not tell Patrón Puentes you were there…that you saved him by telling me."

John's grip loosened and he forced a shrug. "I often go for a run when I cannot sleep."

The guard nodded enthusiastically, "Yes, you were sweating very much when I saw you." His tone was void of any suspicion.

John saw his window of opportunity. He let go of the gun altogether and withdrew his hand from his bag.

"Maybe you should have gone for a run as well," John said playfully. "You were very sleepy when I saw you." He gave the most innocent little wink he could muster.

The guard's eyes went a little wide then, and some redness flushed his cheeks. John noted again how young he seemed, even in his uniform and while holding one of those deadly Remington TAC-14 shotguns. Some things couldn't disguise age when one looked closely.

"Yes…I…" The guard swallowed and took a half-step toward John. "Did you say to anyone that you were there? Or that you saw me…yawning?"

John frowned and shook his head. "No, of course not. That would get you in trouble, no?"

The guard's face betrayed some of his relief. He almost whispered when he spoke. "Yes. I would greatly appreciate it if you did not speak of it to anyone. Especially *Patrón* Puentes. You saved his life, thank Maria, but he would be upset with me if he knew." He looked down at his feet, ashamed.

"Do you think *Patrón* Puentes would kill you?"

"Or worse. Please, *Señor* Carpenter." The guard's eyes were pleading as much as his words.

John made a show of thinking about things, then nodded. "Okay. I won't say anything. You may have made a mistake, but you seem like a good and loyal man."

The guard smiled. "Thank you, *señor*."

John's face grew dark then, surprising the guard. "But there are other guards who want to hurt our *patrón*."

"No," the guard said, confusion and shock painting his face.

"Yes, but I am only a tutor and I need help from a guard I can trust to stop them."

"Tell me."

John's ears perked up as he heard the pitter-patter of Pablito's feet running down the hallway. The boy's timing couldn't have been more perfect.

"We will talk more of this. Can you meet me for a drink tonight?" John said quickly.

"Um…yes, yes, alright."

"Say, seven o'clock, at the *Timito*."

"Okay," the guard said timidly.

Pablito burst into the room and looked at the guard and then at John. He was beaming.

"I am ready to learn!" he cried.

***

The *Timito* was a seedy dive bar a couple streets over from the main strip of Antigua's downtown. The place was dark, ebbing dark reds and violets from shadows cast off its painted plaster by incandescent light bulbs. A single old man with half his face obscured by a strange blue tattoo manned the bar. John had opted for a dark corner of the *Timito*, sitting on a high stool at a small round table dirtied with stains. It was an ideal place to meet to share conversation that would best be left unheard.

The guard entered, out of uniform and scanning the room. Once he spotted John, he moved over to the table and pulled up a chair. He sat down uncomfortably and leaned forward, hands clasped, looking expectantly at John. John took a slow sip from his beer.

"Why don't you get a drink, *amigo*. It's on me. You look like you could use it."

The guard frowned but then went to the bar. He came back with a *Gallo*.

"*Gallo*? You can't drink *Gallo*!"

"Why not? It is the beer of Guatemala" The guard paused before sipping, then looked at the label. He gave John a questioning look. Guatemalans were proud of their *Gallo* beer.

John didn't care for *Gallo*. It had a bitter aftertaste. He preferred *Cabro Reserva*, a premium beer from the same company.

"This is the beer of Guatemala, that's why." John raised his *Cabro Reserva* and took a swig.

The guard finally laughed, shrugged off his stiffness, and clinked John's bottle when he offered it. The man took a deep drink.

"What's your name?" John asked when the man finally put his beer down.

"Carlos." The man nervously tugged on his ear and looked to the doorway.

"Okay, Carlos. Is everything okay? You seem distracted."

"You said *Patrón* Puentes was in danger."

"Yes."

"Tell me. Who is he in danger from?"

"Americans. Other cartel leaders. Rich political families."

Carlos rocked his head back and forth, disappointed by John's answer. "This is why I guard him. We know these dangers."

"Yes. But…Carlos, this may be hard to hear…"

"Tell me."

John looked pained. "He is also in danger from his own guards."

"What?."

"Yes. Even from men such as…" John brought his voice to a whisper. "Juan. Your *comandante*."

Carlos looked horrified. John waited as he worked up the courage to speak.

"I…there have been rumors but…most of us thought them false…"

John mentally filed away that information. Those rumors would help sow more confusion after Marcela eliminated Juan. "Exactly. And I fear there may be truth in these rumors. You and I both saved *Patron* Puentes' life. Do you know what this means?"

"We are good men."

"Yes. And it means we can trust each other."

Carlos's eyes narrowed and nodded. He took another long drink.

"Let me get you another beer."

Carlos looked at his beer and seemed to consider.

"*Sí. Graçias.*"

John nodded and got the man another *Gallo*. The bartender shook his head and John shrugged to him, jerking a thumb at Carlos. The bartender rolled his eyes and passed the beer over the counter. John resumed his seat.

"As I said. We can trust each other." He clinked the man's new bottle to prompt him. John began to drink. "But we may not be able to trust anyone else. I have heard guards mocking him."

Carlos's eyes were wide. "Mocking him? Mocking *Patrón* Puentes?"

John nodded solemnly. "Calling him a *tonto del culo.*" *Dumb ass.*

"*No.*"

John nodded again, taking a small sip of his beer and letting Carlos's imagination do the rest.

"Where…how did you…?"

"Strong men don't notice a little tutor sometimes."

John was hoping that would suffice.

"I need to ask you something important," John pressed.

"*Sí.*"

"It could be…dangerous."

"*Sí.*"

John stared off for a moment, letting his words linger. "I need to finish this before I go on. Liquid courage."

John gave the other man a quick look, hoping he would follow suit. He did. They tipped their bottles back, drinking the beer down.

"I might need another," John said. He pointed at Carlos, but the man waved him off. "Are you sure?"

"*Sí,* I need to think clearly."

"I sometimes find alcohol helps me do that," John chuckled.

But still Carlos refused.

"I will get you some soda," John said before Carlos could reply.

He went back to the bartender and asked for a Cuba Libre. He thanked the man, made a show of considering, then ordered another *Cabro Reserva* for himself. As the bartender ducked behind the counter for the small fridge, John pulled a small pill from his pocket and dropped it into Carlos's drink. He retrieved the *Cabro Reserva* and sat back down at the table, placing the rum and Coke in front of Carlos.

"I confess, Carlos my friend, I had the barman put a tiny bit of rum in there for you." Before Carlos could refuse, John made a show of how tiny the amount was with thumb and forefinger.

The man smiled reluctantly, thanked him, then took a drink.

John's narrowed his focus. He had followed his script as closely as he could. He had established trust between them, sown distrust for others, and now John needed the man to give him what he needed. The pill was nothing fancy; a simple inebriating agent derived from a cruder agent called PTD, originally used in the Cold War by both sides, but preferred by the Soviets. The original agent put subjects into a dizzying stupor and often knocked targets out cold. The more subtle agent John applied was something not unlike alcohol and had the tendency to loosen lips and aid psychological manipulation. It was difficult to use without lubricating the subject first because it would come on too strong. In one unfortunate case in Honduras, John's amateur use of a pill left an informant uncertain what had hit him and had drawn attention with a trail of vomit. The debrief had commanded all units to now only use the agent with sufficient alcohol consumption.

"Listen to me closely, Carlos. Very soon, I may need your help to protect our *patrón*."

"How?"

John made a show of checking the entrance of the bar, then lowered his tone. "When I tell you, you must convince our *patrón* to leave the compound."

"I don't know if-"

"There is no *if*, Carlos," John said, biting his words off. "He is in danger."

Carlos grew silent and took another sip of his rum and Coke/PTD-derived agent.

"*Sí*?" John asked.

"*Sí*." One of Carlos' eyes twitched slightly and began to droop. "When?"

"I will tell you. Soon."

"*Patrón* Puentes is a careful and smart man. But he is always in danger."

"*Sí*. That is why we must protect him."

"We are the good ones." Carlos nodded as he took another sip. His eyes were dilated now.

John stared at the table for a moment.

"

Señor …this is all…it sounds very dangerous."

John took the man's hand and let him continue drinking with the other. "Yes. Yes it is. But we must…our *patrón* could be killed."

Carlos seemed to mull that over for a moment. His eyelids fell then flew back open again, as if he were awoken from a nap.

"How do I do this?"

John made a look of thinking. "You will take the *patrón*'s car." He pulled out a scrap of paper and pencil, wrote the address of the safe house, and slid it across the table. "Take him there."

Carlos's eyes widened a bit as he read the address, his pupils tiny pinpricks in a sea of bulging veins. He tucked the paper away and drew himself upright. "Juan is quite fearsome, John. And this may look suspicious."

"Don't worry about Juan, Carlos." It may have been too much to say that.

"I don't know if I can…"

"You can, Carlos, and you will. And I will help you. Don't forget that. Promise me you will do this."

Carlos let out some air and finished his drink. "I promise you."

"Good." John let go of his hand. "And promise me one other thing. Just as I did not tell *Patrón* Puentes about you yawning at the summer house, you cannot tell a single soul about what we spoke about today. *Entiendes?*"

"*Entiendo.* I understand, *señor* Carpenter. It is only us we can trust."

"*Sí,*" John said sadly.

"*Señor…*"

"Yes, *amigo?*"

"I think I need help getting home."

John laughed. "Sure. That's the least I can do for you."

It was getting dark out. John paid the bartender, hailed a cab, reminded Carlos what to do and what not to say, then saw him off.

He didn't have much faith in Carlos, but he had faith in his own ability to seize opportunities when they presented themselves.

CHAPTER 17

Blackthorne, known to agents like John and Marcela simply as 'the Firm', had an extensive portion of its training on psychological warfare. Candidates underwent brutal reshaping to steel themselves against the weight of annoying human imperatives that could be unpredictable, like emotion or morality.

The reasoning was twofold. On the one hand, it made agents impervious to external pressures, such as interrogation efforts or the simple stress of social isolation that was often imposed. It also ensured individuals were able to carry out vicious actions that most would balk at. In one case, an agent had reportedly claimed killing someone had the same emotional value as cutting a slice of cheese.

Obviously this had to be monitored. Things had changed since the experimental phase of the 50's and 60's. No LSD, for one thing. They were more careful now.

The other aspect of the training regime was its use in the field. Agents were slowly and painfully stripped bare of their egos and personalities, opened up and laid bare for what some referred to as 'spiritual vivisection'. Agents were broken down into the simple parts that made them up, while instructors tinkered with different traits and desires, revisiting and amplifying important experiences, and ultimately sewing agents up as new and stronger people. It also meant that they became experts in applicative psychology and the emotional makeup of a person. Their knowledge and ability was firsthand.

It remained an intimate case study of what could be imported as a field-option. In any given situation, agents flashed a set of appropriate actions to be taken. Psychological warfare and emotional manipulation were potent tools in each agent's toolkit.

Marcela had passed at the top of her unit's class.

She was particularly intrigued by a theory of emotional state championed by one of her instructors. She once knew all the intimate details but now only concerned herself with the general idea that targets were most vulnerable at their emotional peak. Whatever emotion it was — anger, sadness, happiness — didn't matter. There remained a gaping hole in one's reasoning ability when eroded by emotional extremity. Therefore, targets should be wound like a coil, wrung like a wet rag, and squeezed until that peak point was nearly reached. Suggestion could be slipped in right before the climax, and, as the theory went, the suggestion would associate with the output.

Opponents of the theory argued that as reason took hold, any suggestion would be wiped away, and Marcela was aware that the whole thing wasn't very academic, besides. But she had field-tested it and gotten great results. It wasn't really all that complex after all. It was like sex. Or like men. Simple.

"I'm horny, *querido*," she said, tugging on Juan's sleeve.

She had gathered her purse and followed him carefully through a couple halls until he made his way to his room, probably for a *siesta* or to get away from business. When she had made herself seen slinking around a corner, he hid a smile and waved away the guards standing outside his door.

Marcela and John needed to ship Pablo out to the safe house. They had met briefly last night to exchange any outlying information and confirm the plan. They went over the data found on the wig and John had further described what he had seen lurking behind the Mayan calendar. Apparently he may have also worked a guard too. She grudgingly admitted she was impressed.

The first thing on her end would be to remove Juan, leaving a flimsy security situation in its wake. She couldn't help but feel frustrated that they couldn't use Juan more. She had been working him for almost her whole time here. But his usefulness had probably ended. Either way, she knew how she'd handle things.

She moved to business.

She wrapped her arms around him and kissed him, but he pushed her away, albeit lightly.

"No," he said. "Please. This is trouble."

His hands lingered though, petting her hips lightly, unable to let her go.

"This is trouble? No, my Jaguar, *I* am trouble." She pulled one of his hands up away from her hip and onto her breast. He began to caress and squeeze.

He shook his head and looked up above his doorway. A red light blinked against a metal frame.

"The cameras," he said.

Marcela laughed then, loudly. "You are head of security!"

"And others see them too."

A sheepish look washed over him. Marcela pouted at him, then changed tactic, deciding to push rather than pull. She tossed his arms off her and folded her own.

"Who checks them, Juan? Really? Tell me, does anyone check them?"

"I don't know. Sometimes.. No. Not really."

She held her gaze on him and watched him teeter on the brink of pulling away and succumbing to her. It reminded her of what she had learned when fishing with her father.

'Set the hook, Chela, that's it. Not yet, no. Don't pull yet. Wait for the fish. You already have the hook, now you must wait for the fish. Feel it nibbling? Good, Chela…now!'

Juan rolled his eyes and broke into a grin. He moved in to kiss her again, sliding his tongue into her mouth. He opened the door and stumbled inside, half carrying her, then slammed the door shut and pushed her against it. She pulled at his belt and considered, for a moment, how the action reminded her of tugging at a fishing rod.

"We will have to be quick," he said, breathing hard in her ear.

Her heart beat fast despite herself.

"I can be quick."

"And quiet. We will have to be quiet."

She undid one of the buttons on her shirt and looked him in the eye.

"I don't know if I can do that."

She loosened his buckle and her hands slowly found their way inside.

***

They lay in bed when they were finished, naked and tired, neither wanting to leave the soft comfort and warmth of doing nothing. Juan may have been a capable lover, but he returned to his awkward stiffness after the fact, leaving her to caress him gingerly. He didn't so much as put an arm around her. But this was who he was. An awkward man pretending to be a soldier.

Unlike him, she didn't pretend. It was too easy to pull a small knife from her purse left at the side of the bed. It rested against her leg now, under the sheets.

"Juan," she whispered.

He grunted in response. Then turned his head slowly to face her.

She gripped the knife firmly and with the care needed for effective movement. She tapped the blade with her thumb, deciding if she could squeeze anything else from this man. She loosened her grip.

"I am concerned about you."

He grunted again. "Why?"

"Because," she said, tracing one of his nipples with her other hand's finger. "You are your father's son. But you are treated like your uncle's."

As impossible as it seemed, she could feel his body grow stiffer.

"Don't. I don't want to talk about that."

"No, Juan, you have to. It is important. It is who you are."

"Stop."

"Okay, fine, forget about your uncle. I want to hear about your father. Tell me."

"Tell you what?"

She pulled him in for a kiss. She made it long, pressed her lips hard against his, and moved her tongue slowly. They parted with the light sound of moist skin.

"I want you to tell me about your father. Your *papá*."

He was silent for a long moment, and Marcela thought he would fall asleep, or simply ignore her. But then she heard him clear his throat.

"I always knew my father, my *papá*, would die one day. We all die. It is something he would say. When I was younger I thought it was a joke. When I was older I realized it was a creed. You see, the thing we all fear is death. But we all die. So my father would remind himself of it. I guess. I don't know. It sounds stupid."

"No," Marcela said softly. She pulled his arm around her. "You said he was smart."

"Yes."

"Tell me."

He sidled up closer, losing some of his rigidity.

"He was a brilliant businessman, Marcela. Because he knew business was business. Because…if something was wrong, he didn't believe in burning it to the ground. Like so many of the rebels and revolutionaries from before. When others called for destruction, he sensed an opportunity for change. He could turn anything to his advantage."

That made Marcela feel sick and grow hot with anger. "Is this why you are okay working under your uncle?"

He tensed again.

She kissed his cheek. "Sorry. It just…seems to make sense to me."

He adjusted himself but didn't move away. "I guess so. Yes. My *papá* would try and work with anyone. He could turn corruption into industry. He could take the most insane person and channel their abilities into perfect and steady action. The way a fire tempers steel. He would make steel out of brittle iron."

"Like…" She felt at the metal in her hand again.

"Yes, like Pablo. My father could just…make good product out of nothing, you know? An opportunist, sure, but a measured one."

"I see. But now, with your father gone…"

He sighed. "Yes. My father is gone. And now my uncle reigns like a mad king."

She let him see that she opened her mouth to speak, then made a show of hesitating.

"What?"

"No. I…no. It's nothing."

"What?" he asked more forcefully.

"Well, do you think he killed your father?"

Silence.

He sat up then, back straight as if he were up against a wall. The sheets fell from his shoulders and pooled around his waist.

"No."

"No you don't think he killed your father, or no, you don't want to think about that?"

He flinched then turned away from her, reaching for his shirt, strewn next to his pants on the floor.

"It just seems to make sense to me, Juan. I mean, Sandor must have given so much to Pablo in the will he left."

"He must have." Juan shrugged.

Must have?

Marcela paused. She thought for a moment about how to proceed, then decided to try a different angle. John be damned, she could work this target. If he could work a target — a *guard* — she could get at Juan. Elimination was such a waste.

"Juan."

"Yes."

"Did you see the will?" she asked.

He was standing up out of bed, buckling up his pants now, beginning to adjust his hair with a comb. He was hardly paying her any attention.

"The will. Your father's. Did you see what he left you?"

Juan scrunched up his eyes as he made sure his hair was combed properly.

"What? Yes, he left a will. My mother took care of all that."

Marcela sucked in air. She caught herself from making it noticeable. Luckily Juan paid no heed.

Isabella.

The woman who had married Sandor had later married Pablo. From the outside, it seemed that Pablo was playing patriarch, claiming the woman who had been with his brother, placing a flag of ownership on her, sending a message to everyone else — *I am the rightful heir of everything.*

From the inside, from someone like Juan or Isabella, it wasn't just tolerated, it was gracious, maybe even expected. He was taking them in, keeping them close and safe, making sure others didn't greedily encroach upon the tragedy.

But Juan not seeing his father's will? Isabella 'taking care of it'? Juan being bullied by his uncle-now-stepfather? He was still captain of the guard, but some days it didn't feel like it. And Pablo didn't trust him enough with the kill switch.

No, this was a yarn ball of potential intrigues. Pablo may have killed Sandor outright, a disagreement in management. Or a simple takeover? A crime of passion? He could have had an affair with Isabella? Who's to say Pablito didn't belong to her? And again, there was Isabella. She could have killed her previous husband. Or her and Pablo together? Was Pablo consolidating power, or was she?

It was a mess of ideas. Usually, this would mean she would have to find the thread of truth in the ball of unknowns. In this case, however, it didn't matter. In fact, it worked better. She could leave that to Juan. His imagination could take on the legwork. And if this was what she was able to come up with in a short span of idle thinking, what could his heated thoughts summon up?

"Juan, I know something that you don't. It is important. It will hurt you. But it will also make you stronger. It will make you a man, instead of a little boy."

A heaviness fell on the room. He turned slowly. The movement was more menacing than anything she had witnessed in the compound. She buried her fear the moment it dared to appear.

They locked eyes.

"You don't want to be a little boy, do you?"

She could tell he wanted to hit her then. But her eyes flashed dangerously, enough so that it made him reconsider. She saw him mull over the truth of the question, as he moved his tongue around his teeth, contemplating.

"No."

Marcela leaned over the side of the bed and slipped the knife she held back into her purse. She pulled out something else and showed it to Juan.

It was her phone. With pictures of the will John had sent her.

He looked at it carefully and she beckoned him over to take a closer look.

CHAPTER 18

Graveyards always felt cold, regardless of Antigua's chilly mountain air.

After his time with Marcela, Juan wanted to be left alone with his thoughts. He had waved off his guards and taken a walk to the graveyard where his father was buried. The time alone hadn't helped him as he thought it might. His thoughts were noisy and annoying, shouting over one another. There was no semblance of the peace he had hoped for.

"I thought I might find you here."

His mother's voice was usually sharp, but today it held a softness that made him want to cry out to her, hug her, love her. That made him irritated. He didn't want her here. Juan held himself firm, like his father would have wanted. He stared at the lavish gravestone and statue of the *Virgen de Guadalupe*. The name *Sandor Puentes*, cut deeply into the grave marker, carved into his mind.

Some men may be great, but all men die.

"Did you see *Fuego*?"

Juan didn't pull his gaze away from his father's grave. He felt numb.

"Juan."

"Yes."

He had seen it. Smoke had begun to surge from the active volcano *Fuego*. The word meant 'fire' in Spanish. A fitting name. Juan wished he had something like that. Something that fit. He never felt like he belonged. He was supposed to be his uncle's right hand man, his Jaguar warrior. But he was still treated like a boy. He wanted something of his own.

"Do you remember when you were learning about volcanoes? When you were little, *mi hijo*?"

Juan shrugged.

"There had been an eruption, and lava swallowed some people and buildings. Everyone was talking about it. You asked why people would build a life on the side of a volcano? It does seem a stupid thing when you think about it. You were such a smart child. Asking questions." Isabella gave a sad smile and looked at where Sandor slept. "I told you that Mayans believed volcanos held the great *dualidad. Duality.* Life and death. The volcano may breathe fire, but because of this it creates the most fertile soil. That is why they built their cities on the sides of volcanoes. And this is the same reason they are burned."

Juan thought about this for a moment. The imagery of a village engulfed in fire turned green and lush in his mind. The price paid for a good harvest was great turmoil.

"But that is life," he said aloud.

Isabella nodded. "That is life."

A cool wind blew, rustling the white cedars surrounding the small graveyard. He thought he smelled sulfur on the wind.

"Do you think," Juan asked slowly. "That my father was really killed by an American assassin?"

Isabella's brow furrowed at Juan's abrupt question and she gave him a strange look.

"What? Juan, *mi hijo*, we know he was. It was a sad thing. And now Pablo is punishing them."

"Yes, he is. Yet it is still bothering me."

"That he is punishing them? The people who killed your father?"

Juan looked at the lingering clouds above. Further west they were streaked dark with soot.

"No. I don't think they did." Juan looked her in the eye. "My father was working with them. I know this much. So why would they kill him?"

"Juan, you know how messy these things are. Americans hate each other and work against one another all the time. Just as cartels war with one another. A rival group sent the assassin, or maybe even the group he was working with. We don't know."

"And then they killed each other."

"And then they killed each other. Yes."

She began to rub his shoulder, but he pushed her arm away.

"My father had security, like my uncle does. And this is was a trained professional. DEA, or something like that. Not some *idiota*."

Isabella let out a breath, as if to say 'go on', but she didn't seem to be particularly engaged in what he was saying. Juan ignored her, walking in a circle and trying to add appropriate actions to his thoughts.

"Security should have dealt with the agent. Guards, cameras. But they did not. Fine. The man is a professional. But then when coming face to face with his target-" He mimed a gun, pointing it at the grave. "He is also shot. The two die together."

It was hard talking about his father's death with such cold and detached reason, but it made him feel stronger. More powerful. The leader he should be. The man he should be.

"I accepted this. Perhaps I was too scared to consider anything else. It doesn't matter. Coincidences happen. But then even with this coincidence, Mother, I consider my father's will." He spun on her. "I did not get what was mine, did I?"

Isabella froze. She tried to hide it by giving Juan a look of confusion. But he had seen it. He had seen it there, even if it was a small and subtle thing.

"Juan, you are your uncle's *comandante*, and you control much of-"

"I was supposed to have it all, Mother. By my father's own wishes. By your *husband's* will." He let the words linger, growing more furious as silence poured from his mother. "It is too neat and tidy. You even have a new convenient husband."

He saw her anger begin to bubble. "You said you didn't want to see the will. You told me to take care of things. You said you didn't care about your cut."

"I was upset!"

"You were acting like a child."

"How dare you hide my *papá's* words from me!"

Isabella slapped him, hard. Juan grew silent, shocked. He shrunk before his mother, even if only a fraction.

"You were given some of the business. And I have always remained discreet about you running it the way you wished, *mi hijo*. I even remained silent about you stealing Pablo's mistress. Marcela is quite something, no?"

Juan clenched his teeth until they hurt. His face washed with shame.

"I suspect Pablo knows. We hold no secrets." She took him by the shoulder. It felt threatening at first, but then turned into something consolatory. Motherly. "Yes. It is convenient. And yes, it cost you some of what you should have inherited. But there would have been struggle, just as there was between the brothers before. We both know the money that comes from moving drugs and women. And the power! It was too much for you, you weren't ready. I wanted you to learn from Pablo."

Juan's mind was at war with itself. There were too many thoughts, too many betrayals, too many questions. He could trust no one but himself. Even then he didn't know what he could do. He thought about what his father would do. That didn't give him any answer. He thought of what Marcela had whispered to him in bed, before all this pain was let out.

He looked at his mother, for the first time in a long time, he *really* looked at her. He forced himself to remember when his mother had gotten sick. So sick that she was sent away for a number of months to get treatment. He hadn't been able to see her because of her condition, he could only speak to her on the phone to make sure she was okay. Shortly after she had recovered, Pablo had celebrated the birth of his baby son. Pablito. Juan had been so worried about his mother. But what if he'd been fooled? He had always suspected. But he had never brought the words to his lips.

"Are you Pablito's mother?" He asked evenly.

She moved to slap him again, but Juan caught her by the wrist. Staring her down. He made up his mind. About everything. He would take what was his.

"I don't care." He let go of his mother's wrist. "I know that Pablo killed my father. And now I am going to kill him."

Juan stormed towards the villa, leaving his mother yelling at him from his father's grave.

"Pablo didn't kill your father, Juan! *Mi hijo*! Come back!"

"The volcano gives life, but also takes it," he whispered to himself, drawing his gun.

CHAPTER 19

John sat with Pablito at the kitchen table. His phone buzzed. He looked at the message displayed on the screen. It was from Marcela.

```
Secondary target has left nest.
Will disable switch.
```

John was surprised she hadn't eliminated Juan. His concern mounted and he punched a quick response.

```
Secondary target status?
```

The reply was instant:

```
Unstable — threat to primary target.
Intentional.
```

She must have worked Juan after all. He allowed himself a grim smile as he typed out his response.

```
Confirming all.
En route to birdfeeder with primary.
```

He hit send.

"I'll be right back, Pablito. Keep working on those animals!"

Pablito didn't look up from his dot-to-dot book. He redoubled his effort at John's words, a tongue sticking out a corner of his mouth expressing his tough work.

John was embarrassed at how much he cared for the boy. But maybe it was a good thing. Something he needed. He could look back at this later and be happy. He ruffled the boy's hair, snagged a handful of small crackers left in a dish on the kitchen table, and let his mind move into the calm, ready state that settled upon him before a plan sprang into action.

There was work to be done.

CHAPTER 20

Carlos had been in the service of the Puentes family for four years now. He had always liked Pablo. It was a good job. The hall was silent and empty as he stood vigilant outside the master bedroom. It was another day in the gorgeous Puentes compound.

Yet he shifted nervously. A few days ago he'd been a nobody, happily serving under

the protective paycheck of the Puentes security detail. A simple red beret. Juan was his *comandante*, Pablo was his master. All the guards knew the money came from their *pátron*, but Juan would give out assignments, positions, and logistics.

When Pablo requested Carlos for his personal security, Juan could only agree. His red beret was switched for the coveted black of Pablo's personal guards. It was a position many had their eyes on. But Carlos had seen the reluctance in Juan, the discomfort of not having full control over his troops. It was understandable, but Carlos's loyalty to Pablo was unshakeable.

But then came the mistake. A few too many *Cuba Libres* after visiting *Maximón,* and a few more back at the summer home. He liked drinking with his *amigos*. One had insisted he drink a tall glass of tomato juice and *Brava*, a *michelada.* Normally, this would have been fine. Sleep it off and go to work. His father had always said, 'You can drink with the boys at night. But you have to work with the men in the morning'.

Unfortunately, Carlos had drawn the short straw and was required to stand guard in the dead of night. Carlos had stood straight and breathed slowly, trying his best to summon sobriety.

Then came the attack.

Carlos had found that he now had a second person he could trust, someone loyal to his *patrón*. Perhaps not as trusted as his *pátron,* but enough that he made sure his prayers to the *Señora de Guadalupe* included another name.

John Carpenter had saved his honor. Carlos had been given another chance to prove his worthiness. He had already decided to drink less, although apparently even with *señor* Carpenter he had let himself go. Repentance was a long and heavy road. He was determined to walk it.

But the more pressing concern was what John had said about Pablo being in danger. Danger from his own men. Carlos had been watching every single guard — red beret or black — with precise and steady caution. Guards heard everything. Saw everything. No secrets.

"Carlos."

He had no idea how John had snuck up on him.

"I fear the time has come," the *gringo* said in perfect Spanish. Carlos's irritation of being caught off guard was washed away by the pleasant reminder at how elegant John's words flew. But a torrent of concern flooded his thoughts.

"What has happened? The *patrón?*" He felt his eyes go wide. If anything bad had happened to *patrón* Puentes…

John nodded stiffly. "He is fine. For now. But the time has come for us to act."

The relief Carlos felt was short lived. He turned his attention fully to John.

"What do we need to do?"

"You know." John's eyes were piercing. "Go find the *patrón*. Tell him he has to go somewhere safe. Drive him to the address."

Brief hesitation haunted Carlos as he felt the paper John had given him in his pocket. What John was asking was dangerous in itself. He wasn't authorized to give such commands. How did he know Pablo was in danger? And where did this address lead? His mind was abuzz.

"I can go to Juan," Carlos said.

If John's eyes had been knives, they would have cut flesh.

"*No*, Carlos. Go to the *patrón*. Drive him. There is no time."

Carlos couldn't deny he owed John at least some loyalty. Some trust. Something clawed at the back of his mind, some sixth sense that compelled him to do as John said. But he knew nothing of the man. He was supposed to be a tutor. Maybe he was something more. Suspicion began to creep into his thoughts...

The sound of a shotgun blast tore through the air, not a hundred feet away. It was muted by the many rooms and walls of the estate, but it was unmistakable. Carlos nearly jumped a foot off the ground in surprise.

John held his gaze as if he had been expecting such a sound. As if it had been planned.

Carlos took the paper and crossed himself quickly.

"We are the good ones," John said softly. "Now go!"

Carlos nodded with grim determination and bounded off to the courtyard. He was sure Pablo would be there.

He and John. They were the good ones.

***

Marcela removed her newest pair of shoes, not looking at the guard posted in the bedroom with her. She was expected to spend most of her time in the spacious room, a place of honor for the people Pablo deemed special or those who had curried favor with the man.

"It's so hot, and my feet get so sweaty," she said to herself, but loud enough for the guard to hear. She rubbed them to emphasize the point, then stood up and stretched. She ignored the ball of discomfort forming deep in her belly, nervousness beginning to pour upward and encourage adrenaline to flow. Instead, she took it as a sign that she should get moving.

She grabbed her handbag and shoes and left the room. She walked barefoot, yet confidently and without her eyes wandering. The best way to make someone think you weren't doing anything suspicious was simply to make it look like you knew what you were doing. No uncertainty.

She wasn't supposed to be wandering through the estate. Not really, not without any good reason. Because many of the guards had begun to realize she was sleeping with Juan (how could such a thing remain a secret?), few dared to intervene.

"*Señora.*"

Few. Still some.

The guard in the sitting room she was passing through took a few steps toward her, away from his post against the wall. Marcela turned slowly and brought a confused look to her face.

"*¿Sí?*"

"Where are you going?"

She rolled the fingers of her right hand impulsively, ready to kill the guard in a single move if it came to that. It wouldn't be good to leave a body in the middle of the room.

"I was going to find *señor* Puentes." She pulled her shirt down so the fabric stretched tightly across her breasts and revealed the outline of a lacy black bra. "Thought I'd give him a surprise." She winked.

The guard flushed and nodded. "Ah. The *pátron* is a, uh, very... lucky man."

Marcela winked again and turned without another word. She could feel the man's gaze follow her, but she knew it would be lustful rather than suspicious now. She thought about how pathetic so many men were. But then her mind focused again. She was through the room, hitting another hallway and turning toward Pablito's bedroom.

As with most of the Puentes's estate, Pablito's room was far too big and extravagant for what it was used for or what was needed. She hoped that would play to her favor, giving extra space to move about. Unlike most other rooms, there were three guards here instead of one or two. One on the outside, two inside. She began to see why.

The sightlines were bad. She couldn't focus on the guard outside the room because then she'd have two on her immediately. This doubled her resolve to get inside first and deal with the guards after.

Again, the best way to take your enemy off guard was to make it seem like you were exactly where you were supposed to be, doing exactly what you were supposed to be doing. She strode boldly to Pablito's room, not stopping for the guard at the entrance.

"*Señora…?*"

She dropped a shoe as she crossed the threshold, and made her way to the guard posted in the corner. Another stood across the room

"*Mierda!* Would you mind grabbing that for me?" She called to the entrance guard. He was following her, about to ask another question, but bent down to grab the shoe she'd dropped.

It was the extra second she had needed.

The guard in the corner was looking at her with raised eyebrows, not sure why she was approaching him. She didn't give him a second glance. She flipped the remaining shoe in her hands upside down and slammed it into his neck.

They were high heels. High heels with three-inch stiletto heels.

Before he had the chance to cough up the blood that was pooling in his throat, she'd already reached into her handbag and pulled out her knife. She threw it across the room and it stuck into the other guard who was only now beginning to shoulder his shotgun. The knife burrowed its blade firmly into his belly, the guard's arms dropping the gun and moving protectively to the wound. The gun pulled on its sling and swung backward, creating enough momentum that made the man stagger to the side and lean against the wall, shocked by the sudden pain.

The entrance guard who had entered and had graciously picked up Marcela's shoe stood up, confused.

"Thank you, *señor*," she said to him as she sidled up beside him. Her hands grabbed either side of his head. "You are too kind."

Her father had shown her a firm twist of the neck was the best way to kill chickens. It worked well on people, too.

***

Juan stood straight as a rod, the Remington shotgun he held pointing up and resting against his shoulder. It normally felt heavy, but today it was light as a feather. Smoke curled lazily from the barrel. He considered firing another shot, indulging in the display of power. But then his father's voice came, soothing in his ear.

"*No, mi hijo. Just find Pablo. End this.*"

Juan suppressed the urge to cry, allowing a few tears to fill his ducts before blinking them away. A second later, shotgun pellets fell from the sky, scattering in a nearby pacaya palm tree.

"*Comandante?*"

Guards dotting the side entrance of the Puentes's estate were coming forward, concern covering their faces, many sweeping guns left and right in search of a threat. He looked at them and smiled when he saw so many soldiers with red berets. They might be simple soldiers, but they would follow him. They would be loyal.

"Where is my uncle? Where is Pablo?"

"He should be in the courtyard, *comandante*."

Juan motioned them to follow him. The soldier who had spoken couldn't hold his tongue.

"*Comandante*, has something happened? Is Pablo in danger?"

Juan's expression didn't change, but his mouth twitched slightly. It was hardly noticeable.

"Yes, *amigo*. Pablo is in great danger. We must find him. Tell the others."

Many of the guards picked up their pace upon hearing such news. They split apart to cover more area, shouting at guards they found and waving hands to follow.

"And," he said yelling as they moved. "All of you will only listen to your *comandante*!" A vicious smile crept across his face, but the twitch remained, making it an ugly thing. "All of you will only listen to *me*!"

***

"*Patrón!*"

Carlos was trembling as he flew toward Pablo across the courtyard, eyes hanging heavily on the blood speckling his *patrón's* shirt. Before, he would never run at his *patrón* in such a reckless fashion. He'd always observed the respectful tones and gestures worthy of such a man. But now his life was at stake, and Carlos would die before he saw the *patrón* hurt.

"*Patrón!*"

Guards and servants stared as he tore through the courtyard. Carlos saw the remnants of a man's body being collected and taken away from a bloodied table. There were bits of flesh and bone scattered about, making servants bend over and pick through the otherwise perfect grass. They were bundling everything together on the tablecloth to take it all away. Already, servants were arriving with soap and water buckets to clean blood that had stained some courtyard tiles.

At first he thought Pablo was dying, already bleeding out. But Carlos quickly realized it must have been a regular occasion of swift and fair justice. Carlos breathed a sigh of relief, but the feeling didn't last long. The air rang with the crack of another shotgun blast from across the estate.

Pablo was still in danger.

The *patrón* was patting a servant on the shoulder when he looked up to see Carlos. His eyebrows rose, surprised but not taken off guard. Pablo could never be taken off guard. He seemed to know everything.

A few of the men put themselves between Carlos and Pablo, giving Carlos a cold, hard look. But Pablo pushed them away.

"Do you not see his black beret? This is one of my trusted men. He helped save my life when the Americans attacked me at my summer home."

Carlos flushed with embarrassment at this, but Pablo's face suddenly grew twisted with rage, a shade of red creeping through his complexion.

"My summer home, of all places! He is a hero. I will hear him speak."

The guards stepped aside sheepishly. Pablo looked at Carlos expectantly.

He froze. He didn't know what to say. It took a moment for his tongue to find any words.

"*My p-patrón.* You are in danger. I must take you somewhere safe."

The words may as well have been said to a brick wall. Pablo kept his eyes on Carlos, as if

he was expecting the man to go on.

"*Patrón?* I have to-"

"Thank you for being so concerned, Carlos, *mi amigo.* Truly, *graçias.* But I am always in danger."

"Yes, but-"

Something flashed in Pablo's eyes. Something that cautioned him and told him not to say

anything more. That he'd already overstepped. What was he supposed to do? How could he convince the *patrón*?

Another guard ran toward them. Carlos recognized him. Vinicio. One of the other guards that had accompanied the *patrón* to Santiago and his summer home. Carlos didn't know the man well, but he was another one of Pablo's favorites. Black beret. Besides, anyone who survived that battle at the summer home could be trusted, Carlos was sure of it.

"What is it?" Pablo said.

A hint of feeling had crept into his voice. Was it concern? Caution? Carlos couldn't figure it out. But it hadn't been there a moment before.

"*Señor,* Juan is gathering the men. He is looking for you."

"What?"

Silence fell over the courtyard. It was an ominous thing. The courtyard was the heart of the compound. It was always bustling with activity, if nothing more than gardeners weeding and servants pouring drinks. But now they stopped, one by one, realizing something was amiss.

A deep boom pounded against the sky, rocking the courtyard's walls and reverberating in everyone's chests. The earth shook, causing a guard to lose his footing and a pot to smash against pavement. Gardeners and servants and guards alike spun their heads, looking for where the sound had come from.

Everyone but Pablo. He looked to the sky.

"*Maximón,*" he said, barely audible.

The rumbling continued for a moment, then was laid aside by whatever forces had ordered such a thing.

Pablo looked at the man who had told him about Juan, and then looked to Carlos.

"Okay. We will go. No one else."

Carlos snapped himself out of his reverie, blinking and forcing his wits to come about. He broke into a stride, setting an aggressive pace for his *patrón* and his colleague.

He dared not slow when he saw smoke curling up from the north. *El Volcán Fuego* volcano had erupted.

***

"Sir."

Barker practically pounced on Mike as he stepped off the elevator. The op was going down, finally. Mike had rushed to the office as soon as he'd gotten word. He had been thinking hard about his meeting with Locklee and its repercussions, even if it meant another sleepless night. He still hadn't come to a decision over what to do. If he turned the man in, Mike would also be implicated in a serious breach of authority, as well as unauthorized use of Blackthorne assets. But if he didn't and Locklee was lying, he'd get away with cartel collusion.

"Can you give a man a second to get in? Jesus, Barker."

"Sorry, sir, this is important."

Mike was going to snap at the man, but then remembered that his assistant was incredibly good at his job, even if he reminded him of an earthworm.

"Of course. What is it? Have they disabled the kill switch?"

"They're working on it." He gave Mike a folded newspaper as they walked into the command room. "Read the headline."

Mike froze.

'CIA Officer Paul Locklee Found Dead in Office, Suspected Suicide'.

He read the headline a second time, and a third. It was as if he couldn't quite understand what it meant. In many ways, he supposed he didn't. He felt his gut wrench.

He lowered the paper slowly and led the way to his personal office. They both stayed silent. As soon as Barker closed his door, Mike turned to him.

"I need you to get Locklee's office on the line."

"Locklee's…office. Yes, sir." There was a long moment while the man punched in the number and extension, and waited. It was taking too long. Mike felt like an idiot as he practically twiddled his thumbs. Finally his assistant piped up again, phone held against his shoulder.

"The line's busy."

"What do you mean, the line's busy?"

"It's making that *boop-boop-boop* sound." A bead of sweat crept down the man's forehead as he tried to keep eye contact with his increasingly furious boss. "Sir," he added quickly.

Mike exploded. "This is the CIA! Line's aren't busy in the CIA!"

Barker rung his hands together nervously. "I can try-"

"Forget about it." Mike sunk in his chair for a moment, then stood up. Barker was giving him a look of uncertainty. He was trying to figure out what was going on. Mike gave him a quick dismissing gesture with his hand. "Never mind. Don't worry about it. We have an op to run."

"Yes, sir." He moved to open the office door but paused. "Sir, would you like me to do some digging on this…suicide?"

Mike thought for a moment. The way his assistant had said the word 'suicide' made it sound like a question. It was subtle. But it was there.

For all his greasy hair and pimpled skin, Mike could appreciate his assistant for being a damn fine intelligence officer. The least he could do was protect him.

"No. Thank you, Barker. That will be everything."

Mike opened the door, donned an earpiece, and smacked his hands together as he paced in front of his team working diligently at their computers.

"Get me a sitrep, people. Now!"

***

"Where's Pablo?" Juan bellowed a second time. His voice rang in the silence of the courtyard. Servants hung their heads, scared to make eye contact. Even a few guards anxiously avoided his gaze. He could feel their confusion, their shame, their *noncompliance*.

Could he stand here yelling all day? He could. But it would undermine his authority.

"*Comandante.*"

Juan spun so fast on the guard that the man flinched.

"Speak."

The guard had been in the courtyard before Juan had arrived. He took a deep breath. Juan silently commended him for remaining so calm. He would have to remember this man. Yet he wore a black beret.

"*Patrón* Puentes left. In a bit of a hurry, soon after the volcano."

"By himself?"

"No, *comandante*. With two black berets."

The man's eyes flicked away, glancing at a number of men in the courtyard who also wore black berets. Juan knew almost all the men behind him wore red ones. As he glanced around, it seemed the black berets were beginning to move closer to one another. He had seen a couple whispering to one another on his way across the compound, and some of his own men had struggled to explain the situation to others wearing the black.

The black berets would not follow him. They were loyal to Pablo. They wouldn't help him in his mission. They would know the danger to Pablo was right in front of them.

They would stand in his way.

"Anyone wearing a black beret," Juan shouted for all to hear, making sure each word was crisp and powerful. "Put your gun down. Now."

The silence deepened, air thick with tension. No one moved.

Three of the men with black berets slowly unslung their Remingtons and began to bring them to the ground. A few more looked nervously at the others, uncertain. Red berets looked to Juan for reassurance, then looked at black bereted men, realizing they were standing right beside one another.

Again Juan bellowed, "Black berets! Put your guns down!" His voice clear and strong.

A mourning dove cooed and took flight from a tree, crossing the sky and leaving the compound. A light veil of smoke drifted through the walls and foliage, caressing everything it moved through. A low rumble ran through the ground. *El Volcán Fuego* was angry.

Life and death, thought Juan.

He raised his shotgun.

"The *comandante* wants to kill our *patrón!*" Someone yelled.

The sound of the first shotgun blast was drowned out by the reply of a dozen others.

***

Marcela spent a few seconds standing in front of the stone Mayan calendar that hung on the wall of Pablito's room. She couldn't deny that it was a gorgeous piece of art. Intricately detailed serpents and birds adorned the stone, with individual scales and feathers lovingly cut into its surface. The glaze shone over a dazzling rainbow of painted colors swirling together and bringing it all to life.

She looked over her shoulder at the small pile of dead bodies that she had pushed into the corner so nothing would seem suspicious from a passerby in the hallway. She retrieved her handbag just in case she would need any tools, and then, brushing a wisp of hair out of her face, she got to work.

She lifted the calendar gingerly off the wall, feeling a piece of cord hanging on a screw keeping it afloat. It was heavy. As she pulled the calendar away from the wall, she felt something still attached behind the face. She uncovered a small wall safe, just as John had said. It was flush against the wall, the combination lock a flat dial in a revolving metal disc. The numbers were small, but she could make them out. Nothing seemed out of the ordinary, except for a thin green cord attaching itself to the calendar's back.

Sweat began to creep out of the pores on her forehead and temples.

Further inspection showed that the calendar had a small translucent pad sticking to its center. The small and flat metallic chip there was unmistakable to the trained eye, and trained she was.

A pressure pad.

Her first thought was that the whole thing was rigged to blow. But that would make little sense. It should have already activated. A timer, then? A delayed explosion? Or a warning, perhaps. She'd have to get inside to deactivate it or confirm her demise.

She heard boots stomp through the hall outside and froze in place, not sure how she would deal with the threat if they barged into the room. Luckily, the sounds of the patrol faded. She realized she'd been holding her breath.

She had to get moving.

The safe seemed normal. The pressure pad was strange, but didn't reveal any obvious dangers. Not immediately.

Unconvinced, she pulled out a custom stethoscope from her bag, precariously balancing the giant calendar on her thigh as she stood on one foot. She put the ends of the stethoscope in her ears and brought the round amplifier up to the safe's face.

No ticking (although bombs didn't usually make that clichéd Hollywood sound). There was some soft whirring, which meant electronics, but none of the telltale signs that it was a dirty safe.

Her spike of concern was replaced with relief and then childlike excitement. She had once disarmed a bomb-rigged safe in Nicaragua with thirty seconds to spare. This was nothing more than a fun activity before they could make their escape.

Mierda. It's too easy.

She tucked the stethoscope away with a grin and pulled out one of her favorite tools. She'd only been able to use it twice in-field.

It looked like a portable computer mouse with a simple LED screen on its face. On the device's back sat a disk with four small suction cups arranged in a ring.

She eyeballed the safe's combo lock, shrank the disk accordingly, and lined it up carefully. Still wary of some sort of pressure-bomb, she pressed lightly at first, then harder, letting go and making sure the mechanism stuck. It didn't come loose, only spun slightly as her hand left its back.

She tapped the screen and it came to life. In actuality, it was fairly low-tech. The equivalent of the first iPod screen with basic touch controls. But, like an old friend, it still brought a smile to her face.

She selected the standard safecracking program and set it running.

Suddenly, the wall and floor rumbled.

At first she thought a bomb had gone off. Then, seeing the bed slide and doorway shiver, she realized it was a tremor. They were common in Guatemala and Antigua. She hopped on her foot, trying to adjust the calendar's weight on her leg. It wasn't too heavy to carry, but it was becoming unwieldy.

The soft whine of metal grating on metal was barely audible under shouting coming from across the compound. Marcela cocked her head, hoping the safecracker wouldn't take too long. It had to make slow and full rotations to be sure it plugged in the proper numbers, but it beat doing everything manually by stethoscope. Plus it always made her feel like a proper American spy.

The sound of gunfire nearly made her lose her balance and drop the calendar. She gripped it firmly, hearing the sound of shotguns rock the estate.

She tried to figure out what was going on out there, mentally calculating what had changed in the last hour. She thought about Juan and pursed her lips.

It appears I may have overdone it. Again.

Boots stomped through the hall, but again she was left unbothered.

I hope you've gotten Pablo out of here, Carpenter, because once I'm done here I'm sure as hell not staying.

***

Pablo rode in the passenger seat of the Mercedes as if he were on a leisurely drive to *Cerro de La Cruz*, that peaked hill that provided a gorgeous view of *Volcán de Agua*. He gazed out the window, hands resting calmly on his crossed legs. In contrast, Carlos's hands gripped the wheel hard as he drove, fingers turning white. He looked in the rear-view mirror to examine Vinicio. The man moved his eyes and head side to side, scanning the windows like an impatient dog, searching for threats.

"*Fuego*," said Pablo softly, to no one in particular.

"Yes. We should be okay, *patrón*," said Vinicio, just as quietly.

It was hot outside of Antigua so Carlos had kept the windows down, but it was too dusty to keep it that way for long. Pablo turned on the air and Carlos wasn't sure if he saw one of Vinicio's eyebrows raise. It was a strange luxury neither of them could get used to, air conditioning in a car. The sweat on his back made his shirt stick to the seat. At least the tint of the windows helped to calm some of his nerves, providing some semblance of safety.

They hit a bump in the road and everyone bounced in their seats. Carlos cringed as they hit the road again, hard, and shot a quick glance to Pablo, expecting some sort of admonishment. But Pablo only sighed and continued to stare out the window.

Pablo's phone began to ring. He bolted upright as chattering came through the phone when he answered. Carlos couldn't make it out. He looked in the rear-view again and met Vinicio's eyes. The man gave him a look of concern. It was the briefest connection before both turned their eyes back to the road, but Carlos was momentarily thankful that he could share his worry with someone else.

Pablo hung up, called someone else, and was in the middle of a yelling match by the time they reached the location John had provided Carlos. It was a small two-story apartment on an out-of-the-way street, near downtown but far enough that it wasn't frequented.

"What is this?" Pablo asked, his hand covering his phone's receiver.

Carlos clenched his teeth and tried to blink away his anxiety.

"It is a safe location, *patrón*."

"Is it now?" Pablo looked to Vinicio.

Carlos was hoping he could count on the man to help convince Pablo, but he only shrugged and looked at the building warily.

"I don't know this place, *patrón*."

Pablo turned slowly to Carlos, suspicion beginning to creep across his face. He opened his mouth to say something, and Carlos was already beginning to cringe and figure out what he would say in turn, when someone else interrupted him.

John Carpenter, seeming to materialize out of thin air, was standing before them.

"Follow me," he said.

***

Juan ducked reflexively for a second time as a chunk of plaster and rock tore off from the wall just behind him. His adrenaline was pumping hard, but he forced himself to stand again and fire his shotgun at a man hiding in a section of the garden. He could just barely make out his black beret among the oleanders.

He pumped and fired, then pumped and fired once more just to be sure the spray penetrated. Unfortunately, a gardener fearfully running away from his hiding spot was clipped by the shot, a leg blown out from under him and shoulder whipping back from the blast.

It was chaos everywhere. No matter where Juan looked, the bloodbath engulfed the courtyard. Chunks of flesh smeared plants and tiles, and spatters of blood stained the walls.

Red berets and black berets had turned their shotguns on one another; whoever pulled the trigger first at point-blank range became the sole survivor of a terrifying duel. The split-second reaction times of well-trained men had been overshadowed by those who looked over their shoulders for reassurance and found someone else preparing to fire. The guards fought to find cover or a place to hide, oftentimes ducking behind precarious and desperate things, such as other people. Many of the servants and gardeners had become casualties as the fighters vied for control of the courtyard.

It wasn't as simple as red beret versus black beret. Many made the mistake of simply trusting the same color, only to get into verbal arguments that turned into short-lived death-matches. Sometimes guards were killed before a single word was uttered, some refusing to even discuss if they supported Pablo or Juan or some other objective altogether. Most of these more chaotic clumps fell to infighting if they didn't solve their problems fast.

The nervous individuals left over were willing to make wary unspoken pacts with one another, forming broken squads huddling in corners or holding strategic points in the courtyard. Juan and his group dominated the entrance into the house and had pinned down a perimeter. The front gates should have been open to anyone who wanted to leave, but some of the guards and servants had managed to slip away in the middle of the conflict, shutting the gates behind them to delay any pursuit. No one was able or concerned enough to chase them, but the problem remained that the gates were shut. Anyone who wanted to leave now would have to take the time to open them, and that would only mean a swift death from behind. The man lying face down at the gates was a testament to this fact.

The pot-shots had been waning for a while now, the last of the stragglers picked off and a silent agreement of ceasefire sinking in. Groups were yelling threats and slurs and questions of loyalty at one another, giving rise to a new chaos of verbal assault where before had only been gunfire.

It was going nowhere. If Pablo wasn't found, Juan suspected the men would decide one way or the other who they should ultimately side with. On the one hand, Juan was here, now, an imposing force. A dominating presence. It was hard to disagree with their *comandante* in the flesh, who had already unloaded twenty-odd rounds into those who disagreed.

On the other hand, Pablo was their employer, the man they were paid to protect and serve, and their beloved *pátron*. He may be missing, but that didn't mean their loyalty disappeared with his absence. At any moment, for all any of them knew, he could return in a blaze of gunfire and ruthless justice on his traitorous stepson. Those who were at the summer home knew he was prone to appearing in the thick of battle. Those who saw him every day in 'court' knew he was not to be trifled with.

A solitary shot brought down a runner and Juan saw another black beret go down with grim satisfaction. He decided a different course of action was needed. Juan turned to the man beside him and saw it was the black-bereted man who had told him Pablo was missing. Juan was surprised he had sided with him instead of retreating to one of Pablo's groups. It wasn't as if the man were simply staying for safety; he'd jumped into the fray and taken down a few opposing guards, nearly receiving lead as payment. He wasn't sure what truly motivated the man but he'd put him to use.

"*Amigo*," Juan said to him, putting a hand on his shoulder.

The man turned his head to face Juan. "*Si, comandante?*"

"I am going to send you inside. Take a few others with you."

"*Si, comandante.*" The man nodded, peaked over the low wall topped with *monja blanca* orchids, then looked at the door. It was a short distance, but under the circumstances it could be deadly.

Juan needed to do something that would cripple Pablo forever. Something that would destroy him inside and make him never want to come back. Good leaders made bold choices.

He tapped a couple more men on the shoulder and they turned to listen to him. He pointed to the black beret.

"Go with him."

They nodded. He pulled another one of his more trusted men toward him.

"*Amigo*, you will go and start the helicopter."

His eyes betrayed no fear. "*Si.*"

Juan grabbed the forearm of the black beret. Gunfire was breaking out again and they all ducked as shots flew wide from their position. Guards further down the line returned fire.

"Are you with me?"

The man's mouth became a tight line. His nod was firm. "My brother Mateo was killed at the summer home. I'm with you." He grasped Juan's forearm in kind.

"Go into the house," Juan said, jerking his thumb over his shoulder and ignoring a burst of gunfire slamming into a potted herb garden ten feet from his foot. "And get Pablito."

***

The safe door finally unlocked with the satisfying *click* of the last digit entered by the cracker. It was a sweet sound, but Marcela took no time to revel in it. The booms and pops of gunfire had been echoing down the halls too long for her liking. It wouldn't be long until the action moved inside. She glanced at the doorway of the room, then back to the safe. She pulled her safecracker off, hearing the light pop of its suction cups, then placed it back in her bag gingerly.

The safe was ready to be opened.

She took a quick breath then pulled on the small handle.

There was a timer. And it was counting down.

The little space of the safe held a short stack of American money, a handgun, and a small laptop. The screen was on and displayed a timer set with just under six hours remaining.

Marcela let out the breath she was holding. There was still time, however this kill switch worked.

She shifted the calendar on her leg, relieving some pressure from where it was digging into her thigh. Her eye followed the thin green cord and saw that it attached to the laptop.

The computer was plugged into both an internal and external power source. There was a socket providing regular power, and a backup battery that charged while plugged in. It was smart. If the power cut out, the laptop would use the backup until power returned. Then the battery would simply recharge again. An ethernet cable coiled out through the back of the safe.

Curious, she leaned an elbow in the safe and went to the touchpad on the laptop. There were several programs open. She scrolled over the first and found an email containing a single attachment.

There was a burst of gunfire and yelling, still far away. She did her best to ignore it and keep her focus, but it was still disconcerting.

She was running out of time and she still had to figure out how to disable the timer.

The email had a preselected list of names as recipients if it were sent. They were American names. She recognized a few of them, reporters and political activists. It appeared the Firm was up against publicized blackmail. It was easy enough to deal with.

She quickly located the attached file, then scrapped the email. She opened a new browser, opened her own encrypted email, and attached the file. She fired it off to an email Esteban used for sensitive information retrieval while they were in-field.

Pleased with this bit of success, she moved to the program she suspected was connected to the cord and calendar. It didn't take long for her to find that she was correct about the pressure pad on the back of the calendar. What she was surprised by was what the pressure pad did.

Marcela looked at the timer, then at the calendar. She reached around to the front of the giant disc and looked for where the pad lined up to the front. It was right in the centre, the round face of *Tonatiuh*. What was more, the face was moveable, carved separate from the rest of the stone. Pressed up against the wall of the safe it would easily activate the pressure pad if someone were to push it.

So she did.

She looked to the timer. It had changed, resetting to two-four-zero-zero, then counting down.

She pushed the face again, and it reset.

A twenty-four hour timer, resetting every time the pressure pad was activated. As she browsed the program, she understood: it looked as if when the timer hit zero, the computer was programmed to send its mass email.

The whole kill switch was downright simple, but cleverly hidden. All that remained now was a simple deactivation. It was a small comfort that she could take twenty-four hours if she needed to.

The sound of boots made her perk up. They were coming too close for comfort, not just passing by this time. She removed the pressure pad from the calendar now that she was confident how it worked, then moved toward the doorway, holding onto the giant stone disc with both hands. If someone entered the room she'd be able to bash them with it.

"Pablito's room is here!" A man's voice yelled. He moved to the doorway.

Marcela tensed and lifted the calendar slowly over her head. She'd have to get the timing just right.

"He is in the kitchen, *amigo*!" Came another man's voice from farther away.

She could hear the man hesitate at the door frame for a moment before retreating, presumably going to meet the other man in the kitchen.

Marcela let out a short breath, put the calendar on the bed, then returned to the safe. A little digging at the software assured her she could simply unplug the laptop and end the countdown. She did, feeling somewhat anticlimactic about the whole affair now that it was over.

She picked up the calendar and reattached the pressure pad so as to keep up appearances until the safe was reopened. Before she shut the safe, she eyed the stack of cash bills, shrugged, took a couple, and then closed its door. She hung the calendar back on the wall, smoothed her dress, and walked out the door, not giving a second glance at the pile of bodies that still sat in the corner.

The kill switch was disabled.

***

Mike's phone pinged and he saw that one of Blackthorne's more sensitive accounts had just received an email. He opened it and saw it was from Marcela. There was an attachment there. The message itself contained nothing but a colon and bracket smiley-face.

He frowned.

"Sir."

His head snapped to Barker. He was holding a phone out to him.

"It's Linda."

The director of the Special Operations Group. It wasn't unheard of for the director to get involved in operations, calling in for a quick progress report to get an idea of how things were going, or relay certain changes in intel. Or to interfere.

He nodded sharply and accepted the phone. Barker took temporary control of the operation, relishing in his power by snapping his fingers at a nearby jockey and saying something harsh.

"Mike." Linda's voice was firm, businesslike.

"Linda. What can we do for you?"

"You've just received an email from one of your agents in-field."

He stiffened. "Yes, I just opened it."

"The attachment?"

"No, just the email."

He thought he heard her give out a sigh of relief. "Okay. Mike. Don't open the attachment. It's a harsh virus that can penetrate some of our toughest cyber-defences. All it needs is a doorway."

Mike didn't know what to say. "That was fast," he said after a moment, feeling stupid.

Linda didn't miss a beat. "Cyber-security got a warning light after the email sent and told me to get you on the line right away."

"I'll delete the email."

"No…no. Forward it to me and then delete it on your end. We want to take a look at it. See if we can't poke the bear without making it growl."

Mike's eyes narrowed. "Okay."

She hung up.

Mike looked down at his mobile, where the email sat displayed. This was the information Pablo was blackmailing them with. If Locklee was telling the truth, it would detail Sandor's involvement with the CIA, and appear to all be linked to his late colleague through bribery.

He stared at the attachment symbol for a long moment. Then he forwarded it to Linda. Maybe he could dig through it himself. If it did have a virus, he was sure he could get someone to work it for him. But his inbox would be snooped soon enough and Linda would know if he had held onto it against her orders. He thought of what Locklee had told him in the car as rain poured, so loud he had to almost yell his darkest secrets. Mike could just find out the truth of it all, it was right there in his hand…

Then he thought of Locklee, dead in his office.

He hit delete.

***

"And what the fuck are you doing here?" Pablo asked, fury beginning to overtake the calm in his voice.

John could sense the man's confidence was waning. He couldn't blame him.

"Getting you out of there." He jerked a thumb over his shoulder toward Puentes's estate. "This is where I live, Pablo. It's the only safe place I could think of."

Pablo looked like he was about to say something, but Carlos spoke quickly.

"He is right, *patrón*. It was his idea to take you here."

He had no idea how John had gotten here so fast, but Carlos wasn't about to say anything else to upset the *patrón*.

Pablo narrowed his eyes. He looked between the two men. Then he looked at Vinicio. The last man spread his hands, declaring ignorance of the plan.

"Where else should we go, *patrón*?" John asked. "You are in danger."

And like that, something changed in Pablo's entire demeanor. John couldn't say what it was. But when their eyes met, at a guess he'd say it was understanding.

A trap is still a trap, even if the prey knows.

Pablo turned to Carlos. "Get me my gun." Carlos went to the trunk of the car and retrieved an AK-47.

"Vinicio, pat him down," Pablo said.

Vinicio checked John over with his hands. Carlos gave Pablo the AK-47. Pablo wasn't

looking at Vinicio or Carlos or even the gun as he took it. He had his eyes locked on John. It wasn't until Vinicio gave Pablo a nod of approval that he motioned to the apartment.

"Lead the way, *profesor*."

It was a good play, John had to give the cartel boss that much. If John were trying to lead him into a trap or kill him, it would be difficult with three armed men at his back.

And so he had no choice but to enter the building and begin up the steps. A passerby on the street crossed their path to the building. The young woman was looking at her phone, she suddenly stopped in her tracks as the strange entourage caught her eye. She gawked at the two uniformed guards and Pablo's assault rifle.

"*Buenas tardes*," John said calmly.

The woman walked quickly past them, not making eye contact and not replying to John, breaking into a run once she was past them. The others entered the building and climbed the stairs without comment. They reached the third floor and John led the way down the hall to the safehouse room. He opened the door. There was a faint *click*. The kind that one would only notice if they'd been listening for it.

The stove-trap was armed. He'd have to close the door twice to disarm it.

One minute...

John held the door open for the others. Pablo glared at him.

"*Pasa, señor,*" Pablo said. *After you, sir.*

John shrugged and walked inside.

Vinicio entered after John, looking side to side, the ever-vigilant guard. Pablo entered next, leaving Carlos to follow last.

John slipped behind the door and slammed it into Carlos just as he was taking a step inside. The door closed shut.

Vinicio whipped around, shotgun swinging into a firing position. John sidestepped toward him, snapping his arms up and stopping the remaining momentum of Vinicio's motion on his forearms. Vinicio fired too soon, expecting to have had it levelled at John, eyes wide with surprise that John had moved closer to him rather than away. John gave a quick chop to the man's throat and Vinicio made a choking sound as he collapsed against the wall.

Pablo backed away and held up the AK-47, ready to fire. Hot fury burned in his eyes. He pulled the trigger, and the gun made a soft *click* sound.

John ignored him as the door was kicked open. John just barely managed to raise a leg to stop it from flying into him, taking the brunt of the force on his left knee. Carlos barreled inside, pistol in hand, apparently deciding it would be a better weapon than the Remington slung on his back. A bad spray could hit his boss. His nose was bleeding down his face in two messy streams, thick red blood covered his mouth and chin.

It took a split second for him to locate John. In that time John grabbed the man's gun hand and raised it, feeling a bolt of energy as Carlos let off a round. John delivered a sharp fist to the man's solar plexus with his other hand, then swung it around again quickly at the man's arm, still held high.

Carlos had just enough time to match eyes with John. His eyes were shocked, frightened, angry. John wasn't sure what his own eyes said. It didn't matter.

He made a fist and struck at the man's raised elbow and pulled down with his other hand that held the man's wrist. The arm cracked in half at the joint, bones poking through the bleeding skin.

Pablo grunted in frustration as he tried to fire his AK-47 again, to no avail. John continued to ignore him, taking the gun from Carlos's hand and pointing it at Vinicio, who was behind him. The man was trying to push himself up from the floor with one hand and a scrambled leg, the other hand clutching his throat in pain. He finally managed to catch some air just before John shot him twice in the chest, then once in the forehead.

He turned the gun back to Carlos.

Tears were leaking down one of his cheeks as he tried to sit up. His eyes were sad. Pleading. His arm was pooling blood on the floor at an alarming rate. His bloody lips opened to speak.

"We were…supposed to be…the good ones…"

"No," John said. "But you were."

No one would have noticed the briefest of hesitations in John before he gave Carlos the same treatment with the handgun as he had Vinicio.

The third and final shot seemed to hang in the air as John turned to Pablo. John closed the door with his foot, disarming the stove-trap. The fight had lasted less than a minute.

Pablo was pulling the trigger again and again, but the AK-47 refused to fire. It was arguably the most reliable assault rifle in the world, able to fire even after being slathered with mud.

But no gun works without ammunition.

"I emptied the magazine," John said, stuffing his handgun into the back of his waistband.

Pablo looked at John and then the assault rifle in his hands as equal parts confusion and horror washed over his face. He raised a finger and released the magazine. It clattered to the floor, hollow and empty.

"When?" Pablo asked, taking a step backward and lowering the gun. "How? I always keep it-"

"I was in the trunk, Pablo. Of your Mercedes. Now," John said, grabbing a chair. "Have a seat."

***

"Sir? An agent is reporting in."

Mike looked to the jockey and nodded. "Patch them in. Full audio."

"Yes, sir."

There was a brief pause as the encrypted line was established and then put on the speakers for the room to hear.

"Esteban?" It was Marcela.

"I'm here. Report."

"The kill switch is deactivated. I repeat, the kill switch is deactivated."

A cheer went up in the command room. Barker flashed Mike a grin, and he couldn't help but smile as well. But then he turned to business.

"Do we have Pablo?"

"I believe so. John should have him at the safe house."

Barker received a printout from an aide and passed it to Mike. Mike scanned it briefly.

"And Marcela, we've had reports in the area saying there's been gunfire coming from the Puentes estate?"

There was a brief pause.

"Yes, Juan has declared war on Pablo."

Mike rubbed his forehead. He knew Marcela too well.

"And did you have anything to do with this?"

"Yes, yes, I'm sorry. But to be fair, I think this was a long time coming. He…"

She was cut off by a loud *whooshing* sound.

"Marcela, what's that noise? I can hardly hear you."

"Oh shit…up…copter…"

"Marcela, can you-"

"…have Pablito…"

"…*mierda*."

The line cut out.

The smiles on the faces of everyone in the room dropped. Mike thought they'd lost her for good, but then the call came back in.

"Esteban?"

"*Yes.*" Mike almost yelled it. His heart was pounding.

"Sorry. They just launched their helicopter. They have Pablito. It looks like Juan just kidnapped Pablito."

"Okay. Are you able to get out?"

Pause. Then, "Yes. The front gates and courtyard are under fire, but they don't have the back of the property properly guarded."

Mike heard the sound of a gunshot.

"Marcela? Marcela?"

"Like I said, not properly guarded."

Mike sighed. "Head to the safe house and meet up with Carpenter."

"Okay."

She ended the call. Mike had another jockey activate John's line.

"Esteban?"

The voice was cold. Hard. It gave Mike a chill.

"Yes. Report."

"I have Pablo here. We were just about to start our chat. Do you want a cup of *café*?"

Mike was about to tell John no, why would he ask him if he wanted a cup of coffee, when he heard someone in the background yell some profanity in Spanish. He realized John must've been talking to Pablo.

"Carpenter, the kill switch is disabled. See what you can get out of him and then you are good to eliminate the threat."

"Yes, sir."

He heard a loud smacking sound, and then a cry of pain.

"Sir, is there anything in particular you'd like me to ask him?"

Mike opened his mouth to answer and then he closed it. Silence filled the room. Most of the jockeys were looking at him, waiting for an order. Waiting to hear what he said.

"One second." Mike turned to Barker. "Patch him through to my office. I'll talk to him. See if you can get some eyes on the situation and monitor any more reports on this Puentes's civil war if you can."

Barker nodded, but his expression was surprised. "Yes, sir."

Mike went to his office and was about to open the door when he felt Barker close behind him. Too close.

"Sir?"

Mike turned. They were out of earshot of anyone else in the room.

"Sir, do you not...trust us?"

Mike looked at the young man sadly. Barker's greasy face gave him the creeps on a good day. He was too excited about, well, everything a normal person would avoid. But Mike could see pain in his eyes.

"Oh, Barker. I trust everyone in this room. I trust you most of all."

Mike put a hand on the handle of his office door.

"Then why-"

"Because," Mike said, not meeting eyes with his assistant. "I don't want anyone else to be responsible for what happens next."

He entered his office, leaving Barker and everyone else outside. He lifted his office phone and accepted the line.

"This is Esteban. Carpenter, I need you to find out some things for me."

***

"Yes, sir," John said, ending the call. Esteban had laid out a few clear questions. It was up to John to get the answers. Interrogation was fairly straightforward. It wasn't his first time.

He walked over to Pablo, who was sitting in a chair. One of his cheeks was developing a bruise and coffee was dripping down his face. The rest of it sat in a nearly empty mug on the table. He wasn't tied up. He wasn't gagged. But John would be sure to make Pablo understand there wasn't a thing he could do but talk. John calmly set his phone on the table and set it to record.

"*¡Chupala!*," Pablo said, his tone biting. *Suck my dick!*

John didn't react. He loomed down on Pablo.

"My employer needs to find out a few things. You are going to tell me."

"Your employer. You mean me?" Pablo spat on the floor.

John didn't reply.

"Or do you mean the CIA?"

"I mean what I say, Pablo. I have some questions. You will answer them."

"Or what? You will kill me? Do you not realize that if you kill me-"

"Your kill switch has been disabled," John said softly, sitting down in a chair by the table, resting his elbows on it. He pulled a gun out of his waistband and placed it flat on the table, pointing at Pablo. "The Mayan calendar. The safe."

That silenced whatever the cartel leader was about to say. John watched him change his mind and say something else.

"*¡Ándate a la verga, estúpido!*" *Go to hell, asshole!* "I trusted you," he said.

Pablo was going through the standard motions of someone realizing they were losing power. Threats didn't hold weight. They appealed to emotion instead.

"No, you didn't. You just didn't think anyone would be able to get at you. Let alone a *gringo*. You didn't even trust Juan."

Pablo's face darkened. "That *hijo de puta.*" *Son of a bitch.*

"Is that any way to speak of your wife, Pablo? Of Isabella?"

"You know nothing about Isabella."

John didn't answer. He reached into his pocket.

"Do you see this?" John held up a small pill in between his fingers for Pablo to see.

Pablo looked at it but didn't say anything.

"Have you ever heard of truth serum? *Suero de la verdad*?"

Pablo's eyes narrowed. "If it makes me tell the truth, *señor* Carpenter, why don't you just use it?"

John didn't miss a beat. "Because it is incredibly painful. And largely untested. I have to consider how much you'll be able to say before the pain receptors in your brain overload your speech capacity. I show you this so you know I will get something out of you no matter what. But I'd rather you just talk."

Pablo didn't reply. For a moment, it seemed as if he would do just that, making a face like an egg about to crack. But instead, when he opened his mouth, he spat in John's face.

John raised a hand quicker than Pablo could register. The glob of saliva and phlegm collected in his palm and he slapped Pablo with it. Pablo tried to throw a punch, but John just shuffled backward in his chair.

"My men will kill you!"

John looked at the man.

"And where are they?" John asked.

Pablo opened his mouth to answer, but John cut him off.

"Where are they?" he asked again.

"They are-"

"*Where are they*?" John yelled.

Pablo looked away. When he finally looked back at John, he might have had something prepared to say. But the calm on the John's face shocked him into silence.

"No one knows where you are," John whispered. "And if they did? Your men want to kill you. Your own stepson is bringing down your empire as we speak. You have nothing."

"I have-"

"Nothing."

Pablo tried to get up from his chair.

"I have-"

"*Nothing.*"

John reached over with both hands and forced the man back into a sitting position.

Pablo struggled hard against John's grip. His thumbs were beginning to pierce through the skin under his shoulders.

"I have honor. I have a family. I have-"

John plunged his thumbs in all the way. Pablo shouted in pain. John watched him for a moment, then pushed Pablo's chair over with his foot. Pablo crashed to the floor, hitting his head on the floor, sputtering.

"What do you-"

John drew himself up and stood from his chair. He took a couple steps until he was standing over Pablo. He wiped his bloody thumbs on Pablo's pant legs, still angled over the chair's seat. John placed a shoe over one of Pablo's arms as he tried to get up, the man visibly wincing from the two bleeding holes above his chest. When Pablo was finally able to meet his gaze, John's face had contorted into something ugly. Something dark and terrifying. Twisted, even. John leaned forward slowly.

"Those things you would do in your courtyard? Cutting off hands and shooting people?

"Justice," Pablo managed.

"You were sending a message," John shrugged. "You might think I'm doing no different. But, *patron*." John's tone was admonishing. Chastising. "Think for a moment. You never needed to get information. You could do whatever you wanted. I have to be more calculated. It is like…well, like teaching. When you are a teacher, you make sure the student understands. So they can give you a good answer."

John tapped the man's hand with his foot.

"Call me traditional. I always start with the fingers."

John began to snap his own fingers like a metronome, looking at each of Pablo's digits as he made the noise. He moved the shoe and let it graze Pablo's ribs.

"These next. They crack with very little pressure in the right spot."

He moved low until his shoe stopped, resting on Pablo's genitals.

"And of course, *los cojones*," John said, smiling. "No pressure at all."

He locked eyes with the man and lowered his foot slowly, until Pablo gave the smallest

flinch. A twitch of the eye. A quiver in the lip. John's eyes showed no hint of malice. They were content. Curious.

"None of these are lethal, Pablo. There are so many parts to the human body. I spent the time to memorize them all. A hundred of the most useful ones. I use them on *cabrons* like you. All the time. And you know what? I sleep like a fucking baby afterward. Every time."

Pablo simply stared. His scowl was beginning to show the fear hiding underneath. John took his foot off the man's crotch and reached down to pull Pablo's chair back up. John expected the man to make a move then, but he didn't. He only pushed his feet a bit to help John lift him and the chair back up.

"In the movies, interrogations are overdramatized," he said, not a hint of strain in his voice as he pulled Pablo and the chair effortlessly off the floor. "Lots of torture. People pretending to hold out. The torture continues. Elaborate methods. American audiences find it entertaining." John patted Pablo's shoulder, making him wince. "But in reality, everyone has a breaking point. They just don't know when or where it is. It doesn't go back and forth. It's a science. At a certain point you hit it and…"

John brought a fist to Pablo's face and the man drew back, squeezing his eyes shut. There was no blow. When Pablo opened his eyes he saw that John had stopped the blow an inch from his face. John spread his fingers from the fist, like a blossoming flower.

And so Pablo, vicious cartel leader and *patrón* of Antigua, seemed to concede in his mind. John read it on his face as easily as he would from a book.

"The carrot and the stick," Pablo said softly, frowning slightly.

John smiled, brightness changing his face. His eyes nearly twinkled. "Yes, there you go! The carrot and the stick." He laughed for a moment and then let the moment die. His face matched it. "Was your brother Sandor working with someone in the CIA?"

The question sparked an inkling of resilience in the cartel leader.

"I would think you would be the one to know that. *Gringo*. American spy."

John slapped him hard across the face.

"Was your brother Sandor working with someone in the CIA?"

Pablo caught his breath. "I don't know."

John grunted. He'd made a bet with his interrogations trainer years ago who insisted subjects always said 'I don't know' at least once. John mentally subtracted another point from his tally. He had been in debt for years now.

He slapped Pablo.

"Was your brother Sandor working with someone in the CIA?"

Pablo's tone was more respectful now. "My brother…was working with many different people…*señor* Carpenter."

John looked at the man. Waited a moment. Then he slapped him.

"Was your brother Sandor working-"

"I think so! I think so…"

John's hand was already brought back for the swing. "Don't interrupt me."

He slapped him.

"Was your brother Sandor working for someone in the CIA?"

Pablo held his tongue and his breath until John gestured for him to speak.

"I think so, *señor*. I think so. I know they were Americans. I'm sorry, I cannot know for sure. He didn't share that information with me."

"Why not?"

Pablo slowly reached a hand up to his cheek, watching John to make sure it was acceptable. John didn't say anything, so Pablo rubbed it.

"He wanted to keep me in the dark. That's what Isabella said. She said Sandor thought I was too…*imprudente*. That I was unwilling to make deals with enemies. So I could not be trusted."

John's eyebrows rose as Pablo spoke. "Isabella?"

Pablo caught the gesture. "Ah. You do not know about Isabella."

"What about her?"

"Isabella was the one who told me that my brother had a deal with some high level American. She found a CIA phone number in my brother's files. She's the reason I know anything. You should be talking to her if you want information."

John put it on his mental to-do list. But he couldn't interrupt his momentum. He was getting somewhere.

"What was the deal?"

Pablo frowned. He didn't answer.

John's eyes filled with rage, suddenly snapping at Pablo's failure to answer.

"What was the deal?!" he roared.

"I don't know!" Pablo screamed. "We don't know. Isabella and I both. Something…high up, CIA…Isabella searched through his files, but…" He splayed his hands open, frantically trying to find other words to say, panting with fear and surprise.

John grunted. "Why would she betray her husband to you? Were you having an affair?

Pablo began to calm down. "Isabella may have been his wife, *señor*, but that does not mean she liked it. She was a product, before. Sandor liked her so much he wed her. She had no choice. You know our business."

John put it together.

"Trafficking. She was one of them? One of the girls?"

"There is a saying you have, *'no cagas donde comes'*, no? *Don't shit where you eat.* It is like with work and family. Do you see me sniffing my product?"

"So she didn't like Sandor. Why go to you?"

"Because I didn't like trafficking. Never have. I was against that addition he made years ago. It is wrong. It has no honor."

John stifled the comment he wanted to make about a drug lord talking about honor and morality.

"What did Isabella want?"

"She wanted revenge on Sandor for his treatment. He took her life away, so she wanted to destroy his trade through me."

"What about Juan?"

"Yes. That is the other reason she did it. She loves her son, even though he is a *maldito traidor!*" Pablo yelled. *Traitorous bastard!* John waited for him to continue. "Juan was born from a mother who was a slave to sex, but he never knew. He didn't know this is where his mother was from. And he was so determined to run his father's business. She couldn't persuade him to stop. So she changed Sandor's will. She would do anything to stop him from inheriting it. She was convincing me to put it to an end."

"Did you?" John took a sip from the remaining bit of coffee from the mug sitting on the table.

"I was going to. She had given me Sandor's empire. That was the deal. But Americans threatened me. Told me to *cuidado.*" *Be careful.*

John narrowed his eyes.

"What do you mean?"

"When I began to shut down operations, I had Americans threaten me. I don't know how much clearer I can be, *señor*. It is the reason I had to do something more *extremo.*"

John felt disgusted. He thought of Brian. He thought he was beginning to see the tip of the iceberg. The bit that Brian might have seen, the trail he might have followed. John had finally picked up the scent.

He put the coffee down abruptly and stood. Pablo tightened his lips, intimidated but not yielding.

"And so you made a kill switch."

"For protection against these Americans. Isabella did most of it, honestly." Pablo chuckled nervously. "I am quite bad with computers."

"What was the blackmail?"

"Everything. All of Sandor's business and linking it to Americans. Isabella was convinced it was CIA because they knew about the agent sent to kill Sandor. There was money sent from my brother's account to a CIA man. So I called him and blackmailed him and said we were done *jodiendo*. Immunity, *señor*. Invincibility. I could finally end the trafficking."

John took a breath. He collected his thoughts. He had enough for Esteban. Now it was time to ask his own questions.

"The American agent who was sent to kill Sandor." John cleared his throat. "How was he killed?"

"Sandor killed him."

"How?" John couldn't control his tone.

"A handgun."

John drew his hand back to slap the man harder than he had before.

"Oh! Oh, I see. My apologies, *señor*. You mean *how*. Sandor received a call that an *asesino* was coming for him. Detailed exactly how it would be done. He said the tip came from his American business partner. I argued with him about it. We told him how dealing with Americans led to death. The agent came and my brother killed him. He was so panicked and we argued, then Isabella picked up the gun lying on the floor and shot him. It was easy to say Sandor and the agent simply killed each other."

They'd have to find Isabella. She could continue the blackmail. But John was thinking about the American who had tipped off Sandor. Of all the dirty things to happen... John's suspicions were confirmed. Brian hadn't botched the op. There had been a leak from the inside. And now John had that information. He knew the truth. He could finally move forward instead of lingering in the past.

Sandor may have killed Brian, but he was dead now, and it had been a petty act. But whoever leaked the information that Brian was coming — that was what John was after. *Who* he was after. He didn't think he'd get this lead. Now that he had, there was no satisfaction in it. Brian was infatuated with truth and justice, but John was just scratching the surface. He'd have to find the person who'd called Sandor and hunt them down. He would hunt them to the ends of the earth. Then he would end their life.

John picked up the gun resting on the table. He cocked it and pointed it at Pablo. The man looked like a scarecrow after a torrential downpour. Pablo gave a smile of resignation through the bruises on his face.

"You are a shitty man, *señor* Carpenter. But you are a good teacher, no?"

John didn't reply. He didn't need to.

He shot Pablo twice in the chest and once in the forehead.

CHAPTER 21

John stood silent, watching blood ooze slowly out of the bullet holes in Pablo's body. It lay limp in the chair, sad and empty.

He didn't take much time to savor the moment. He pulled out his phone and placed a call.

"Esteban?"

"Go ahead."

"Pablo is dead. I extracted the information. I'm sending you a recording now."

"No. Wait." There was a long pause. John heard the telltale clatter of keys, but that was his only clue to what Esteban was waiting for. "Carpenter, don't send the recording to me. Or anyone. Even if they have authorization. Do you understand?"

John blinked. "Yes."

"Good. Play the recording for me. Then delete it."

"Sir?" It didn't take an expert to know this wasn't normal procedure. A sudden break from Esteban's normally unwavering adherence to process suggested a severe internal breach. If Pablo was telling the truth about Sandor working with Americans and it was someone in the Firm…

John thought about what Marcela had asked him as they sipped coffee on the rooftop, as they'd planned this operation.

"Do you trust Esteban?"

"I trust him to give us orders."

"That's all you need?"

The words echoed in his mind. He had sidestepped the question. He had implied before that it didn't matter if he trusted Esteban. But now he was willing to answer that question. Now his answer was clear.

No. He didn't trust him.

Pablo had said that someone on the inside tipped off Sandor. Someone who knew Brian was coming. Now that John had the evidence, Esteban was asking him to allow him to review it, and then destroy it?

Could Esteban be the man who had gotten Brian killed?

"Carpenter? The recording."

His reflexes snapped back into action. "Yes, sir," he said automatically.

He played the recording, but he hardly heard it. His mind was spinning.

A phone began to ring somewhere in the room.

It sounded familiar, but John couldn't place it right away. He had heard it once or twice around the Puentes estate.

Of course. Pablo's phone.

He found the cell hidden in Pablo's jacket. It was Juan. The recording was still playing for Esteban. John made his way to the bathroom, away from his phone on the line with his handler.

He accepted the call.

"Pablo, you *puta madre*. I have your *pequeñito* son. Do you hear me? I have him. And I will kill him if you do not meet me at home. It is mine now, by the way. I have it. I have it all."

John didn't say anything. The line stayed open for a few seconds before Juan hung up.

John stood there, staring at the phone, not sure what to say or do. Juan's voice was full of rage. John met it with his own. How dare he take Pablito? The boy was innocent. He was a good kid. Just a good kid in a bad family. Powerless. John's hands began to shake, his jaw visibly quivered while deep inside his gut something turned. It wasn't rage anymore. He wasn't sure what it was. Something he had tasted when Brian had died.

John was tempted to sit down on the toilet seat, or wash his face with water, anything to wake him up from this feeling that was settling in. He took a couple moments to lean on the door as a compromise. He heard the recording softly playing in the other room. He gave himself more time than he should've needed, then slapped himself lightly on the cheek and went back to his phone sitting on the table.

"...*Sandor received a call that an* asesino *was coming for him...*

Footsteps coming up the apartment stairs. Stomping around the floor below. More than one pair. It sounded like at least two pairs of heavy boots.

...*told him how dealing with Americans led to death.*

Shit.

...*came and my brother killed him. He was so panicked...*

John moved to Carlos's body, stepping around the blood that had pooled and was slowly soaking into the floor. He retrieved the Remington shotgun from the body's back and checked the magazine.

...*picked up the gun lying on the floor and shot him. It was easy to say Sandor and the agent simply killed each other."*

John picked up the phone.

"*You are a shitty man,* señor *Carpenter. But you are a good teacher, no?*"

He killed the recording just as the first gunshot sounded through the speaker, then plugged in a pair of earbuds as he moved toward the door. He had an increasingly uncomfortable feeling that he was being set up, just like Brian had been. He shook the thought away. He wasn't done here. He had to focus.

"Esteban. Pablito has been apprehended by Juan."

"Yes. Marcela said he was put in a helicopter."

John's tone grew chilly. "You knew. Juan just called Pablo and threatened him." He couldn't keep the ice out of his voice.

"Alright. We're not sure what Juan is-"

"Esteban. Is it mission complete?"

"What?"

"The mission. Deactivate kill switch. Extract information from Pablo. Eliminate."

"Yes…Carpenter what's going on?"

John tucked the phone into his pocket and opened the door. He cocked the shotgun once, making sure it was primed.

"I'm going after Pablito."

***

Mike ended the call and exited his office.

"Everything alright, sir?" Barker asked.

Mike became aware of the scowl that must have been on his face.

"Peachy. Pablo has been eliminated."

A half-hearted cheer went up from the agents and jockeys. Mike gave a grim smile, nodding in approval, hastily ending his celebratory handshake with Barker before it could last too long in the younger man's clammy hand. He wiped his hand on his pant leg. "Now. Patch us into Marcela. Speaker."

"Yes, sir."

Marcela's voice filled the room. There was no sound of gunfire or helicopter blades in the background this time. Instead, the soft sound of a small crowd, a car moving down a street.

"Esteban?"

"Yes. Where is Isabella?"

"Isabella?" Marcela sounded unsure. "I'm…not sure. I know she had left the property after Juan…before the fighting started. I was disabling the switch. No idea."

Mike sighed. "Okay. Do your best to find her."

"Got it. Do you want her dead?"

"No! No. Just find her and follow her. Detain her if you can.

"Okay."

"Thank you Marcela."

"*Ciao.*"

The line disconnected. A couple jockeys raised eyebrows at her choice of words. Blackthorne agents were painfully reminded to refer to their superiors as 'sir' or 'ma'am' when they slipped up.

Mike ignored them. He was thinking about the recording. About what Pablo had said. He knew he couldn't trust anyone, not even Linda. She had said the email from the kill switch contained a virus. For all he knew it did and Pablo was lying. But Pablo had confirmed everything Locklee had said. Linda had said she was contacted by cybersecurity, so she might not even know that the email held collusion evidence between Sandor and the CIA…

Everything was becoming about as clear as mud. But if there was anything good that came out of all this back channel bullshit, it was that Mike was learning to play along. He'd get to the bottom of this business one way or the other. It might just take a while to dig it up.

Cream rises. Crap sinks.

He didn't remember where he'd heard the saying. He turned to his assistant. "Barker, give Linda a call. Tell her it's mission complete. I'll give her a full report in my office."

"Yes, sir, but-" Barker raised a hand like he was a schoolboy asking a question.

"But what?"

"John's going after Pablito? And Marcela is now pursuing Isabella." Mike was already entering his office.

"Yes," he said over his shoulder. "Neither of which change the fact that it's mission complete. If Linda wants more, she'll have to ask. That's how Blackthorne works. It's mission complete." Mike waved his hand dismissively and entered his office in a huff.

"Yes, sir," Barker said pointing at someone to get Linda on the line. No one heard him as he spoke softly under his breath. "I guess it just doesn't feel that way."

***

As John exited the safe house room and moved into the hallway, the sound of boots reached the top of the steps. His floor. He carefully closed the safe house door, opened it, then closed it again, as Marcela had shown him. Then he pointed his shotgun at the wall where the men were about to appear, and fired.

The cluster of pellets attacked the wall, taking out chunks of plaster and cinder block. Someone had been just about to step around the corner. They drew back hastily, shouldering against the wall, deciding whether to make a move. Waiting. There were some harsh orders given in Spanish. Then whispers.

John didn't give them any more time than he needed to. He barreled through the door across from his room, using his shoulder to burst through.

Whoever was using the room wasn't there. Some clothing was strewn about, the rest sitting in travel suitcases. He closed the door as best he could against its broken hinges. Then he moved quickly across the floor and threw open the doors to the balcony.

A cloud of smoke hit him full in the face.

El Volcán Fuego had blown and thick gusts of gray-white smoke blew throughout Antigua in reply. John shielded his eyes and tried to listen, looking toward Pablo's compound. He heard the faint sound of a helicopter. He could just barely make it out, but the smoke blotted out so much of the sky.

He looked down. There was another balcony below, then the ground.

Someone yelled *'Vamos, vamos!'* from the hallway. John swung his shotgun's sling onto his back, then pulled himself over the railing of the balcony. Aiming for the balcony below, he dropped down, landing badly. He swore in pain as his ankle rolled underneath him. Gingerly, he flexed his ankle as best he could. The stupidest things happened from the simplest tasks. He knocked over a potted plant in his effort to stand properly.

At least it isn't broken, John thought as he forced himself over the balcony. Dropping again, this time to the ground, he was careful to put all the weight onto his good foot.

A couple of passersby looked at him with wide eyes, startled at his sudden appearance. John glared back. To the ones who felt it was necessary to keep staring, John said, "*Sigue caminando.*" *Keep walking.* Seeing his slung shotgun was enough for them to comply, except for some *gringa* tourist in a flower dress who had her cellphone pointed at him. John spotted what he was looking for, pushed past her, and sent the phone clattering to the ground and crushed it under his foot. He ignored the woman's shocked protests, moving towards his new target. A young man stood next to a motorbike, wearing a helmet and texting on his phone. He had probably just come out of one of the shops lining the street.

John limped over as the man mounted the motorbike. He put his phone away just in time for John to hoist the man by the armpits and fling him off the bike. He went crashing to the sidewalk, flustered and flailing. He pulled himself up hastily and yelled something incoherent through his helmet, already swinging in with a punch. John swatted the fist away as if it were a mosquito. Then he looped a hand under the helmet and gave the man a hard shove. The man fell again, his cries of indignation becoming louder as the helmet peeled off his head. John put the helmet on and mounted the bike. The key was in the ignition. John liked when things worked out nicely. He hadn't wanted to beat the man to get the key from him.

He looked up and tried to spot the helicopter. The smoke cleared for a brief instant, just enough time for him to pick it out. He slapped the visor of the helmet down, turned the key, and revved the engine.

***

Marcela ducked into an alley as she saw more uniformed men run into the apartment building where their safe house was. She didn't know if they were working for Juan or Pablo, but it hardly mattered.

Pablo's Mercedes sat obnoxiously on the street. It was only a matter of time before they found where John had taken him. She scanned the street, planning to move over to the next in search of Isabella, when another Mercedes pulled up to the apartment. Curious, Marcela stayed where she was to watch.

Guards jumped out of the car and opened the back door. Isabella stepped out and was escorted inside the building. Marcela's heart pounded in her ears. She moved down the alley, away from the apartment. She called her handler.

"Esteban?"

"Go ahead."

"I've spotted Isabella."

"Good. Where is she?"

"Heading into our safe house. I'm outside. On the street."

"Can you get to her?"

"No. There are too many men here. I'm Rambo."

"Understood. Tail her. We'll see if we can get her once she leaves."

Marcela made a face. "Esteban. I'm sorry, but that won't be happening."

A pause. Then Esteban's voice was stiff. "Clarify."

"You told me to take every precaution with the safe house when I first got here," she said slowly. "I'm afraid Isabella is-"

The ensuing explosion made whatever she said next inaudible.

***

John looked up and tried to spot the helicopter again, but he had to bring his eyes back to the road. He swerved around a couple who had wandered into the street, narrowly avoiding them. He managed to bring the motorbike back into the middle of the road, and exited the downtown core of Antigua. He passed under the Santa Catalina Arch welcoming people to the city, passed the last few shops, and hit the countryside.

It was easy to see the hulking mountains surrounding the valley out here. *El Volcán Fuego* pumped smoke steadily out of its mouth, blotting out the sun and smothering the sky. It looked like snow, albeit dirty snow. Sand and grit blew forth, and ash was everywhere. John spotted the helicopter swerving erratically through the mass of grime. He had flown a helicopter before. These were less than ideal conditions. Only an idiot or a madman would fly in something like this.

He revved the engine to a higher gear and was greeted by a boom that he could feel in his chest. For a moment he thought the motorbike's engine had exploded, but out of the corner of his eye he saw something bright, like a spark. He looked to the volcano. It spat a small geyser of lava, leaving a dribble curling down its face.

He looked back to the road, making sure the bike was righted, then searched for the helicopter.

It was nowhere in sight, but not because of the ash and smoke. He should still be able to make it out based on where it was last. It should be…

His heart dropped in his chest.

The helicopter was going down.

It was low to the ground and losing altitude fast. John's first thought was that it had been hit by lava, but that was ridiculous. Maybe the pilot had decided to land because of the sky's conditions. Maybe they had taken a lungful of smoke and passed out. Maybe the grime of the volcano had damaged the engines.

It didn't matter. It was going down.

The road came to a bend. John looked to the helicopter, then the road, then made his decision. He steered the motorbike straight, hopped the gravel shoulder, and landed on the grass of the field in front of him. His breath came short and shallow as he sped closer to the volcano, into the smoke to where he had last seen the helicopter. He had lost it outside a cluster of trees. He steered beside them, praying Pablito was okay.

He broke past the last few trees and turned into a clearing.

The helicopter was there.

It was turned on its side, blades bent upward against the ground. The only way out the doors was up. He sped toward the scene.

A small figure was flying across the dead and patchy grass and dirt. The way he ran was familiar.

"Pablito!" John yelled, but the boy couldn't possibly hear him from so far, or over the sound of the engine, or through his helmet. Still he yelled. He raised his helmet visor and saw a man hopping out of the doors, running after him. John slammed the visor back in place and sped straight for Pablito.

As he drew closer, the man chasing after Pablito stopped and turned. He pointed his shotgun at John. He was two hundred or so feet away.

He knew the effective range of a Remington TAC-14. The man was too far away to get the shot.

Even so, he wished he had his special bulletproof backpack.

The man's shotgun blast roared.

Whether it missed or the shot fell short, John couldn't say. He didn't care. He closed the distance, and began entering into kill range.

The man fired again. This time, John felt impact: something hard bounced off his helmet, he felt a hot prick against one of his legs, and he heard the sound of metal on metal as his motorbike roared through a hail of shotgun pellets. He patted his calf where he'd been hit. His pants were torn, but the damage to his flesh was no more than a scrape.

The next shot, however, would probably kill him.

John kept closing the distance. He could see the man pump the shotgun for the next shot now. He was closing to fifty feet…

John leapt off the bike and reached over his shoulder, grabbing his own shotgun off his back. He swung it forward as the motorbike continued to speed toward his target unmanned.

John hit the ground and fired.

The man crumpled; a second later the motorbike bumped over his body. The impact caused it to veer off course. It continued for a few more seconds, wobbled, and collapsed. John looked for Pablito.

He wasn't far from him. Pablito was frozen in place, petrified by fear. John tore off his helmet and pointed to his face, waving.

"*Profesor* Builder!" His tiny voice hardly pierced the air. John's heart sang;, he wasn't too late.

Pablito began to run toward him.

But John had spent too long on the man pursuing Pablito. Out of his peripheral vision, he spotted a second figure crawling out from the helicopter's doors.

John waved his arms at Pablito.

"No, Pablito! Keep running away! Turn around!"

Gunfire erupted in the clearing.

Pablito's small frame collapsed into the dirt.

Darkness swept over John. An icy rage. It became focused calculation in an instant. He reflexively drew his pistol from his waistband and ran toward the helicopter.

Most overestimated how easy it is to fire at a moving target from far away. The assailant had probably been trying to hit John, but instead he hit Pablito. Instead, he had killed him. A small, innocent child was dead because someone had been trying to kill John. He wanted to go to the boy. But the man was still a threat.

John could see the man saddled above one of the helicopter seats, handgun pointed. He'd have to close the range again.

John's moves were textbook. He raised his own pistol and took a shot, missing the man and expecting to at this distance, then ran forward ten feet. Stopped, aimed, took a shot, ran forward ten feet. The shots forced the man down and each time he tried to come up for his own attacks, John drove him back down. The man had no choice from his saddled position. He crouched lower and lower, hunkering into the passenger area of the helicopter.

After a few attempts at trying to shoot John but finding himself under fire each time, the man decided to raise the gun up by itself, not popping up from cover, and fired blindly out onto the field. As soon as John saw the gun come up, he swept in a wide arc. The shots went wild, the closest landing a couple feet away, exploding in a puff of dust.

John checked his pistol, sensing he was out of bullets, and confirmed the bad news. He tossed the gun aside. It didn't matter.

He sprinted another ten feet. The distance was closed, but the hard part was rooting the man out. He had the high ground. John drew his shotgun and came up against the helicopter's broken frame.

There was a pause. The man would know John was below him now. He would have heard him. John listened and heard the man reloading, so he moved.

The man came out hard and fast, gun blazing. He emerged from his crouch and cover, shooting before he presented himself, hammering his trigger and unloading his gun at where John had been a moment before. By the time the man saw, dumbfounded, that no one was there, it was far too late.

He swung his head around wildly. Horror spread across his face as he realised that John was in the helicopter, standing behind him, face cold and twisted into a snarl. He had slipped around the back.

John's shotgun blast connected with the man's chest at point blank range.

***

Pablito's body lay face down in the field, unmoving. John rushed toward him, already trying to isolate any feelings of sadness he had, and putting them far away in his mind. He knelt next to Pablito's body, searching for wounds.

The boy was breathing.

Joy and panic swept through him. He flung the boy over, prepared to perform CPR if he had gone into cardiac arrest. Or maybe he'd bled out from a severe flesh wound. Or maybe he was in a coma…

"I went to cover when I heard the gun!" Pablito cried through terrified tears.

For the first time in a long time, John felt genuine surprise, and relief, as emotion sweep over him. He picked the boy up, tucked his head into his shoulder, and held him tight as the boy cried.

CHAPTER 22

"You know, Mike, I was surprised that you wanted to meet with me."

Sara Burnes had climbed the ladder in the PAG faster than most. According to what Mike knew, she was a mover and a shaker, and wasn't too interested in the status quo. Mike suspected she wanted to make a name for herself. She wanted a power play. She was a good candidate for what Mike was looking for. More importantly, as Mike reminded himself grudgingly, she was probably the only person in PAG that he had any real rapport with. There would be no do-overs here.

"Our departments don't normally come in close contact with one another," she said as she tucked in her skirt and sat down across from him. "At least, not until recently."

Sara was beautiful and classy. That probably had a disarming effect on most men. Hell, it had an effect on him. But Mike recognized power when he saw it. The way she smiled with her perfect red lips concealed a voice that had brokered deals to topple governments. The way she tilted her head, hinting at a mind that ticked with the complexity of a Swiss watch. Even the way she ordered her mineral water and grenadine, commanding authority through sweetness. She was fascinating. She was dangerous.

The restaurant he had chosen was far too expensive for anything his taste. But he was schmoozing. He was in the field. This would be his new identity. This was his op. He was running the show now. He had to play the game.

"I know, and what a shame that is, really. Did you hear the news from our end?"

"What news is that?"

"Paul Locklee?"

"Oh. Yes. We heard about that. Sorry, Mike, I didn't know you were close…"

"Oh, we weren't. Don't worry. Man was an asshole."

It pained Mike to speak ill of the dead, but at least the last part was still truth.

Sara laughed. "I'm glad I don't have to pretend otherwise."

Mike mimicked her with a chuckle. "And besides the whole getting-paid-off to get an agent killed thing."

Sara grimaced. "Well, I know you two were working the Antiguan op together. But the more recent allegations are chilling."

Mike shrugged. "He was a damn headache. Kept steering us all over the place."

"Oh?"

Mike shrugged and accepted the bottle of beer he'd ordered from the waiter. Sara's drink was placed in front of her and the waiter ducked away, sensing his intrusion into their conversation.

"Just a pathological liar. It doesn't matter. What's done is done."

"Did he say anything…strange?"

Mike frowned. "Locklee? Like what? What do you mean?" He took a sip of beer, quelling the nerves bunched up inside him. It'd been a while since he'd worked someone.

"Oh," she waved her hand at a fly pestering her drink. "I mean, if he had hinted at anything that might've tipped you folks off sooner. About him being bribed by Puentes. Anything like that."

"Oh. No. Well, sort of. He said all kinds of weird things. He didn't mention being bribed by a drug lord though, I can assure you that much."

"Ah. Sounds like he was reaching out and trying to prime a defence. Trying to sow the seeds of doubt, build his case before he was found out."

"Well, yeah, like I said, he told me a few conspiracy theories, but we're not taking them seriously."

Sara's eyes flashed. Then she smiled sweetly. "So what was it you wanted to talk about?"

"Right to business, eh?"

"Call me curious?" She batted her perfect eyelashes, the small lines at the corners of her eyes bunching together as she smiled.

"Well, after this last op, and having one of my colleagues completely screw us, I'm concerned about some of the affairs I'm overseeing. I'm wondering if we can join some of our efforts in the near future." Sara leaned in, mixing her drink with its straw. "I've got big ideas for Blackthorne, but it helps to have an ally. Especially in a different department."

"I see…well, I've always been fascinated by Blackthorne's abilities. Just incredible what you are able to pull off. Unfortunately, you folks are so restricted being under SOG. I can't imagine Linda wanting us buddying up. But…what are some of your ideas?"

I want to infiltrate your damn department and tear it down from the inside. I will find out who Sandor was working for. I will find who set up Brian, who killed Locklee, and what you bastards are hiding. I want to burn your whole department to the ground.

Mike didn't need to force himself to grin.

"Well, I was thinking of opening up our unit to others under Special Activities. Maybe even turning some of our assets internal if it's possible. I want to make sure we don't have any more Paul Locklees lurking about."

Her eyes widened and she stopped sipping her drink. Then she smiled the smile of someone who had just been unabashedly and pleasantly surprised.

"Mike, that is quite…provocative. I mean, it's a good idea, but Linda wouldn't go for it."

"Oh, I wouldn't ask Linda. I'm asking you."

Mike simply held her gaze. He didn't waver. When she didn't take the chance to speak, he frowned.

It had taken him a long time to figure out what to do about everything that had happened. It only came to him after he had debriefed the op for Linda, talking about how difficult Pablo had been, choosing to contact his enemies and establish a kill switch. Sandor had played ball with the CIA and it had gotten him killed. Pablo resisted, but was reckless. Between their actions and Locklee, Mike had figured the best play would be to deliver Blackthorne into the lap of PAG. It seemed counterintuitive at first, but this way he could prove himself ignorant of anything other than Locklee's guilt. It would make him seem a compliant ally as opposed to a restrained enemy. And besides, maybe this way Mike could avoid his own corpse being found by Barker and labeled a suspicious suicide. But most importantly, it would get him close to his enemies.

Linda would throw a fit, but he couldn't tell her what Locklee had told him. If she was a part of it, maybe she'd show her hand. If she wasn't — and he prayed she wasn't — maybe it would silently tip her off and she'd start her own inquiry.

Sara would, of course, see it as a favor. If Locklee was right and the PAG was as fractured and bloodthirsty as he said, Mike could play them against one another. He would be able to run an internal hunt under all their noses, right inside the damn department. Locklee would've torn him apart for making such a decision. But Locklee was dead.

"Are you interested or not?"

Sara's face smoothed over in an instant. "Oh, I'm in. I have some colleagues who would love this."

And others who would hate it, I suspect. Well, hopefully we're on the same side. If not, you're going to give me my ticket into the PAG either way.

"*Bueno.*" Mike raised his beer. "Cheers, Sara."

They clinked their drinks and picked up their menus, deciding what to order for their far too expensive lunch.

***

"You sure he will be okay?"

John looked to Marcela through pained eyes.

"Yes, John. Pablito will be fine. I have known this organization since I was a child. They're the ones who helped me during the civil war."

He thought about that. The group looked after high-risk children and smuggled them out of the country to safer relatives or friends with absolute privacy and off-the-record movement. He suspected it was also the way Marcela had come in contact with Americans who had recruited her to fight the rebels. But right now, anything was better and safer than Pablito staying in Guatemala.

They were standing in a playground on the outskirts of Antigua. Pablito was running around the jungle gym with a group of other children. They were playing tag, but it looked like whoever was 'it' was required to also act like a monster. Pablito was particularly good at it. He ran at John and collided into his legs.

"Rawr!"

John looked down at the small heap that had collapsed in front of him. He frowned.

"Rawr!" Pablito said again.

"Rawr," John replied.

Marcela smiled and walked away, giving him some room to talk to the boy before they left. John knelt in front of Pablito. Pablito met his gaze.

"I know my *papá* is dead, *profesor*."

John was surprised. "Yes," John said, sadness in his voice, but not hiding from the truth of it.

"Do you know how he died?"

John looked closely at the child. He would probably never see him again. He could say whatever he wanted. Even the truth. That's what Brian would do.

John took a deep breath. "Yes. I know how he died. But I won't tell you."

Pablito looked like he was trying to make up his mind about something. His eyes began to well up with tears.

John spoke quickly. "I know your father didn't like secrets."

"Yes!" Pablito said. "But even he had a couple, I know!"

"Yes, he had a couple. And they were dangerous. Knowing how he died…even some of the things you know right now. These things are dangerous. So we're going to keep them hidden. I'm going to hold onto some of these secrets for you. You don't need any more to hold onto. Okay?"

"I loved my *papá*!"

"I know," John said. He gave the boy a hug.

Pablito's tiny eyes searched John's face for something. Then he ran off, screaming like a monster at the other children. They laughed and ran away.

John watched for a moment, then went to meet Marcela. They began to wander the streets. The smoke had thinned and people were out cleaning and sweeping the layers of ash off cars and terraces, but even that had begun to settle down. The crowds were on edge, but most were optimistic that *El Volcán Fuego* had calmed itself, at least for a little while.

"Esteban said it was mission complete," Marcela said after they had been walking for some time in amiable silence. "So I'm assuming you got information out of Pablo?"

John eyed the road uneasily. "No. I decided to use a truth serum pill. Unfortunately, it melted his brain to pudding. Couldn't get a damn thing."

Marcela smiled, sadness in her eyes. She knew just as well as he that there was no such thing as a truth serum pill. Which meant he was hiding the truth, but letting her know.

"And the wig I gave you?"

John looked up at the sun, squinting. "Taken care of. Disposed of it."

She eyed him warily. She could tell he hadn't destroyed it. He had told Esteban he'd delete the recording of Pablo's interrogation off his phone. He hadn't done that either.

That meant John had two pieces of volatile, classified intelligence. The interrogation of Pablo recorded on his phone proved that Sandor had been working with someone high up in the CIA. The wig had Isabella's entire hard drive. He had dug up the will that had set events into motion, but John had a pile of more data to sift through.

He wasn't supposed to be holding onto either of these things.

It was the first time he had outright disobeyed his orders. He had a feeling that it wouldn't be the last. A long dangerous road waited ahead for him.

Marcela stopped abruptly, leaving John a few steps ahead of her. "You don't have to do this alone," she said softly.

John lowered his shoulders. He didn't realize how much tension was there.

"I know, Marcela. But I want to."

When she didn't say anything, he made a rare move. He turned around and sidled up to her, put his arm around her shoulders and drew her close. He gave her a quick squeeze. It made him feel awkward, but Marcela accepted the gesture and didn't make fun of him, thankfully. They continued their walk into town.

"Esteban says he wants me to link up with Juan. Play the ignorant and helpful mistress. I already suggested he destroy the day's security camera recordings. He agreed. Less trouble that way."

"For us, or him?"

"Both."

"What's the op?"

"You know I can't tell you that," she teased with a wink. But then her expression darkened. "No, seriously, I don't know yet. That's it for now."

"Seems like nothing changes."

John peered at the sky. It was still full of floating ash, puffs of smoke still lingering from the eruption. He hoped it would grow into a beautiful day soon. Even if he wouldn't be around to see it.

"And you?"

"Don't know yet."

Marcela sulked. "Off the hook for now, it seems."

"For now."

Neither of them mentioned how dangerous it was for her to be going back under cover with Juan after their op had just finished, and in such a violent way. She wasn't supposed to have told him. He wondered if she was telling him on purpose. A safeguard. Have at least one person know where she was, and what was happening. Brian had done the same thing. It made him think of Pablo's kill switch.

Or maybe Marcela just bent the rules. He wasn't sure. This op with Pablo had changed things. More gray areas. It left John with a sense of purpose he hadn't expected. He found it strange.

"Well, I could go for a beer and a fuck. How about you?"

John couldn't help but smile. He knew she was joking. Pretty sure, anyway.

"Marcela, you still haven't managed to seduce me. But for all your effort, the least I can do is treat you to a *cerveza*."

Marcela pouted. Then she pulled out a small wad of American bills and gave them a little shake and winked at John again.

"*Cervezas* on Pablo!"

***

Juan was overseeing the collection of bodies and general cleanup of the estate. It was a mess. It would probably be a week until everything was properly sorted and back in order. It was a shame. The place was beautiful. It didn't deserve such a beating.

There was still the niggling problem of any men who were uncertain about his leadership, and Any loyalties remaining to Pablo. Juan encouraged any he suspected of this to go to the apartment in town, where Pablo's Mercedes had been found. Emergency workers had cordoned off the area so they could continue monitoring the situation and finish their body count. Juan hoped that sent a strong enough message, even though he hadn't been the one to set such an explosion. In truth, he had no idea how everything had happened. But he was putting together small pieces as they came through. He was trying to channel his father's patience.

Unfortunately, he kept thinking about his mother. He wanted to grieve, but he couldn't, not in front of his men. He was ashamed that his last moment with her had been an argument. That she had been disappointed in him. He was mad at her, but he didn't know the reasons for what she had done. He would never, even on his worst enemy, wish a mother dead. Sadness turned to rage and turned back again into sadness. The feelings came and went like tides.

He heard the sound of a vehicle approaching the estate's driveway. It interrupted his thoughts, and he broke his gaze from the cleanup to see one of his guards approaching him.

"*¿Señor?*"

"*¿Sí?*"

The man looked nervous, but he spoke quickly, knowing not to waste Juan's time. "*La Policía Nacional Civil.* They want to know what happened here. They want to investigate."

Juan sighed. He pulled out a stack of American bills. He handed them to the guard and he ran off to bribe the officers. It hadn't been the first time that day. He suspected it wouldn't be the last, either.

He turned to one of his other guards.

"Any word on Pablito?"

He shook his head sadly. "No, *patrón.*"

He finally held power, just as his father had. Seizing it was messy. It was proving more difficult than he'd imagined, being the man in charge. Pablito's unknown whereabouts were getting on his nerves. For all the repeated annoyances of the day, he was met with a surprise when his phone rang. The number was unlisted. He hesitated as it rang again, then answered.

"*¿Sí?*"

"Hello, Juan."

Something about the voice chilled him. He didn't know why, but it did. It was a woman's voice..

"*¿Quién es?*" he asked evenly. *Who is this?* He tried to keep the bite from his voice. He imagined his father tapping his shoulder, tempering him. The thought made him jump with surprise. The woman spoke.

"A business partner. I used to work with your father."

Juan eyed his servants and guards working about in the courtyard, and moved inside. He waved a couple guards off as they followed. He walked through the halls toward the master bedroom — *his* master bedroom, as he spoke.

"And what, you want to negotiate something?"

"Sort of. Sure."

Juan's temper flared again. This *gringa* had the audacity to call him after he had taken

power and lost his mother? Trying to sneak in like a thief? He knew how to deal with such people. Both his father and his uncle had shown him that much, at least.

"You want to try and buy me out now that my father, uncle, *and* mother are dead? You think I'm some pathetic child trying to run away? I own this now. It is mine."

There was a brief pause on the other end. Then the woman spoke again, her tone controlled and full of unshaken confidence. "Oh, I'm sorry Juan, I think you misunderstand me. I simply want the same business arrangement I had with your father, before he was so unjustly killed. Before Pablo ruined everything."

Juan blinked. Then his eyes narrowed.

"Tell me, *señorita*. I'm listening."

Enjoyed This Book? You Can Make a Difference

Thank you very much for purchasing this book, Ghosts of Guatemala.

I'm very grateful that you chose this book from all the other wonderful books on the market.

I hope you enjoyed reading it. If you did, please consider sharing your thoughts on Facebook, Twitter, LinkedIn, and Instagram.

If you enjoyed this book and found value in reading it, please take a few minutes to post an honest review on your favorite site. Reviews are very important to readers and authors — and difficult to get. Reviews don't have to be long: even a sentence or two is a huge help. Every review helps.

While on your favorite site, feel free to vote for helpful reviews. The top-voted reviews are featured for display, and most likely to influence new readers. You can vote for as many reviews as you like.

Thank you for your support,

Collin

Author's Note and Acknowledgements

This book is the product of a partnership my father and I share. A few years ago, Dad decided to take me on a father-son road trip to Chicago. Amidst Chicago-style pizza and Dad speaking Spanish to people in elevators, he asked if I would write him a stage play.

I am like most creative types and artists, which means I'm the worst. I have a backlog of unfinished stories, unedited creations, and plenty of notebooks filled (or unfilled) with utterly brilliant ideas. I was acting and writing amidst my university degrees and while my parents have always been supportive, they are also firm believers in hard work. They wanted to see some product.

Dad said he would support the project financially and see it to completion. The catch was, of course, that I had to write *his* idea, not my own.

Since that fateful day in Chicago, Dad and I have created two stage plays: *In Real Life,* performed in London, ON in 2015, and *LoveSpell,* in the Hamilton Fringe in 2016.

As I struggled to get more serious about writing, Dad decided it was time for another project, this time a book. His idea, his marketing, my writing. A CIA spy-thriller about a guy who is like my dad (but definitely not like my dad), and it takes place in Guatemala because Dad goes there for months at a time.

Oh boy.

When I say my father and I wrote a book together, I sometimes get asked who did what on the project, and I think it's important for people to know. I wrote the book, but it's also my dad's book. My dad provided ideas for main characters, a few scenes he wanted to play out, some basic theming, and went so far as to write half a chapter. He also went through the work and made sure all the Spanish is accurate and all the cultural and regional details made sense. Credit where credit is due.

And of course, a book is something that so many others are a part of, and this is the part I finally get to thank them all properly.

Thanks to my two beta-reader groups for their generous time, honesty, and feedback: Alex Colvin, Bill Scott, Brian O'Riordan, Dave McAdams, Louis Castrogiovanni, Michael Shumacher, Nathan Olmstead, Ross Mosher, and Tom Kehoe.

Thank you to my line editor Rebecca Heath, and my book formatter Ruslan Nabiev.

I thank all my friends and family for being supportive, but particularly my mom, who often mitigated arguments between Dad and I, and provided an editing intervention one ugly night at the kitchen table. A big thanks to my girlfriend Shawna for supporting me, even through the times spent in writing isolation, and not leaving me when I spoke like my characters in public. Thank you to Ross, my good friend and stylistic editor who, amidst rock-solid editing, made my awkward phrasing sound professional, and who created a timeline so I knew when things in the story were actually happening. A shout-out to Nathan, my good friend and roommate who spent plenty of time not working on his PhD so he could hear me whine about plot holes instead, who knew the answers always lay in a cup of coffee between friends. I'd also like to thank my incredibly supportive coworkers — my entire Chapters Fairview team — for asking how John was doing. Writing can be hell, but all these people helped to keep the temperature a little bit lower.

Thank you.

About the author

Collin Glavac is a Canadian-born actor and writer who lives in the Niagara region. He has written, directed, and acted in two original stage plays: *In Real Life*, and *LoveSpell*. He completed his Dramatic and Liberal Arts B.A. and M.A at Brock University.

Ghosts of Guatemala is his first novel.

Collin loves hearing from readers, so please don't hesitate to contact him by email at: collinglavac@gmail.com